HOMECOMING

SUSIE STEINER

FABER & FABER

First published in 2013
by Faber and Faber Limited
Bloomsbury House
74–77 Great Russell Street
London WC1B 3DA
This paperback edition first published in 2014

Typeset by Faber and Faber Limited
Printed and bound by CPI Group (UK) Ltd, Croydon, CR0 4YY

The right of Susie Steiner to be identified as author
of this work has been asserted in accordance with Section 77
of the Copyright, Designs and Patents Act 1988

Extract from *Home Electrics* by Julian Bridgewater,
copyright Julian Bridgewater, 2004, New Holland Publishers Ltd

Extract from *Unless* by Carol Shields first published in Great Britain
by Fourth Estate in 2002. Copyright © 2002 Carol Shields

A CIP record for this book
is available from the British Library

ISBN 978-0-571-29664-4

FSC
www.fsc.org
MIX
Paper from
responsible sources
FSC® C101712

2 4 6 8 10 9 7 5 3 1

For Tom

2005

—

NORTH YORKSHIRE

OCTOBER

— The start of the farming year —

Joe closes his back door, his feet cold inside his boots as he steps out into the yard in the dark. He can smell the rain coming and digs into his pocket for his phone.

'Yep?' says Max.

'Let's lift this beet then, shall we?'

'I thought I was sorting it,' says Max.

'So did I. Ted Wilson brought a machine over last night.'

'I was going to call him,' Max says.

Joe listens to the fat cooing of a wood-pigeon somewhere over by the hay barn.

'I were waiting for a break in the wet,' Max says.

'Well, you'd have a long wait then, wouldn't ye? I've done it now.'

'It's set to tip it down,' says Max.

That boy. Always looking for the obstacles.

'We'll just have to do best we can,' says Joe, careful of his tone. 'How soon can you get down here? You'll need to hitch the trailer to the John Deere. I'll meet you over on the in-bye.'

He pulls himself up into the harvester's cab. The brown seat is frayed and sagging and he can taste the age on her: a diesel leak, worn metal. The dust off other farmers' boots. First time he's not been able to afford Wilson's lads to lift the fodder beet for him, and here he is, pushing sixty, trying to drive a clapped-out harvester he's never set eyes on before.

3

Joe starts the engine and pushes his foot gently down on the gas, feeling for its bite, keeping his eyes on the rear-view mirrors which are big as tea trays. Then he's easing the harvester out through the farmyard gate with his mouth hanging open from the concentration of it; turning at a stately crawl, sharp right past his own front door.

Ann'll be waking.

'Shouldn't you be lifting the beet?' she'd said, more than two weeks ago. But the rains had never ceased, the ground as sticky as a clay-pit. So they'd waited. And she'd been on at him, too, about the money – how much he'd have to get at Slingsby to make the next rent payment to the water board and whether the stores would fetch more than fifteen pound a lamb this year. She wanted out. He knew she did. Wanted 'a retirement', she said, that wasn't all watching the weather and getting up at dawn. She was pressing him to hand over more to Max, so he'd said it was Max's job to sort the beet. And then he'd watched him as the days passed and it didn't get done.

He's gaining the feel of the harvester now: her weight against the gas. Marpleton village green slides by to his left and he glances across it at his slow roll: sees the Fox and Feathers unlit, and beyond, in the lightening dawn, Eric and Lauren Blakely's house – a former rectory which stands taller than the workers' cottages around it. Eric with his indoor shoes and his Nissan Micra, his farming days behind him. Alright for them, they'd owned their land. They weren't tenants like him and Ann. All that work – farming a hundred acres, tending five hundred Swaledales on the moor, and what would they have to show for it? They were worth less every month, even with all the love and care that went into them and the patience they gave back, standing out on the moor in the harshest winters. No, they couldn't be left. Max wasn't ready.

Joe pulls off the road onto a dirt track that crosses the in-bye and feels the comfort of looking out across the lowland where his forage crops are grown and grass for hay and silage; fields penned by dry stone walls, where rams are put to the ewes at tupping and where the lambs are born. He marvels that he's grown to love it so – when it was a thing foisted on him, not chosen. And who'd keep this in order if he were gone? Handing it on to Max – well, look how that was going. Couldn't even organise for the beet to get lifted.

The sky is thundery and low as he pulls up beside a wall and jumps down from the cab. He looks across the field at the green tops of the fodder beet stretching away. The ground giving up its treasure to him: it was a beautiful thing. He pictures the soil and the layers – the substrata – brown then red, then glaring orange, reaching down to the earth's core where it was hot. And him on the surface, gathering its riches up – drilling goodness and filtering it into trucks. This was what a man was meant for. What did she want him to do, if not this?

Max presses the red button on his phone. He's standing next to his Land Rover in the yard outside his farmhouse, not five miles from his father's. He can feel the energy drain out of him. Joe had only said a week ago – about lifting the beet – and already he's fallen short. Maybe he could've got round to it sooner, but he was caught. Never knew how much to spend or which was the right way. If he'd scrimped, Joe would say he should've been bolder. If he'd paid full whack and got in Ted Wilson's boys, Joe would've asked him if he thought they were made of money. So he'd put it off, waiting for a break in the wet and to see if the answer might come to him.

He gazes at the farmhouse where a light is coming on. It casts a weak glow over the yard and the front door opens. Primrose is standing in her nightgown with her wellingtons on. Her nightie is see-through and her thighs are silhouetted in the yellow of the hall. 'Sturdy,' Joe had said of Primrose, when they announced they were to marry, and Max wasn't sure if this was a compliment or another gibe.

'Going over to the in-bye,' he shouts to her across the yard. 'Lifting the beet.'

'In't it too wet?'

'Aye, well. He's hired a machine off Ted Wilson, ha'n't he. So it's got to be today.'

'Right,' she says. 'I thought you were s'posed to be sorting it.'

'Doesn't matter who sorts it, does it?' he says, turning away from her and opening the car door. 'S'long as it gets done.'

She walks into the kitchen. The lights are on and their claustrophobic glow creates a feeling of night abutting wakefulness. She puts a kettle on to boil and hears a thunder-clap outside but no rain. The air is charged with electricity, warm with it. She prepares her tea and toast with the same ritual she follows every morning.

Primrose opens her DIY manual on the kitchen table and hunches over it, her tea in one hand, her toast in the other and the metal overhead light casting a cone from above. Within minutes she's lost in a labyrinthine task involving earth terminals and flex and circuit-breakers. She examines a diagram of a ceiling rose, following, with dogged precision, the pathways of each wire and their connectivity: the ones that must be broken, the ones that must not be touched. '*Loosen the two or three terminals that hold the flex wires,*' she reads. '*Remove the wires, taking care not to disturb any of the wires entering the rose from the circuit cable.*' She stifles a yawn and is surprised at how hard it is to stay awake this morning. It isn't like her, Primrose being one of those people who accepts being awake as an indisputable fact.

Ten minutes later she is easing flesh-coloured bra cups over her breasts. She flinches and rounds her shoulders. They are too tender, like when she's on the blob. Her belly has the same over-ripe feeling. She looks in the mirror but she looks the same. She finishes dressing and washes her face with a cracked bar of Imperial Leather soap.

Out in the yard, she creaks and rustles in her anorak as she mounts her bicycle. The light is dusk-like under the lowered cloud and on the journey, the rain starts to plop in fat drops onto her shoulders. By the time she reaches the Co-op in Lipton two miles away, she is soaked through.

She's first in. She unlocks the door and turns on the lights. They flicker on with a plink-plink, so that she sees flashes of the empty green plastic boxes for veg and the aisles of jams and tins and Mr Kipling cakes that last in their boxes for years.

She's just taken her place on the high stool out front, with the cigarettes behind her – has lifted the stiff cover off the till, folded it and stowed it under her feet – when Tracy and Claire clatter in through the door in mid-conversation.

'So what did she say?' Tracy is asking Claire as they make their way past the till.

'Hiya Prim,' says Claire, smiling at her.

Primrose smiles back but doesn't reply. There is a metallic taste in her mouth.

'Come on,' she hears Tracy saying at Claire's back as they walk down to the staff room, past the mulligatawny soup. 'I won't say owt.'

She can't hear Claire's reply.

Primrose shifts on her high stool. She slouches, then straightens. She puts a hand on her lower belly.

Ann's fingernails are painted with pink pearlised varnish which flashes and sparkles under the gloom of her umbrella as she hurries up Lipton High Street. Perhaps she shouldn't have sent that email to Bartholomew. Toned it down a bit. 'Your dad's lifting the beet by himself – hired some rust bucket off Ted Wilson. Oh I do feel sorry for him, doing a job like that at his age, but he won't stop. Won't slow down. You'd think Max would step up.'

Her expression beneath the shadow of her umbrella is crumpled. She's prodding her youngest for his usual response. 'Sell up, mum. It's too much of a strain at your age.' And then she can argue against him, as if it's some internal refrain she's wanting to play out. 'Sell what? Lamb prices are on the floor, house prices going up every week. We'd have nowhere to live.'

She wears a beige mac, darkened by the wet at her elbows and at the base of her back. Hanging from the crook of her bent arm is her handbag, large and practical. She is stooping, her feet taking quick steps on the pavement. They'll be having a right job getting the beet up in this, she thinks. Joe's been glued to the weather reports these last weeks – standing beside the kitchen radio, craning his ear, looking at his shoes. You were so

8

at the mercy of the weather, farming. Like some poor referee between a low sky and the sodden earth. But Joe, he'd tell the clouds where to blow if he could.

The rain subsides, as if some hand has turned a celestial dial round to 'off'. Ann slows her pace and stops outside Richardson & Smith, Residential & Farm property sales. Her umbrella and mac are reflected in the glass. Hovering just above her indistinct shoulders is a square panel containing four pictures: a farmhouse, some outbuildings, fields and a line map of the land. Frank and Joan Motherwell's farm. She'd heard they were selling: millions, that land would go for. Cashing in on the bull market and moving abroad to start over. Somewhere hot, Maureen Pettiford had said yesterday, as Ann handed her coins across the counter in return for *The Times*.

'Joan can't wait to see the back of the place.'

'And Frank?' Ann had said.

'He's not taking it so well.'

Somewhere hot. She'd made Joe go on a holiday once. Long time ago, when money wasn't so tight. Never again. The fidgeting. The deep sighs, then heaving himself off the lounger to call Max.

She'd said to him, only last week, 'Max managed alright then, didn't he? When we went to Málaga that time?'

'If doing nowt is managing,' Joe had said.

'Oh come off it,' she'd said, but he'd shot her a look, like she was trespassing where she shouldn't.

'Slowly, slowly catchy monkey,' Lauren had counselled, when she'd gone across the green for a cup of tea.

Ann begins to feel the wetness that has slid off her umbrella; a cool patch at the base of her spine. She is taking in the sunflower-yellow colour on Joan Motherwell's kitchen walls and the patterned blue curtains which look like a toddler's defaced them. She grimaces. Her own house wouldn't come off much better, mind. Bet Joan can't believe her luck. She thinks of the desultory yard at home, a mess of machinery parts and ripped hessian sacks; the pole barn for hay and straw, clumps of it strewn into the mud.

'That's a fair old price is that,' says a familiar voice at her shoulder. Ann spins round. It is Lauren, her face smiling out from beneath a giant floral umbrella. 'Makes Eric and me wonder if we shouldn't have held on for a bit longer. Market seems to go up every week.'

Ann nods. She pats her collar-bones. They both peer at the Motherwell farm details.

'I know they've had to struggle,' says Ann, 'what Joan's been through, tearing Frank away from the place, but still, that'd take the edge off.'

'She still has to live with Frank,' says Lauren. 'Frank without a farm. Wouldn't wish that on me worst enemy.'

Easy for Lauren to say. Ann and Joe, they'd be lucky to get enough for a two-bed flat on the trunk road out of Malton. Above the Chinese. Perhaps it was better to press on, like Joe said: stay in the big house where her bairns were born. Wait for things to get better.

Lauren is rubbing her shoulder. 'Don't think on,' she says. 'There's nothing you can do about it so don't think on. Lamb prices'll pick up. Here, do you fancy darts tonight – at the George in Morpeth-le-Dale? It's just a friendly – they haven't chosen the league yet, but between you and me, I think the captaincy's in the bag.'

'I don't know,' says Ann, patting her collar-bones again. 'I don't know the rules.'

'Don't be daft. I can fill you in. I'll pick you up at seven.'

'Alright then, yes. I'd love a lift.'

'Get that wrist action going,' says her friend as she walks backwards away from Ann, her hand nodding with an imaginary dart, her face drenched in red from her umbrella.

Lauren has, over twenty years of friendship, taught Ann the value of hobbies – ladies' darts, the WI, flower-arranging, church committees, life-drawing classes – and Ann is continually surprised by the richness these diversions bring to her life. On the face of it, they provide contact with others which Ann, well, she'd be shy about it normally. More than that, they bring her a singular involvement in the moment: herself, up against all these new things, even if it was only poking a delphinium into a damp block of oasis. Often she showed no discernible talent – her pottery was shocking. But as she got older this seemed to matter less. The vanity of youth – what a liberation it was to be free of it. It is age, too, that's taught her a kind of dogged tenacity. She's realised, late in the day, that the stringing together of small things, and keeping going – above all plodding on – is what makes a life.

Nevertheless, she has to fight resistance at her core – her inner sod – which pours scorn on her hobbies and plays on her desire to stay cocooned at home, instead of grimacing at the cold night like a physical shock and some draughty hall full of strangers, or worse, acquaintances, to whom she must present herself, jollied up with a sweep of Yardley lipstick. She dreads the navigating of the difficult few among the genial whole: those women who were barbed or envious or who presented to her a perfect life. Lauren didn't seem to suffer the same reluctance, though age had also taught Ann that you never really knew how hard people were paddling beneath the surface.

At any rate, Lauren seemed to have the knack of being happy.

She'd had her moments – especially after Jack, when she'd not got out of bed for what seemed like a year – but generally, she put the effort in, never appearing to ask herself the question of whether it'd be alright to give up. Yes, Ann felt she was fortunate in loving Lauren.

Max is tired after three hours lifting the beet. He jumps down from the tractor's high seat, into the mud.

'That's a good job, son.'

Max can hear the satisfaction in Joe's voice – not just at having lifted the beet, but about setting him right.

'Bloody miracle, I'd say,' Max says, his hands in the small of his back. 'I was sure she'd clog up halfway down.'

'Good job we didn't leave it any longer,' Joe says, and Max thinks to say, 'How do you know? Weather might be dry tomorrow.' But he keeps quiet. Easier to let Joe congratulate himself.

'Have you got the tarpaulin?' Joe is saying. 'We'd best cover them up.'

And even though Max is dog-tired, he jumps into his tractor cab and pulls the bright-blue plastic out from behind the seat. He knows better than to keep Joe waiting, not with him so watchful, like he's always testing and Max always falling short. He begins fixing the tarpaulin over the trailer with rubber spiders.

'Need to start bringing the ewes down off the fell soon,' says Joe at his back.

Max stops and rolls his eyes, then pulls down harder on the tarpaulin.

'Auction's first,' he says. 'Let's just get through that, shall we, before you bring on next year's lambs.'

'Can't let the grass grow,' says Joe.

Max feels Joe's hand on the back of his neck and his father shakes him as if he were an apple tree. Max submits to it.

'Come on,' says Joe. 'Let's see if your mother will cook us a bacon butty.'

⌒

'I knew it'd be bad, with the weather against ye,' says Ann with her back to them. She has a tea towel over her shoulder and Joe watches her bottom jiggle as she ushers the eggs off the bottom of the pan. He and Max sit at the table with towels around their shoulders and cups of tea before them.

'It's not bad,' says Joe. 'It's fine. We'll be done by end of today.'

'And then we'll go to Slingsby and get tuppence-ha'penny for those wonderful lambs and Barry bloody Jordan will drag me over hot coals,' she says. The room is full of sizzling and steam and the smell of bacon.

'Arh, Barry Jordan,' says Joe. 'It's no business of his.'

'It is when he's balancing our accounts,' says Ann. 'Anyway, you're not the one has to go and see him.'

'You'll live,' says Joe. 'I'm going to ring Bartholomew. See how he's getting on.' He walks out to the hall and comes back holding the entire telephone unit, dragging the long wire behind him. He sets it on the table and sits down.

Bartholomew picks up, just as Ann sets a bacon-and-egg sandwich down in front of him.

'Bartholomew!' says Joe, over-loud.

'Hello,' says Bartholomew. His small voice seems such a long way away.

'We're all here, so we thought we'd ring you!' bellows Joe.

Bartholomew jerks his head away from the handset.

'Hello,' he says, bringing it closer but still not touching his ear. He's standing at the counter, looking out of the warehouse window to the car park where he can see a van pulling up. The driver, a bald man with a pencil behind his ear, gets out then opens the van's double doors before going round to the passenger seat. He picks up a clipboard and examines it. Bartholomew casts around the room for Leonard.

'You're all there, are you,' he says into the phone, craning to look down the corridor.

'We are, son. Here, your mother and Max want to hear you too.'

'Just don't put me on spea—'

He can hear the echo already. The line fills up with the sound of clattering plates and frying.

'There you go, love!' shouts Ann. 'You're on the speakerphone!'

They always did this – called him when they were all together and he wasn't. As if it was their great gift to him – the sounds of family life speeding down wires the length of the country, north to south, thanks to the technological brilliance of the speakerphone. For them, he supposed, it was a way of having him at the table. And they couldn't understand why he'd be itching to get off the line.

The delivery-man has approached the counter, ignoring the fact that Bartholomew is on the phone. 'Where do you want your bare rooters?' he says. 'I've got fifty cherries, and . . .' he looks at his clipboard, 'various apples. Hundred in all.'

Bartholomew scans again for Leonard, puts a hand over the mouthpiece and nods at the corner of the warehouse. 'Just drop them over there.'

He returns to the phone call and its white noise. He can hear cutlery on plates, chairs scraping, his mother saying, 'Another slice, Max?'

'Lift the beet alright did ye?' he says, hearing his voice repeat down the line.

'Nearly there,' says Joe. 'No thanks to your brother. Says he were waiting for a gap in the wet.' His father laughs. 'Had to sort it myself in the end.'

Bartholomew can picture Max reddening.

Joe seems to realise he's gone too far and quickly says, 'It were no bother. We'll finish by end of today, won't we son?'

'If she doesn't clog,' says Max. 'You should see the rust bucket he's hired off Ted Wilson.'

'Must be hardgoing,' says Bartholomew. 'It's bad enough driving those things in the dry.' He pictures Joe, small and hunched, and five hectares of fodder beet in the melting land to lift.

But Joe is snorting. 'Nah, it lifted those beet like it were hoovering up crumbs.'

There was no helping him when he was bluff like this. There was no helping him at all, not from way down here.

'How many lambs are you selling at Slingsby?' Bartholomew asks.

'More 'an two hundred,' says Max. 'Right fine they are too, the girls.'

'And another two-hundred-odd stores,' says Joe.

Bartholomew watches the delivery-man bring in the last of the saplings, each about four foot high, their roots wrapped in hessian sacks like Christmas puddings. Bartholomew signs the docket, mouths 'Thanks' and watches him leave.

'Any news about Maguires?' Ann shouts, from somewhere in the kitchen, probably the stove. 'Are they still opening up near you?' He'd only told her about it a week ago and now she's wanting hourly bulletins. 'Maybe you could get a little job with them. Something nice and secure.'

Bartholomew doesn't bother responding. The spattering down the line is giving him a headache.

'How are the petunias?' asks Joe.

Max is quick to join in: 'Has the bottom fallen out of the pansy market yet?'

He hears his mother saying, 'Shurrup you two.'

'Fine, can I go now?' says Bartholomew. He's always letting this one go. Joe has never visited the garden centre and their conversations about it end badly.

'OK son,' says Joe.

'Bye lovey!' he hears Ann shouting in the background. 'And let me know about Maguires.'

He puts the phone down before she's finished and marches to the back of the warehouse, peering down the dark corridor at the end of which is a door with a mottled glass panel. A light glows dimly from the room and he can make out the outline of Leonard, who is sat with the newspaper open, elbows on knees. He'd seen the headline earlier that morning. 'Councillor Brands Shopping Trolleys "a Menace"'. The perfect marriage of man and reading material.

Bartholomew hears a distant flush and Leonard emerges from the corridor, newspaper folded under his arm.

'These need putting outside,' he says to Leonard. 'I don't know why I got him to bring them in. Would've helped if you'd taken the delivery.'

Leonard has returned to his stool behind the counter and his shanty town of order books.

'God it's cold,' says Bartholomew. 'Have you lit the stove?'

'And what did your last slave die of?'

'The burner's right next to you,' says Bartholomew.

'Well it is *now*. Looks like you've got a visitor,' says Leonard, and they both look out of the warehouse window to see Ruby's pea-green coat at the main gate. Her hair is the colour of marmalade shot through with sunlight. Bartholomew hurries towards her.

She sees him coming round the side of the building, walking towards her energetically in his bottle-green fleece and heavy boots. He looks lovely and outdoorsy, she thinks. Lovely curls. Unbrushed. And immediately she regrets last night. He'd been sat there hunched over his laptop for what seemed like hours while she'd twittered on about this, that and nothing. And she'd got fed up of him not responding, especially when she was treading so carefully, fighting so hard not to mention Christmas and whether they were going to spend it together, tiptoeing around it in her head and forcibly stopping herself from saying, 'I might go travelling actually. Round Asia.' Because there was always a risk she'd have to go and she can't think of anything she wants to do less. She wants to watch *Only Fools and Horses* together and eat his mother's turkey dinner. Walk across the fell holding hands. It'd been such a gathering strain, not saying all this, that she'd exploded with the words: 'I'm going back to my flat if you don't get off that bloody laptop.'

And he'd looked up, bewildered, saying, 'Sorry, I was just reading an email.' But he'd been distracted the rest of the evening, like he was somewhere else altogether. In the night, he'd thrashed about, fighting wildly for the duvet, throwing her off when she tried to curl her body around his back.

'Hello,' he says, smiling at her.

'There was a letter for you this morning, so I thought I'd drop it by.'

'Thanks,' he says.

'Who's it from?' she asks, peering at it.

'Dunno, looks official.'

He puts the envelope in the back pocket of his jeans. They stand for a moment and then he points over his shoulder with one thumb.

'I've got a lot on, Rube.'

'OK,' she says. But she doesn't shift. 'Shall we go to the pub later?'

'If you want.'

'What's wrong with you?' she asks.

'Nothing's wrong.'

'You seem moody.'

'I'm not moody. You're moody.'

'Alright, calm down.' The wind blows her hair over her face and lifts her hood, which only adds to a feeling of general discomfort. 'OK, well, see you later.' She hunches her shoulders, waves a cramped wave and walks out of the garden-centre gates.

He walks down the central path to the lower boundary and looks out over the rough and the rolling downs that fall away at the bottom of his land. Benign fields, like a sea without surf. He can see the beauty of it, this garden of England, but it doesn't stir him the way North Yorkshire does.

He takes the letter out of his back pocket and tears at it with his thumb. It is from Maguires suggesting a meeting to discuss its expansion plans.

Maguires does not believe in aggressive marketplace domination. We believe there is room for all kinds of enterprise, offering customers a diversity of experience – from small independents such as yourself, to the bigger chains. We believe your business can thrive alongside the new 100,000-square-foot garden and DIY destination due to open next spring at West Tilsey. Please come to our Powerpoint presentation at our head office, where we will fully inform you of developments, and share a glass of champagne with regional centre manager Carl Snape.

Nice, he thinks. Happy to wine and dine me while putting me out of business.

'Excuse me, do you work here?' says a voice. Bartholomew looks up to see a woman in a woollen grey coat and brown boots, with sunglasses on her head.

'I do, yes,' says Bartholomew. 'Can I help with something?'

'Can you advise me what I can plant now? Or do I have to wait until spring?'

'No, not at all. There's lots you can put in now – some wonderful hardy perennials.' He begins to lead her to a trough filled with rows of black plastic pots. 'Here we've got geraniums and pelargoniums. Or there's columbines or bear's breeches. Put any of these in now and they'll get a head start before spring.'

The woman is frowning. 'But these are just pots of earth.'

'Well, yes, it looks like that. But they'll come bursting up in spring.'

'I'm not paying good money for a pot of earth.'

'They're not pots of earth, they're perennials.'

'Still. I want something that looks nice. And something that doesn't need looking after. Something neat.'

Bartholomew sighs. 'Come on, I'll show you the skimmias.'

He leaves the woman at the till with Leonard and walks back down the main path, eyeing up the troughs on either side which are filled with bedraggled stems and desiccated leaves or bare earth. Joe wouldn't reckon much on the place, not if he saw it now, he thinks, taking out a pair of secateurs from his back pocket. He climbs to the back of a bed, towards a tangle of rose stems whipped about by a rampant honeysuckle. He's allowed himself these pockets of planting around the garden centre – his artistic eye at work.

He squeezes the secateurs in his right hand, pulling at the tangle with his left. Perhaps Joe'll visit next summer, and by then he can have it looking better. If he's still in business. He'd known about Maguires of course – had seen the articles in Leonard's Chronicle about planning rows and the campaign against out-of-town giants by pensioners in socks and sandals. 'We'll support you,' his regular customers said, like it was terminal. It was only a matter of time before some local hack called him 'plucky'.

He is pulling at vast canopies of growth, when his phone vibrates in his pocket. Three texts from Ruby.

> Oi, grumpy trousers. How you?

The second says:

> Taken out rage on petunias yet?

What's the bloody obsession with petunias?

> Fancy quiz at Crown 2nite? Starts 6pm.

He hurriedly texts back:

> Can't get off that early. Pint at Three Kings instead?

He puts his phone back in his pocket and goes at the stems again with the secateurs. He is standing awkwardly, one leg in the midst of the plant, pulling and clipping, when his phone vibrates. He curses and climbs out of the bed.

> R: Right u r. Shame. Would hve thrashed you on sport.
> B: Yeah right
> R: Ask me anything

Wearily, he sets his thumbs working.

> B: OK. Here is classic. Swedish boxer, world heavyweight champion. 1959?
> R: Gawd. Ingemar Johansson?
> B: r u on Wikipedia?
> R: Nope, I say Ingemar Johannson to anything Swedish
> B: Good work

He puts his phone back in his pocket and looks at the pile of stems he has thrown onto the path. His pocket vibrates. Bloody hell Ruby, he thinks. Two texts.

> Man at table 5 eating bogies behind FT. NICE.

Then the second one says:

> I love texting

He smiles to himself and begins to text back, just as Leonard walks up the path towards him carrying a mug of tea.

> I know you do

'Ooof,' Leonard says, taking a sip. 'What's that rose ever done to you?'

⌒

A ham is boiling, sending steam into the yellowish light of Max and Primrose's kitchen.

'How was the beet?' she asks, as he walks in from his wet day.

'Like wading through treacle.'

He takes off his Barbour and hangs it on the back of a chair where it drips onto the lino. She wonders if he'll do what he usually does – reserve the gloom for her. But the room is warm and filled with the sweet and smoky smell of the ham and she is happy, standing at the stove, stirring the pan. She wants things to stay nice, knows better than to ask why Joe took the beet job off him. Things'll change now, anyway.

'Dad hired a right hunk o'rust for the job,' says Max. 'You should've seen it. Bloody miracle we lifted it.'

'Well that's good then, that you lifted it in a day. That's one less pressure for the month.'

He has sat down on a chair, his legs spread wide and one forearm resting on the table top. If he'd walked into a bank that day, and shot all the people inside it, she'd have the fewest theories as to his state of mind in the run-up to the incident. They functioned on the practicalities, she and Max: things that needed fixing or buying; a family lunch to go to; starting a family because they were two years into marriage and the time was right. This evening, with a ham boiling and the kitchen's electric light yellow against the grey descending night outside, things are uncommonly content between them. She looks at him, her big man sat at the table. He is saying something else about the fodder beet. His black hair – long and curly – is wet from the rain. She never thought she'd have a big man like that of her own. And she suspects he never thought he'd have a woman for himself. And the achievement, for both of them, is a bolster in a world that seemed to have overlooked them. Like they'd planted their flag in the ground, just like other people. And now this news. She is bringing plates to the table and smiling to herself. She is rich with new information. And everything around her seems new, too: the table she's laying; their kitchen, which only this morning seemed all worn out. She's cleared away her tools – she knows how it annoys him, her wiring – because she wants nothing to spoil the moment. Ever since she'd found out, she'd been rehearsing how she'd tell him and his lines too, adjusting them until he said just the things she wanted.

'It's just a nightmare, is October,' he says over her thoughts. 'And this rain's not making anything easier.'

'No.'

'Is that from Alan Tench?' he says, peering up into the pan on the stove.

He might look at her differently, once he knows. He might touch her differently. With reverence. She's fizzing with it. Because the tingling was something – not just an idea in her imagination. A real thing had happened. And big things – things that changed the course of your life – well, they hardly ever happened.

'Yes,' she says. 'He brought it round yesterday.' She strokes a hand across his shoulder as she turns back towards the stove and he looks up, surprised.

'Looks nice and pink,' he says.

'It's a good one,' she says. 'It were positive. I did a test today and it were positive.'

'Really?'

She can see his mind whirring. There's a slight flicker in his eyeballs, left and right. The news is going in.

'Really?' he says to her. 'It were really positive?'

'It was.' And she waits for him to get up, like he might have done in a film, dance her round the kitchen, his hands on her hips. Or hold her face in his hands and kiss her with a passion he's never expressed before.

'Well then,' says Max, and he is smiling, she'll give him that, but he's still seated. He has sat up straighter and he begins to pat the table top with the flat of his hand. Pat pat pat. Agitated.

'Well,' he says again.

'Yes?'

'I'll ring dad and tell 'im. They'll be cock-a-hoop.'

'I'm not three months yet,' she says. 'You're not supposed to tell anyone until you're three months.'

'Yes, but I'm telling dad.'

'Wait a little bit, will ye? It's very early.'

'When then?'

'Next month. Tell 'im next month.'

'Alright then. I'm going for a wash.'

'OK,' she says. 'Tea's ten minutes.'

He stops in the doorway. 'Prim?' he says. 'It's good in't it?'

'Yes,' she says.

Primrose stands at the counter, sawing slices of bread. The loaf collapses under her hand. He's pleased, she can see that, and maybe that should be enough – a husband pleased to be having a bairn. She sits down at the kitchen table, her mind readjusting itself. It won't be quite the together thing, not like she'd thought. And the disappointment soaks in at the base of her, like yard mud. It'll be a private thing, like all her other private things. This is not us, not really. It's me. And she closes down, as she has so often before, not in a petulant way, but just practical, so the nerve endings aren't exposed. Like insulation tape round a wire.

Some intuitive impulse made her take the test. She'd gone to the chemist in her lunch hour. The shop was deserted and Karen Marshall was looking bored, sat on a stool behind the counter, rearranging nail polishes. Primrose's heart sank when she realised the Clear Blues were right next to Karen, so she'd have to ask. 'Can I have a test, Karen?' she'd said.

Karen had made a point of hiding the test in a bag. 'There you go, Prim,' she'd said, over-mouthing the words in a low voice. So Primrose doesn't know why she's bothered trying to stop Max from telling Joe. Thanks to Karen Marshall, the whole dale would know by morning.

Max walks out of the kitchen and hangs his fleece on the finial at the bottom of the stairs. He takes the stairs two at a time, his heart pounding, to the small bathroom where the door is ajar, its glass panels etched with daisies.

He leans over the sink and looks up at his face, eager to see if it might look different now he's set to become a father. He is smiling still, stupidly, like the joy might burst out of him. He sees Joe's beady black eyes crinkle with pleasure. 'A baby! Ann, Ann! A baby! Did you hear that? Well lad, that's grand.' And he'd get out a bottle of fizz from the larder, one they were saving for Christmas, and he'd pop it. Because bairns, that was what the Hartles did well; that was their strength. He'd seen it in the photos and in all the stories Ann and Joe were forever telling, when they looked at each other in that particular way, full of nostalgia. 'Remember, Ann, that party for Max? You did that smashing picnic in the barn. It was sweltering that day. And we cooled off in Little Beck. Bartholomew went right under, d'you remember?' 'Don't,' Ann had said, patting her collar-bones, 'it still makes me go cold.' But she was smiling at Joe. Now Max is bringing them full circle, he is the first and he will bring it all back for them. He turns off the tap. Joe was always saying that bairns turn things around for a man. Fire up the heart. He could do with some of that. Max scoops up water in his palms, sloshing it over his face and onto the floor. When he looks up again, steam from the hot tap is erasing his reflection, so that only his neck remains.

'I've got to go and see him next week,' Ann says over the roof of Lauren's car. They are outside the George in Morpeth-le-Dale. They slam their doors and their feet crunch on gravel in the dark night.

'Who? Barry Jordan?' says Lauren.

'Yes. God I'm dreading it. He always makes me feel guilty that man, as if buying a fruit loaf from Greggs were some cardinal sin. Lord forgive me, I weakened over a peg bag in Coopers!'

'Hang on,' says Lauren, stopping Ann with a hand on her arm. 'You've got a new peg bag?'

'Drawstring. Fully lined.'

'Be still my beating heart,' says Lauren, and then she's pressing forward again and pushing open the pub door. Ann wishes she could delay her, keep the conversation just the two of them a moment longer, so that Lauren could tut, like she does, and say, 'That Barry Jordan. 'E wouldn't know a peg bag if he were smothered with one.'

But Lauren has gone in and pushed open the second inner door and Ann is already faced with the warmth and noise of the George and all the team over at the bar. Lauren leads the way, Ann behind her like some cade lamb. Lauren says hello to the team: Elaine Henderson, smart twin-set; Mo Dorkin, short and round, with a gold tooth; Pat Branning, tall, face as open as a hay barn. (You could never dislike a woman who smiled as much as that.) Other ladies, whose names Ann doesn't know, are gathered behind Elaine. Ann hangs back in a cloud of Lauren's perfume, with a hand up to any attempted embrace, saying 'I've got a bit of a cold,' to which a couple of the women say 'Poor you'.

'Right,' says Lauren to the assembled group. 'What are we playing? Round the clock or double-in, double-out? Has anyone spoken to the George team?'

'Actually,' one of the ladies says, but then she stops and there is a general shuffling in the group. 'Elaine thought . . .'

'I thought I'd have a bash at captain for the first round,' says Elaine, with military briskness. You'd not want to find yourself on the wrong side of Elaine. Nor Lauren Blakely, for that matter.

Elaine continues, 'You won't mind, will ye, Lauren – letting someone else have a turn?'

'I thought we were getting a league together,' says Lauren, squaring up. 'We've some very inexperienced players,' she says, casting a look at Ann. 'It's important the captain knows who to play.'

'Captaincy's not been decided yet,' says Elaine Henderson, with some force. 'And as you were late . . .'

'Five minutes,' snorts Lauren.

Ann hears in her head the whistling music from that Clint Eastwood spaghetti western. What was it now – *High Noon*? *The Good, the Bad and the Ugly*? That'd be about right. The ladies shift again, like some restive herd. Pat is smiling with all her face, as if this alone might smooth things.

'Double-in, double-out then, everyone?' says Elaine. 'I need eight ladies who can hit the board.'

'Might as well sit down,' Lauren whispers to Ann. 'She'll not pick us for this round.'

Ann exhales with relief.

They buy a round of drinks and she, Mo and Pat follow Lauren to a table. They sit in a line along the banquette, watching women gather in front of the dartboard on the opposite side of the room. The floor is a busy swirl of burgundy carpet, the dark wood pillars dripping with horse brasses.

'Here, Hayley Barnsdale's up,' says Mo. They all look across the floor to an attractive woman in a purple mohair sweater. 'Found love off the Internet, so Karen Marshall says. Madly in love, by all accounts.'

Ann and Lauren shoot a glance at each other.

Mo and Karen from the chemist: the espionage dream team, their periscopes in every bedroom across the dale. There were al-Qaida cells less vigilant than those two.

'Gone on holiday an' everything,' Mo is saying. 'Greece, Karen said. Happen she left her daughter behind. She stopped with the Richardsons a couple of nights, so I hear.'

'You'd know all about it, would ye?' says Lauren.

'Just what I heard,' says Mo. 'Only seven, she is. Well, it's not right, is it?'

'That's it, Mo,' says Lauren. 'You suck the lifeblood out of others' happiness.'

Bit harsh, thinks Ann, watching the two of them. Only human, to be interested in folks' lives. But she can see what it is about Mo that rankles. It's the glee. The feeling that if you were bleeding to death in the street, she'd have more to say about the price of your shoes.

They get in another two rounds, during which time Ann asks Pat about her children. Her son has motor neurone disease. That ever-present smile seems heroic now. All these braveries, Ann thinks, that are hidden in people's lives.

Lauren asks Ann about Ivy Dawson's mobility scooter.

'Don't get me started. That woman's a liability,' says Ann, but a gasp is rippling round the room and all eyes are on the floor. Lauren is straining up out of her seat. She begins a low incantation, through her teeth.

'Don't put Brenda up. Don't put Brenda up. Don't put Brenda up.'

They all look across the room.

'What's happening?' Ann asks Mo.

'It's getting towards the end of the round is all. Scores are low so it's harder to hit the points home. Even the best players —' Mo stops and throws her hands into her lap. 'Well, that's in then. Might as well go home.'

Brenda Farley, who is eighty if she's a day, has taken to the floor. Her toe is on the yellow line, a dart in her hand. She is four foot two and so stooped by a dowager's hump that she can barely see the board. They all watch as Brenda strains her eyes upwards, her brow furrowing hard into horizontal pencil pleats, and then it's as if the stoop gets the better of her and her gaze returns to the floor.

'Oh god, I can't watch,' says Lauren. She has her hand up over her eyes, with two fingers parted to peer through.

'It's just cruel is that,' says Pat.

'There's no point watching,' says Lauren angrily. 'She'll be all week just trying to lift that neck.' She turns to Ann. 'Let's talk about summat else. Have you brought the ewes down for tupping?'

'Not yet,' says Ann. 'Next week or two.'

'What's tupping?' asks Pat.

'It's when you put the rams in to serve the ewes,' says Ann, grateful to be the keeper of some knowledge at last. 'A tup is what we call a ram, you see, for breeding.'

Ann's last words are drowned out by a loud gasp, then another, deeper than the last, and then cheers and clapping as the room erupts, free and strong. Brenda Farley is smiling, though she has allowed her gaze to return floorward. Other team members pat her on the hump.

'Well I never,' says Lauren.

'I don't believe it,' says Pat.

'Just shows you,' says Mo.

'What? What happened?' asks Ann.

'Two doubles and a bully, that's what happened,' says Lauren. 'I'd best congratulate Elaine.'

'Don't choke on it,' says Ann.

☙

'A gimmer,' says Ruby. She takes a fulsome slug of pale ale. 'Hang on, I know this: a gimmer is a female lamb, sold for breeding.'

Bartholomew raises his pint to her. 'Very good. And what's a mule gimmer?'

30

'Oooh, give me a minute. A mule gimmer is . . . a cross-bred lamb. Not a pedigree.'

'And with Swaledales we cross with?'

'The Blue-Faced Leicester!'

'My work here is done,' he says, clinking his pint glass against hers.

'So that email was from your mum,' she says. 'Why didn't you just say?'

He shrugs. Takes another gulp of his pint.

'She's worried then,' says Ruby.

He nods. 'Not the best time to be a farmer.' He is looking out across the room: stripped-oak floors; tongue-and-groove bar painted 'heritage' green; industrial lights. The Three Kings on Cathedral Way is a pub with an eye firmly on itself. Not like the boozers back home.

'So, you're still working on that main bed,' she says.

'Yep.'

'Run this by me again. You're putting more plants in the ground.'

He hasn't told her how much this central bed – his new project – means to him. When his mind is idling, he thinks about it: sketching out the ribbons of oriental poppies, aquilegias and verbascum; the great drifts of alliums and tulipa 'spring green'.

'Just in case someone tries to do something crazy, like buy them?' Ruby is saying.

'I know it doesn't make sense.'

'Is capitalism ready for a visionary such as yourself?'

'I often ask myself the same question.'

'I suppose,' she says, 'you'll be showing off plants to their best effect – showing what they look like in a border.'

'It's not just that. It's what I'm into. Leonard thinks it's point-less, too.'

'Leonard thinks everything's pointless.'

'There's something about plants in those mean little nine-centimetre pots. I want to see them expand.'

'Can you afford it?' she says.

'Arh, businesses don't expect to make much in the first couple of years. If I really want kerching, it won't be from plants, anyway.'

'What d'ye mean?'

'It's the other guff that makes money – your gazebos, those nasty solar lights, plastic toadstools.'

'How depressing,' she says, with feeling. Ruby says everything with feeling. 'I mean, what you're doing with that bed is so much more special.'

He says nothing.

Ruby says, 'I think you should ditch the horrible knick-knacks and go for it on the main bed. Do what you love – find a way.'

He drains his glass.

'What about if you made it a destination – a place people visit and hang out in? So what you would become is a beautiful garden with a nursery attached.'

'Beautiful gardens don't make money.'

'Why not? You could make something really brilliant, Bartholomew. That old lean-to – the glass one – that'd make a great café. Vines in the ceiling, sand on the floor, newspapers on wooden tables. And if you got rid of all the plastic crap, that corner of your warehouse could be a farm shop. Bung in a kids' playground in the lower field.'

'All that takes money. I've got no money, Rube. I've got bank loans up to my eyeballs and piss-all income. That's why the fishing gnomes have to stay.'

She slumps back, jutting out her lower lip. 'Lottery maybe.'

He stands up.

'No wonder you don't have a name,' she says. 'You don't really know what it is yet.'

'I'm going to put some music on. See if I can inject some atmosphere into this place.'

The pints roll on, Ruby downing them as they come. She's a terrible drinker – can't take it at all, because she drinks so seldom, so she soon starts to sway with it, putting her head on his shoulder, laughing too loudly. She was right about a name for the place. In the two years since opening, he'd been functioning under the trade name 'Garden Centre', always with a view to rebranding it eventually – a strategy that drew uniform derision from anyone with experience in business. His mother kept suggesting 'Have a Hartle', which kept him awake at night.

'Have a Hartle! Christ, that's bad!' shouts Ruby, slamming her pint down on the table so that a wave of it sloshes over the side of the glass.

'I know,' he says.

'We can do better 'an that.'

'I was thinking something youthful and urban – just one word,' he says. 'You know, like Planted. Excepted that's taken.'

'Or Soiled.' She laughs. 'Come off it, Bartholomew. One word is pretentious.'

They look out across the bar in silence.

'Worth a Trowel?' says Ruby. 'Pot Luck? All You Need Is Lush?'

'If you're not going to be serious . . .'

'I'm just thinking out loud. Let's think about your stock.'

'Well, um, there's some hard landscaping, you know, paving stones and stuff, bricks, gravel, compost. In the warehouse there's fertilisers and plant food – like fish, blood and bone.'

'I don't think fish, blood and bone is going to draw in the crowds. Tools?' She burps with her mouth shut. ''Scuse me.'

'Spades, forks, aerators, hedge trimmers. This isn't getting us anywhere. And anyway, this is about the tenth time we've gone through it.'

'Maybe we should be thinking elegant rather than cool. It's on Ray Street, Ray of Hope! Hoe Ray Me?'

'Oh god, this is rubbish,' he says.

'No, hang on. Alive and Digging!'

'Alive and Digging?'

'As in the U2 song.'

'Simple Minds actually. No one's going to get that.'

'P'raps not. Dig . . . dig . . . Can You Dig It? Dig When You're Winning! The Dug Out. Diggery Pokery.'

'Please stop.'

'Thanks very mulch.' Ruby is now slurring. And hiccuping.

'Let's get you home,' he says, standing and putting on his padded jacket.

Ann sits heavily down in the passenger seat and enjoys the support against the base of her back. Lauren's car is always immaculate. Still smells of car showrooms even though it's not new by a long chalk. Nissan-something. Not like the fifteen-year-old draughty thing Joe drives. You could be sure of a cold bum and poor visibility in a Hartle vehicle.

'Amazing performance from Brenda,' she says.

'You're telling me,' says Lauren, peering at the road. 'That woman's barely hit the board in a year, and suddenly . . .' She pulls out slowly, both hands on the top of the steering wheel, her body hunched over it. 'Come to think of it, that woman's barely *seen* the board in a year, never mind hit it.'

Ann listens to the rhythmic thrub of Lauren's windscreen-wipers and looks over at her friend, whose face is outlined with a greenish glow from the dashboard. Loose flesh on her cheeks, sagging below the jawline. Crow's feet about the eyes. God we look old, she thinks.

'How's your kitchen coming along?'

'Oh Lord it's slow,' says Lauren, craning forward again, flicking the indicator for a right turn. 'Trouble is, when they're there – the builders I mean – you can't wait to see the back of them for all the dust. And then they're gone again and you're cursing because it's all half done and I'm dying to put all me things away. Sorry, I can really get boring on this one.'

'You let rip love.'

'Well, since you insist. Eric's no help.'

'You do surprise me.'

Lauren laughs. 'Honestly, that man could drive you to drink. He never talks seriously to the builders, always leaves that to me. He's their best friend, cracking jokes, charming their socks off. Then, soon as they're gone, he goes around the kitchen picking at this and that. "They haven't put these hinges on properly. That tiling should be done by now." As if I'm his foreman and I should be following him around with a pad and pen.'

They've had this conversation, or versions of it, for twenty-odd years. They have this saying, she and Lauren, which they say in unison. 'Don't put your husband on a pedestal. He'll only want dusting.'

'It'll be done soon,' says Ann, 'and then you'll love it. You'll forget this bit.'

'I know, but I tell you, never again. Anyway don't let me go on. How are the boys?'

'Their campaign of secrecy continues,' says Ann. 'If they told me owt, they'd have to kill me. Bartholomew is too far away, and Max . . .'

'Not far enough?'

Ann laughs.

'It's always the way,' says Lauren.

'Joe says we have to support Max, pay him enough so he can start a family. But we haven't got a brass farthing. We don't draw salaries ourselves.'

'Well good for Joe,' says Lauren. 'You were always a mean beggar.'

'I am tight, it's true. But why can't Max go and find other work – shearing or labouring or summat? Supplement his income? Joe glories in it – you know, that Max is working the farm with him when most sons would wash their hands of it – but where's the glory in a son as can't think for himself?'

'Arh, he loves those boys, Ann,' says Lauren, glancing at her then back to the road. 'Your Joe, he loves those boys more than any father I've seen. Bartholomew's doing well, in't he? And you liked that girlfriend of his, Ruby, when he brought her back.'

'I s'pose. He's my great white hope, is Bartholomew. But he doesn't tell us anything.'

'That's boys,' says Lauren.

'Ruby's smashing – Joe and I both think so – but he's not marrying her. They've been together a year now and to start with it were all love's young dream but they seem to have gone off the boil.'

'These things do. He's still young.'

'Thirty-two? I had two boys by that age. This generation, they don't commit to anything.'

They have pulled into Lauren's drive and she is pulling on the handbrake. Neither makes a move to get out of the car.

'Well, it's different now. Harder for 'em,' says Lauren.

'And as for Max, I don't know how that marriage works. She's such a pudding.'

'Raw sexual chemistry I expect,' says Lauren and Ann laughs.

'On that note, I think I'll get off. Thanks for the lift.'

'Thursday night for flower-arranging?' says Lauren.

Ann has heaved herself out of the passenger seat. She is stooping to look at her friend who is still seated, gathering her handbag and keys.

'It's a date,' says Ann, then closes the passenger door.

Ruby stumbles on the cobbles of Cathedral Way, under the orange street lamps. Stumbles over and into him, and then drags on his arm. He marches her purposefully up the High Street and past the Theatre Royal. There are still plenty of people about – it's not yet 10 p.m. They've not eaten, apart from a steady flow of crisps and peanuts. No wonder Ruby is rolling.

'I couldn't do it,' she says, hanging on his arm.

'Do what?' he asks. He puts his hand in his pocket so his arm becomes a loop for her to hold onto.

'Set up on my own. Don't think I'm brave enough.'

'Well, it's not for everyone,' he says.

'What are you saying? You think it's beyond me? Good for nothing 'cept serving sandwiches?' Black spidery flicks of mascara have smudged onto her cheekbones, among the brown freckles.

'Course not. What would you do – if you left the café?' he says.

'Dunno. Cooking.'

'You're good at that.'

They walk on, Bartholomew setting the pace. She's a dead weight on his arm, uncomfortable and tiring. They reach Theobald Road.

'Give us your key,' he says and she feels about in her bag for what seems like minutes. She has her feet apart to steady her, but her body sways. She gives him the key and they walk further up Theobald Road.

'So that's what the café idea was all about,' he says.

'Eh?'

'A café at my place – for you to run?'

'I didn't think of that,' she says. 'You want to go into business w' me cos I'm so clever!' She puts her arms around his neck while he tries to open her front door with her key.

'I don't think so,' he says, low and stern. 'I'm not going into business with anyone. I'm on me own. That's how I like it.'

'Jeeeeez, alright,' says Ruby and they fall in, tumbling into her dark hallway.

In the echo of the hall as they clatter up the communal stairs to her flat, he says, 'Watch yourself, Rube.'

She stops on the stairs, looking at her shoes, with one arm on the banister. He is behind her.

'Why are you so paranoid?' she says, suddenly sober and angry. 'You always think I want something from ye, like I'll be sticking a pin in the condoms next. You're not that much of a catch Bartholomew.'

She takes her key off him roughly and opens the front door to her flat, leaving it open for him to follow.

Her place is dark, except for the fairy lights which she never turns off. In the gloom, the purples, pinks and oranges from the cushions and rugs glow, as if they've stumbled into some over-stuffed grotto. She throws her bag down on the sofa and takes her coat off. She is shambling towards the bedroom, prising off her shoes as she goes. He steadies her and leads her to the bed. She sits, then lies her head on the pillow and he lifts her stockinged legs. Her eyes are shut. He hears a snore ring out.

Bartholomew wants to go home but doesn't feel he can leave her just yet. He's been experiencing this more and more lately – a gap between what he should do and what he wants to do – and he wonders if this is how love ought to feel. He goes to sit in the wicker chair in the corner of the room, beside the window where net curtains are filtering the orange of a street lamp, its massive bulb just beyond the glass. He watches Ruby sleep, one hand to his chin, the other on his knee. He sees her turn over with all her body, hip up, face down, and as she does so, she farts.

He'd met Ruby a year ago, at the tea room on Market Street where she works as a waitress. He'd begun to stop there on his way home from the garden centre in a bid to avoid his cold empty flat.

Bartholomew had sat at a table in the darkest corner and watched her as she served the other customers.

Everything about her was rounded: her little belly; the soft slopes of her arms; the milky skin on her chest which rose high with her breath. He was magnetised by the fullness of her. When she came to his table and said – in a gentle Leeds accent which he hadn't been expecting – 'What can I get ye?' he'd said, involuntarily, 'Can I take you out?'

She had laughed, her apple face creasing up with kindness and delight. 'Let's just deal with your lunch order first, shall we?'

'Where do you live?' she'd asked later, when she'd joined him at his table.

'Theobald Road.'

'Now you're being creepy.'

'Why? You asked me where I live!'

'You can't live on Theobald Road,' she said.

'Erm, I can and I do.'

The sight of his frown appeared to make her laugh and this, in turn, seemed to make him happy.

'You are talking about Theobald Road, as in off the London Road?'

'Is there another one?' he'd said.

'Oh Lord.'

'Why, where do you live?'

'Guess.'

'Theobald Road?' he asked.

She nodded and they both burst into laughter, not because it was especially funny – he found it scary – but in part he thought they were laughing because they hadn't even mentioned their Yorkshire accents, that they were two people from another place, a shared landscape, and here they were in a southern cathedral town and living on the same street, and that their voices were each a homecoming.

'What number are you?' she said when they'd stopped laughing.

'Twenty-two. And you?'

'Two.'

'Next to Mr Shah!'

'My new best friend,' she'd said.

'Not just the same street but the same side of the same street.'

'Are you sure you still want to take me out?'

What had surprised him most about their early courtship was its wholeheartedness. He drank her in, unstintingly, telling her he wanted her all the time and she, to his surprise, was neither terrified nor repulsed. She reciprocated and this reciprocity, together with the ease with which she accepted her appetites, was a revelation to him.

In those early weeks, on days when he didn't stop at the café because he was working late, he would get off his bicycle at the bottom of Theobald Road and wheel up the street, wondering if her light would be on. He found himself filled with nervous excitement as he looked up at the second-floor window and then he'd see it lit yellow and the excitement in his stomach would bubble up higher, until he laughed at himself and partly at his own happiness because why would seeing a light on in an upstairs window make him feel so overjoyed?

They didn't spend many nights apart in those days. More often than not, Bartholomew would wheel his bicycle up to his own flat at number 22, prop it in the hallway and go in to get changed, all the while telling himself he was tired: it would be great to read a book or watch some television alone after so much time together. But he'd find himself putting on a clean pair of cords and carefully selecting a shirt and sweater. Then he'd momentarily sit on his sofa, his hands on his knees.

Five minutes later he'd be lolloping down the street. The bell would jangle as he opened the door to Mr Shah's shop. You had to inch sideways through the excessively packed shelves because Mr Shah stocked everything that human existence had ever required: nail clippers; bake-in-the-oven croissants; Phillips-head screwdrivers; fabric conditioner; dog food; nappies.

'Something for Ruby?' Mr Shah would say. The word Ruby sounded even more beautiful when curled around Mr Shah's rich voice.

'Yes,' said Bartholomew.

'She likes the Turkish Delight,' said Mr Shah, leaning forward and over the counter and pointing downward at the chocolate section. 'Fry's.'

'Right, thank you.' Bartholomew grabbed three bars and a bottle of white wine and headed for Ruby's front door.

He was always welcomed, back then. Her face, when she opened the door, was gentle and quietly amused.

'Thought you might need sustenance,' he'd say, or some such other opening gambit. On this occasion, he opened his carrier bag and she'd peered over at what was inside.

'You'll be wanting a hand with those,' she'd said.

'That's why I came to you.'

'You'd best come in.'

She was so unlike his last girlfriend, Maud, who liked to swim in cold rivers in her Speedo suit. 'Show me a river, even in the dead of winter,' she'd say, 'and I want to dive in. So bracing.' He remembered Maud's supermarket own-brand face cream and shower gel. 'It's all the same stuff,' she'd lectured. 'You just pay for the packaging.'

Ruby, though, was all for warmth and pretty packaging. 'Ooh look,' she'd cry, pulling him back as they strolled past a department-store window, her happy face reflected among pink and gold lettering and stripes. 'Lovely! I'm just going to nip in.'

In the heat of his new feelings, when they had been together about three months, he took her out to dinner and over the pop-padoms said, 'Rube, I think we should move in together,' and she had clapped her hands and stroked his face with her palm.

Meeting Ruby, it had provoked life's force in him. There were suddenly no limits to his potential. He wanted to see exhibitions, new films, to try new foods. He found himself loving her with every fibre that he had, like he'd been dunked in it and it was like a pulse, or the rolling forward of an ocean wave.

They visited her family in Leeds, and his school friend Alan, who'd moved there with his new wife Bridget. 'Blimey, you're a changed man,' Al had said, lying on the sofa with his arms behind his head. 'It's the real thing, in't it?' In Winstanton, he and Ruby clung to each other, their social lives embryonic. She had her book group, he joined the squash club at the leisure centre; all of it, at times, a strain. Their intimacy became a lifeboat and even this he came to resent, as if his dependency were some fault of hers.

The moving in had never happened. She'd been so excited, she'd started slowing in front of estate agents' windows, her arm looped through his. Talking about where they'd put the Christmas tree. Maybe it was her enthusiasm that made him pull back, as if someone had to stop them both. Gradually, it became part of the dynamic between them, flaring up at every turn, when she would say 'When?' and 'I might not wait for ye, ye know' and 'Who d'ye think ye are, George Clooney?' in a mock-teasing way. Or else she'd look really sad and he felt he was failing her. He would say 'Soon' and 'When things are more settled' or 'One day'. Occasionally, they really fought about it. He would find himself shouting, 'Stop pushing. You're always pushing!' And he could see he was breaking her heart.

At any rate, after that first forward impulse, something had simply stopped. His caution returned, like the desire to stay in a small room because the big room's just too big.

She has been snoring for half an hour. He lets himself out of her flat and walks back to his.

꩜

That could be me, thinks Max, watching the auction hands hefting sheep into pens. Sweating it for tuppence, or breaking my back on another man's land. But instead here he is, flat-capped like Joe, stood next to him at the Slingsby fence, with one foot on the lower rung. He can't stop smiling on the inside. Because everything's set to change. The prospect of telling Joe his news is all before him, that sweetness undented. He can hardly hold himself back, but he's also savouring the anticipation of it. He tries to pull the corner of his mouth down, but it seems to make the smile more purposeful. The cap shields him at least.

'Here, what are you so pleased about?' Joe asks. 'These prices aren't funny.'

'Not funny at all,' says Max.

'Tell us now,' says Joe. 'If you've won the lottery, I'd like my share.'

'You'll know soon enough. I promised Prim.'

Joe rubs Max's back. 'You're a good lad,' he says, and he doesn't ask more.

Up and down the pens, men stand talking, looking down at the lots. And beyond them, the fields roll away, the mustard-yellow leaves on the trees now starting to shed.

Max and Joe stand together in the circle of men surrounding the auctioneer, and he thinks he can see the other farmers regarding them. Father and son. It was a rare thing to see these days, something to envy. He's puffed up, standing next to his father, because Joe is admired among farmers. Has the knack for breeding sheep, everyone round these parts said so. Always did well at the shows and he's had his share of prize tups that could

44

go for thousands – the ones with strong legs and a sweet head. At least, they did when times were better.

Joe has his eyes on the sheep that are being herded into the pen before them, where the auctioneer stands in his white coat. They run, whipped along occasionally by the auctioneer's assistant.

The auctioneer starts his song of numbers: '37, 37, 37 bid, 39, where are you 39? 39 bid, 39, 39. Sign away.'

A ripple goes around the group. Joe shakes his head.

'Thirty-nine quid. Jesus,' he says. 'Beauties they were, too. Did ye see? That's bad luck, Dugmore.'

'Never seen it so bad,' says Dugmore, who farms over in Westerdale. 'There were store lambs selling last week for eighteen pound. Eighteen pound! Not worth the feed.'

The sold sheep are whipped out through the gate, some jumping three feet in the air as they run.

'Ours is next,' says Max. 'I'll go round.'

He stands beside the pens of their mule gimmers, ready to usher them in. They will run around the perimeter fence, auctioneer at their centre in his doctor's coat, while the farmers along the fence judge them, bidding with a tiny nudge of a forefinger, which the auctioneer won't miss. And Max knows that Joe will feel it in every fibre – the murmuring between his fellow farmers while his animals run the fence.

'That's a bad lot,' says Joe an hour or more later, when the cheques are out and they're settling themselves in the Land Rover.

'Maybe we shouldn't ha' bought them new tups,' ventures Max.

'Arh, but they were beauties, weren't they? And going for a song. Let's hope the mule stores do better next week,' says Joe, lifting himself off the seat and adjusting his trousers. He sighs as he puts the key in the ignition. 'If we can get thirty pound a lamb for the stores then at least the rent's covered.'

Max looks out of the passenger window while Joe takes off his cap and turns to throw it on the back seat.

'In't it glorious, the day?' Max says.

'Are you on the happy pills or summat?'

And the smile bursts out of Max once more, breaking up his face with its unruly joy.

'Come on, lad. Spill the beans.'

And then he can't wait. Not a moment longer. Even though he'd promised Prim. This moment, here with Joe, matters more.

'Prim's going to have a baby.'

'Ha ha!' Joe shouts, leaning over the handbrake to clap him on the shoulder, shaking him. 'Hee hee! Really? Is it true?'

'It is, dad.'

Joe pulls Max's body over roughly for a hug.

'Well done you, lad. Well done you. Wait till I tell your mother.'

'It's early days,' says Max in a half-hearted attempt to dampen Joe's cheer when in fact he's bathing in it. 'I promised Prim I wouldn't say owt.' Joe is beaming at him, and this time, for the first time, it's for something he's done, not because the beet got lifted or the weather was in their favour.

'Ah, that's grand,' Joe is saying, leaning back in his seat. 'A bairn. Best time of your life. It were the best time of my life, when you two were tiddlers.'

He ruffles Max's hair again, gently this time, and Max thinks to remember this moment. He has never before felt such warmth spread through him, right from his belly. For the first time, he's won himself an accolade. All those average school reports; and him never breaking out, like Bartholomew did, to get a job elsewhere – Max had begun to feel lost in the smallness and sameness of his life and now, here was his father, the man who mattered more than any on earth, pinning a rosette to his chest like he was the prize tup. This is what I've been missing, he thinks: the sun on my face.

'It's going to be the best tupping yet,' he says.

'It is, it is,' says Joe. 'You're a good lad, Max. I always knew you'd land on your feet. When will it come?'

'May the twentieth or thereabouts. We'll know more at the scan.'

'And Prim? She alright?'

'She's grand,' says Max. 'Might even pull back on the wiring now there's something else to occupy her.'

'Don't bank on it,' says Joe, laughing.

Max closes his eyes, lays his head back on the headrest. 'Might need a pay rise,' he says, 'if I'm to have a bairn in the house.'

Joe starts the car.

NOVEMBER

— Tupping, and the feeling of looking forward —

'Look at 'im,' says Max. 'He's a look on his face like he's off to creosote a fence, not sow his wild oats.'

'Less of the wild,' says Joe. 'Good tup is that – I've paperwork to prove it.'

They are leaning on a gate, taking a break after a period of hard work. They have driven the ewes down off the fell to the in-bye, dipped them and chosen the right ones for each tup. Joe maintains he has an eye for it – putting himself into the mind of the ram and what he might fancy. Max thinks it's mostly guess-work but he'd never say as much. They have marshalled the ewes into pens of fifty apiece. Most of them – three-hundred-odd – are being put to the Blue-Faced Leicester rams.

Max watches one now as he mounts a ewe and begins thrust-ing into her. Something about his blinking eyes, looking out to the side, gives him a dogged expression.

'Any road,' Joe is saying, 'if you had to serve fifty-odd ladies in a fortnight, you might look a bit world-weary an' all.'

'I'd be ready for action, me,' says Max. 'Prepared to answer me calling.'

'How very manly of ye.'

'She doesn't look like she's having much fun either,' says Max.

'Fun doesn't come into it. How many's he done?'

They look at the ewes' backs. The tup has paint on his chest and his raddle marks are left on the ewes he's served.

'About five,' says Max. 'He's not letting up. Look at that – he's a good tup this one.'

Max looks out across the in-bye. A faint mist swirls around the wintry trees which have only a fluttering of leaves left on them. The bracken is crisp and brown and thick with pheasant. Nowhere in the world, he thinks, more beautiful than this place.

'I've been thinking,' says Joe. 'What you said, about a pay rise.'

'Arh, I didn't mean it, dad.'

'No, no, it's your time. Anyway, I've been thinking on, with you having a bairn an' all. It'll be the making of you, son. I think we should look at you taking over the farm – proper like. Build it up for you and for your son to take over.'

Max hangs his head low, between his shoulders.

'It's what I've always wanted,' says Joe looking into the field. 'To feel the place will be passed on – that it won't come to nothing. All that work – dad sweating his heart out – well, he'd be right pleased.'

Max says what he feels he ought to say: 'I didn't mean . . . I know how tight things are.' His words hang in the air like wet washing.

'It's your time,' says Joe. 'I'm getting too old for this game. I've not got the fight in me. But you – this'll be the making of you. Children make it all . . . Give you a purpose.'

Max feels the pleasure run through him again – that ahead of him, out of the ether, would come his agency in life. He just has to wait for it to happen. He wonders why he didn't do this sooner.

'How d'ye think Bartholomew'll take it?' he says to Joe, his concern a show.

'Ah, Bartholomew expects it,' says Joe. 'He'll have to take it on the chin. He chose to leave. And that's fine. But you can't have both. And another thing. I think we should replace the John Deere. I was going to wait till times were better, but a new tractor'd set you up, wouldn't ye say?'

'It would. If there's money for it.'

'We'll find a way. Beg, borrow an' steal. Come on, can we tell your mother now? It's been murder keeping it from her.' They turn to begin the walk back to the farmhouse, then Joe stops. 'Let's keep quiet about the tractor though,' he says, and he laughs out loud. 'No need to knock her out, eh.' And Max laughs.

'After lambing, too,' Joe says as they walk towards the farmhouse, 'well, that's perfect timing. Perfect.'

Next day, Ann sits on the chair with the wooden arms, her handbag on her knee. Beside her on the floor is a plastic bag, slipping with loose paperwork. Before her is Barry Jordan's desk, behind it his empty chair and beyond that a mushroom-coloured blind, its slats hanging at broken angles. She leans down and gathers the handles of the plastic bag, tries to marshal it upright but it slides down again onto the floor.

'I know what you're going to say,' she says, putting a hand up comically as Barry Jordan enters the room. 'Book that Caribbean cruise Ann! You deserve it.'

'Not quite,' says Barry, as he edges behind his desk. 'I need to go through this change in the subsidies with you. You're aware, I assume . . .' He pauses while he rifles through some papers on his desk. 'Ah yes, here we are. You're aware that the single farm payment comes into force this year.'

He hands her a sheet of paper. She looks down at it: *The Single Farm Payment Explained*. The rest is a blur.

'It's not going to do you any favours,' says Barry.

'We still get a payment though – we've got plenty of hectares, ha'n't we?'

'You have, but you'll not do as well as under the headage payments. Used to be you could farm the brown envelope – keep more sheep and you got more money. But now, with a per hectare payment you'll be down by . . . I've got the figures somewhere. Hilary's got them – she'll give you a breakdown to take away. Trouble is, moorland gets the lowest rate there is, and eighty acres of yours is rough grazing, is it not?'

She gazes at the sheet of paper without reading it. 'Someone up there doesn't like farmers. That's how it feels.'

'I can get you a couple more environmental subsidies – stewardships and such like, but even so,' says Barry.

'Even so what?'

'The best you can hope for is to break even. And you'll be lucky to do that.'

'Can we keep going till lambing?' asks Ann.

'You can keep going as long as you like. I'm just giving you the full picture. You're not the first I've had to have this conversation with and you won't be the last. These are very tough times indeed. I suggest you look at getting jobs off the farm. I know a chap over in Farndale, runs the fire station on the side.'

She thinks to mention that they're soon to be in their sixties, that they're dog-tired, but she worries it would sound like whingeing.

'I know it's hard,' says Barry. 'I've seen that many farmers go under, even take their own lives.'

'Jesus Barry, I don't think we've come to that.' She pauses. 'Our assets, if we sold – what would it get us?'

'You've five hundred Swaledales is it?'

She nods.

'You might be best off hanging on to them at the minute – hope prices recover. Housing market is mad. Goes up every month.'

He clasps his hands together on the desk, smiles at her – a pitying sort of smile.

'Right,' she says. 'Well, I'm sure things'll pick up. Where would we be if farmers gave up every time the going got tough?'

'Where indeed?' says Barry, standing and flattening his tie with one hand to prevent it dipping in his coffee as he leans over the desk to shake her hand. 'I'll help in any way I can, Ann. As you know, my services are paid for by the NFU and that arrangement will continue for as long as you need it.'

'Thank you,' says Ann, rising, realising that she is being ushered out. She turns in the narrow space between her chair and the desk, clutching her handbag and stooping to pick up the carrier bag. 'Right, yes.'

At the door, she raises the plastic bag. 'My receipts. What should I do with them?'

'Leave them with Hilary outside. I'll go through them later this week.'

'Righto, well, goodbye then,' she says.

She sits in the warmth of the car for a minute. The suburban street is littered with curling leaves a foot deep at the gutters. All that build-up and she was out in under ten minutes. She turns on the engine and pulls out from the kerb, towards the myriad of mini-roundabouts which will take her out of Scarborough to the A-road back inland. It's a billowy autumn day, sharp-lit and dry as dust. She is hungry and she faintly needs the toilet but she'd been too distracted to ask Barry if she could use his.

So, there was no getting out now. Not with Max having a baby and lamb prices bottoming out. They'd have to press on, like Joe said. She feels herself adjusting to this idea. It was always bad news with Barry Jordan. Like going to the dentist – you couldn't expect any good to come out of it except the satisfaction that it was over for another while. At least she hadn't had to go through those blessed receipts.

Half an hour out of Scarborough, she pulls into the forecourt of a service station to fill up with petrol. The air has a smoked, woody smell to it; huge clouds skit over the horizon and over the A170 as it dissects the rolling flat countryside. The wind is buffeting her hair and the skirt of her mac as she stands holding the petrol pump's handle, looking in through the window of an adjacent car where a plump baby is playing with his toes. I wonder if Maureen's got a car seat we could have, she thinks. She smiles at the baby. A bairn. To have a bairn around the house again. She'll get some of the boys' old toys down from the loft to have in their lounge, for when Primrose brings the baby over.

She pays for her petrol and resists a Ginsters pasty, even though she's ravenous. Better to save the money and make a sandwich back home. She drives back out onto the road, pulling down her visor against the low sun, shifting in her seat to ease the pressure on her bladder, and thinking about Primrose. Would any woman who took her place in her son's affections disappoint as much as Primrose? Ann had had fantasies, she realises now, that a daughter-in-law would be the girl she never had. But Primrose, she tuts to herself, glancing in the rear-view mirror. She remembers wandering through Lipton market with her, pointing to a floral dinner set and saying 'Ooh Primrose, isn't that pretty?' And Primrose had said, 'I don't know,' in that blank way she had, and 'I'm not much into household stuff.' And she'd looked straight at her, in a way Ann half admired because it never evaded anything. Primrose. She seems to be not quite all there. Absent somehow. What had seemed like a salve for Max's loneliness now seems a rather hasty mistake.

An hour and an interesting episode of *You and Yours* later, and desperate now for a wee, Ann slows the car at the first roundabout on the outskirts of Lipton. She has followed the A170 all the way, its villages strung along it like beads on a broken string. You knew them for what you needed and what they could give: firewood and liquorice at the garage outside Kirbymoorside, pork pies from Hunters in Helmsley. And here in Lipton, their nearest market town, well there was no end to its riches: Greggs for a sausage roll, the hairdressers for a rinse if you were over eighty, scented candles and chopping boards in Coopers, and of course, the Co-op, where Primrose works. Primrose and the baby inside her.

She thinks back to all those years ago, how they worried about Max, and just look at him now. She remembers Joe climbing into bed next to her, saying, 'We're never going to be shot of him. He'll still be here when he's fifty.'

She'd laughed and said, 'I suppose we could move out.'

'He'd find us,' Joe had said, cuddling up to her under the covers.

That's when she'd started the badgering – she blanches just thinking about it – telling Max he needed to 'get a life of his own'.

'Go out and meet some girls,' she'd say to him, rough like, when he was getting under her feet, which was all the time.

She passes Coopers on her way out the other side of Lipton, onto the Marpleton road. The suburban houses peter out, giving way to vivid fields; hedgerows rustling with the grouse. The countryside up hard against them, especially in Marpleton, which had little in the way of entertainment except the Fox and Feathers. And that's where it'd all started – for Max and Primrose. It was after Tony and Sheryl Crowther came up from Essex and took it over. She still thinks of them as newcomers, even though it was five years ago now. The village could talk of nothing else.

'That's a hard-bitten woman is that,' Ann remembers whispering to Lauren, and Lauren had nodded energetically, looking over at Sheryl behind the bar.

'Batten down your husbands,' Lauren had said.

They'd started that quiz, the Crowthers, trying to rev the place up a bit and that was when Max started wearing his best shirt and kicking up a right stink if it wasn't washed in time. Oof, and that deodorant of his, Lynx something. He'd spray it more freely than Round-up, so that she and Joe would waft their hands in front of their faces and grimace as he walked out of the front door. 'Ladykiller,' Joe'd say, winking at her.

She parks outside the farmhouse, slams the car door and races into the house and up the stairs to the bathroom.

When she comes back down the stairs it is slowly, her body relieved. She ambles into the lounge to clear away a couple of mugs she'd spotted there earlier this morning. She opens the curtains and jumps back.

'Ooh god, you gave me a fright,' she says. 'What are you doing here? Shouldn't you be out watching the tups with Max?'

Joe is sitting, round-shouldered, at the computer in the dark corner of the room.

'Just doing some research,' he says without looking round. He is squinting at the screen, then down at the mouse, trying to make a connection between the two. She looks over his shoulder. farmautotrader.co.uk. Joe's answer to pornography. On the screen is a John Deere 5100m tractor. POA.

'Price on application,' she says. 'Or as I like to call it, OMDB.'

He looks up at her.

'Over My Dead Body,' she says.

'It's got leather seats, climate control, telescopic mirrors. And power synchron.'

Ann is standing behind him, hands on hips. 'Oh, well, why didn't you say? If it's got power synchron,' she says. 'What about bells and whistles – has it got those?'

'There's a forage harvester here for fifteen grand,' says Joe. 'If we got one of these, Max wouldn't have to hire one every year. In fact, he might be able to hire it out – make some extra cash.'

Ann has flopped down into one of the armchairs. Strange to be in the lounge with Joe in the daytime. Wrong, somehow.

'Sorry,' she says, 'but do we live on the same farm?'

Joe doesn't respond. She cranes back behind her to look at him. He is staring at the screen, his mouth hung slack like he's catching flies.

'So Ann,' she says, all am-dram. 'How was Barry Jordan? Oh it was fine thanks for askin'. Subsidies going down the toilet, but let's buy a harvester shall we?'

'How was it?' he says.

'Same old doom and gloom.' She leans her head back into the soft back cushion. She can hear Joe behind her head, clicking with the mouse. 'Single farm payment's not going to do us any favours. I can't talk to you when you're on that thing. Can you get off it? I want to email Bartholomew.'

'Gimme a minute. Anyway I'm going to ring him – with Max. Tell him about the baby.'

'If you even think about buying a new tractor I'll thump ye.'

'We've got to build it up for Max.'

'There's nothing spare, Joe.'

'That's why I'm going to turn it round, bring in the lambs. Leave it good for 'im.'

He has stood up, pushing both hands into the small of his back as he straightens. She looks at him. He is impossible, that man. But he is smiling at her as she heaves herself out of the armchair for her turn at the computer. He comes over and puts an arm around her neck so she's near deadlocked. He is chuckling and saying 'A little babby!'

They hug each other and he says into her hair, 'We have to help him, Annie. Max is not strong like Bartholomew.'

She looks at his face up close to hers. It is leathery from a life worked outdoors, his hair grey now. He's improved with age, like most men do. He was always like this about the boys, used to knock her out of the way to get to them after a day out working. And them at the top of the stairs waiting for him in their pyjamas.

He kisses her. 'We always said we'd give them everything we could.'

'Yes, well I've changed me mind.'

'You act all bluff but I know you,' he says. 'You're soft over those boys, just like me.'

'Not as much as you, Joe.'

She looks at his back as he walks out of the room.

It is her great achievement, this marriage. When they were first wed the slightest disagreement would last a week or more. Grievances harboured until she was sore with it. Children soon knocked that out of you. You never solved a fight, she'd come to realise, you just got good at looking the other way and getting on with the next thing. Letting love have the upper hand. If she could give her boys one piece of advice it would be to let it slide – that sense of outrage that it's not better. She begins to type the word 'Bartholomew' into the recipient field and the computer fills out the rest. Her youngest, especially, seems to be still holding out for the perfect thing – the one where there'll be no disappointment to swallow down. Well, he'll have a long wait.

⌒

Bartholomew is lifting the kettle and shaking it to judge its water level when his phone vibrates in the pocket of his jeans. Ruby's passion for texting is beginning to feel like a persecution.

> What time r u picking me up? 5pm? R.

He texts back:

> I'll try. Might be a bit late. Lots to do.

He switches his phone off and puts it back in his pocket, eases out the kettle's rubber lead. As he carries it to the sink, the landline starts to ring. Will she never stop?

'Garden Centre,' he says.

'Hello garden centre!' shouts his father. He can hear a thrashing sound and bleating, and immediately can smell those outbuildings – the dry straw mixed with some kind of chemical, like creosote, emanating from their timbers.

'In the pen are you?' says Bartholomew. He holds the phone between his cheek and his shoulder while he fills the kettle.

'We are,' says Joe.

He turns off the tap and a faucet squeaks somewhere in the warehouse roof. He hears his father shouting 'No Max, he's done that one – look at her back,' and knows that Max must be silently obeying him as usual.

'How's tupping?'

'Marvellous,' shouts Joe. 'We've had some fine rams this year.

We've wonderful news, Bartholomew. Max and Primrose are having a bairn.'

'Ah that's grand,' he says. Struggling for life is a genuine excitement on behalf of his brother.

'Isn't it?' Bartholomew can hear pure joy in his father's voice and feels the stab that he wasn't the source of it. 'First Hartle grandchild,' Joe is saying. 'You and Ruby had best get a move on!'

'Can I speak to Max?'

'I'll put him on. Hang on.' He hears Joe saying, 'He doesn't seem to like that one, we should let her out. Here, your brother wants a word.'

'Hello?' says Max.

'So, I hear congratulations are in order. When's it due?'

'May the twentieth or thereabouts.'

'There's lead in your pencil then.'

'Looks like it.'

'How's Primrose?'

'She's grand. No sickness or anything. Mum and dad are right pleased.'

'I'll bet. Well, sleepless nights ahead then.'

'No worse than lambing.'

'I suppose not.'

'You'll have to visit when it arrives,' says Max. 'If I can prise the baby off mum. She's that excited.'

'Yes, I'll bet,' says Bartholomew. 'Right, well, I'd best go. Give my love to Primrose.'

'Will do. Hang on, dad wants another word.'

'Bartholomew? One other thing,' says Joe.

'Yes?' says Bartholomew, weary with his father again and making it known in his voice. This has become a habit, his shortness with Joe.

'Nothing, never mind,' says Joe. 'We'll talk at Christmas. When you come up.'

Bartholomew hangs up.

He looks across the warehouse at the lagoon of tat which is spreading across the floor, growing ever more garish with the approach of Christmas. Leonard is opening some boxes with a Stanley knife. Beside him is a huddle of statues: a boy with a bit of copper piping for a penis, a cherub with one foot missing, a Victorian lady bending with an umbrella. There are buckets of glass globes and butterflies on sticks; tables groaning with plastic toadstools, random painted figurines, pots shaped like handbags. Oh how it sold.

'Where d'you want these?' asks Leonard.

'What are they?'

Leonard lifts one out of the box – a plastercast dog, nut-brown with a white tummy, carrying in its mouth a large Victorian lantern. Its neck is garlanded with red tinsel.

'Solar-powered apparently,' Leonard says. He holds it away from his body, as if to avoid contamination.

This was the kind of extraneous guff that Maguires excelled in. Last night, Bartholomew had driven out of town for the champagne evening on the outskirts of Guildford and had wandered, glass in hand, through the vast hangar, its aisles empty of people and smelling of sawn timber. He'd marvelled at the banks of children's toys, power tools of every make and model, troughs full of bulbs (all the really suburban varieties). The staff were spotty adolescent boys mostly, and for all their corporate orange jackets, they appeared to have even less energy than Leonard. That pleased him, at least.

'Put them next to the wrought-iron frogs,' he says to Leonard. 'With any luck they'll eat each other. Cup of tea?'

'Yes thanks. Don't leave the bag in too long though. I don't like it stewed. It should just glance the water. Skim it.'

'Right you are,' says Bartholomew. 'We've got a lot to get through in the next couple of days. Can you sort through the bare-root trees and roses and make sure the labels are right and they're priced up?' He approaches the counter with two mugs. 'I was thinking, you know, about our winter footfall. How to get people in the door, and I had this idea for a farm collective, well a shop really. We'd clear all that crap from the far corner—'

'That crap sells,' says Leonard.

'Yes, but Maguires is going to do that stuff on a massive scale. I thought we should go in another direction.' He is hoping he might sweep Leonard along, somehow make of him a 'we' until together they took flight. 'We'd get together a collection of local farmers who'd come in and sell food in a farm shop and maybe people could order veg boxes through us too. It would bring people in during the quieter months.'

'Actually I have to ask you something,' Leonard says.

Bartholomew presses on. 'I'm quite excited about the idea, don't you think? I mean, early days. Thought I'd try to set up some meetings with some farmers.'

'Can I have tomorrow off?'

'Oh god Len, why? There's masses to do.'

'I've got a pair of No-Iron Comfort-Waist Chinos arriving from the Lands' End catalogue.'

'And you have to take a day off?' Bartholomew can't bear to look at him.

'It's due tomorrow. I've tracked my order on the Internet.'

'People don't take days off work to wait in for parcels. Why didn't you just get it sent here?'

'I was worried it would get lost in the system.'

'What system? It's you and me in a shed.'

'And if I chanced it, it could be sent back to the depot, and I'd have to pick it up from there and that would be another day off.'

'Well, not really.' He can hear Ruby's voice saying, 'So how much time is it that Leonard's had off this year? Fifty-two weeks?' And him saying what he always said, 'I don't want to talk about it. I hate managing people.'

'I don't think you're seeing things from my point of view,' Leonard is saying.

'That's an understatement.'

'This parcel's really stressing me out. I've been tracking my order twice a day for two weeks. Tomorrow is D-day, the eagle is landing. I have to be there. For the trousers.'

'Why don't you shop on the high street, like normal people?'

'Because Lands' End does special wrinkle-resistant fabric. And I like the elasticated waist. Can I have the day off?'

'I was hoping we could get these deliveries unpacked. There's a hell of a backlog.'

'I'm getting really stressed about the trousers.'

'Oh d'you know what? Have the day.'

'Appreciated.'

Bartholomew makes for the door, frowning. 'God help us if they don't fit,' he says quietly.

A week later, Primrose is sitting on her high stool behind the till, one hand on her lower belly, filled with the new idea which is making her body tingle.

The midwife had told her it was only the size of a broad bean, but Primrose thinks of the baby as occupying her whole middle, and wonders, when she stoops to pick up a receipt off the floor, say, whether the baby is folded over. Or stooping too.

When she'd cycled in this morning, down the lane to Sinnington and then up the steep incline for the short stretch across the moor, she'd thought about her middle all the way. As if her middle were somehow a thing, brand new. Her legs were pumping on the pedals, her ears were rushing inside her hood and the wind on the moor was blowing hard into her face, but her whole mind was on her middle.

It seemed to Primrose that there were two of them cycling across the moor, two of them switching on the strip lights inside the Co-op. Two of them, together, pouring the change from little clear bags into separate compartments in the till. And so when she finally came to sit on the high stool behind the counter, she laid a hand on her little friend, who was her secret, and served a customer one-handed, half hoping the old lady might notice and ask her when it was due.

'Primrose? Keeping you up are we?' says Tracy in that hard voice of hers. 'You can go on your break if you like.'

Primrose steps out into the bright autumn sunshine. Lipton High Street is peppered, as usual, with a handful of pensioners and a couple of young mothers with children in buggies. She walks past A Cut Above, where an elderly lady is sat under a plastic-domed heater; past the chemist, with its bottle-green gloss paintwork unchanged for decades; past the trays of warm sausage rolls in Greggs' window. She turns down a side road towards Al's Electrical shop.

A bell rings over the door as she inches into the shop's dark, crammed interior. Bulging shelves reach to the ceiling, set with trays of rivets and tacks, and rolls of electrical flex hang from hooks in the rafters. Cable clips. Consumer units. Crimp lugs and heat tape.

'Hello Prim,' says Al from behind the counter. 'Beautiful day out there. The trees are in great colour. I haven't seen them that bright for years. Must be all the rain we've been having.'

'I need another junction box,' says Primrose.

'Right you are. Which type?'

'Thirty-amp. Three-terminal. In brown if you've got it.'

'I'll have a look.'

She stands at the counter, flicking through Al's laminated catalogue while he goes out back.

She stops on a page and reads the text more closely. Al comes back carrying a white cardboard box.

'Have you got any of these in?' asks Primrose, swivelling the catalogue.

Al stoops, putting his glasses on to read. 'Arh, no,' he says. 'Not much call for video entryphones round here.'

'But if someone wanted one, you could order it in, couldn't you?'

'I don't see why not. They're quite fast, this supplier. Would take three to four days to come in, or thereabouts. Shall I order it now?'

'No.' Primrose hesitates, her mind is racing. 'No, not yet. I'll just take the junction box for now.'

Joe's hand guides the steering wheel, turning his Land Rover right onto Lipton High Street. The low autumn sunshine flashes hard, piercing through the smears on his windscreen like shards (he must get that wiper fixed), so he pulls down the sun visor and lowers his head to look under it. He sees Primrose's back, turning off the High Street. Going to Al's no doubt. Sometimes Joe wonders if Primrose should have married Al, but then he remembers that for Al, it's just a business. For Primrose . . . well, Joe doesn't pretend to understand it.

He has a feeling of satisfaction – not just because of the baby. Tupping has been fine this year and it's given him a feeling of looking forward – to lambing and to the kinder weather that comes with it. They've let some of the fattening lambs graze on the beet tops, and defecate on them, and now those in-bye fields are taking the plough, turning this goodness over into the dark soil so that it's brand new again. Wonderful work, ploughing.

The pregnant ewes are staying down-valley, sheltered and fed until their lambs are established inside them. They'll go up onto the fell next month. That was the beauty of Swaledales. Could withstand all weathers. Yes, he has a sense of the future before him, with the farm at full tilt and the baby coming. And then some sadness behind it. He'd been so quick to offer the farm up to Max, that he hadn't considered what it'd mean for him to let it go. As soon as he'd said it, even though it was what they'd always taken for granted, as soon as he said it, he'd wanted to take it back. The image of himself as the grey-haired man on the back seat – well, it didn't fit with how he felt inside, which was still young.

He pushes open the door of Lipton Conservative Club. 'Club' is a pompous term for it. There were no button-back leather chairs and suchlike. It was open to most anyone unless you were a newcomer, in which case you'd be greeted with a raised eyebrow and a wall of silence. Mostly it was for barnacles like Joe and Eric Blakely. Conservative? Well, they didn't like this Labour lot, with their agri-stewardship-whatever schemes. Didn't like change, mostly.

To the club's inner door is pinned a yellowing notice. 'At

the last meeting of the Committee,' it says, 'it was agreed that "tailored shorts" could be worn in the Club at lunchtimes only, and that tracksuits would not be suitable clothing for members to wear. Signed, K. Simms, Secretary.' Joe looks down at his muddied corduroys and even muddier boots, and at the royal-blue carpet of the club hallway, freshly vacuumed. He brushes himself ineffectually, then walks into the 'bar' – a muffled room with red Formica tables, floral curtains and cream-painted woodchip on the walls. Eric stands with Ron Chappell, their pint glasses full. Ron had been a tenant farmer like Joe – same landlord, the water board, which owned most of the land round here. He'd gone under after foot-and-mouth and now he did odd jobs. Eric always bought Ron's pints.

'What are you having, Joe?' says Eric, one arm resting on his belly where he holds his pint, the other jangling keys in his trouser pocket. Joe thinks Eric resembles one of those life-size fibreglass men, wearing striped aprons, which used to stand outside butcher's shops.

'You're alright Eric, I'll get them in,' says Joe.

'Don't be silly man, I'm buying.' Eric smiles, his voice jovial as always. 'A pint for Joe,' he calls to Keith Tindall, who is busying himself in the kitchen to the rear of the bar.

'That was a wet harvest,' says Ron, whose thinness is accentuated by standing next to Eric.

'Mudbath,' says Joe. He takes off his Barbour and hangs it on a wall hook. 'Total mudbath.' He notices that Eric's shoes are new. Smooth brown loafers, unmuddied.

'Did you lift the beet alright?' asks Eric.

'We did, and in a day. The soil was that sticky, but a good harvest it was. Thanks Keith,' Joe says, taking his pint from Keith, who quickly disappears again.

'And tupping?' says Eric, like he's hungry for news of his old life. 'Good tups this year?'

'Very good, yes, very good,' says Joe.

'Those lamb prices at Slingsby were shocking, so I've heard,' says Ron. 'Stores going for under a tenner.'

'It's the cheap foreign imports,' says Eric, shaking his head.

'What can ye do?' says Ron.

They look into their pints.

'Bomb New Zealand?' says Joe, and they all laugh. 'It'll pick up, you watch. Farmers have gone through this type of strife before.'

'Not as bad as this,' says Eric.

'Aye and worse,' says Joe. 'You wait till lambing and you'll both be round mine, rubbernecking over the fence at my prize gimmers and tups.'

'At least I'll not be up against ye at the shows, Joe,' says Eric. 'I could never beat you.'

'You nearly killed yourself trying. You and your tweezers.' And Joe thinks back to the Fadmoor show, must have been eight-odd years ago now. Their rivalry was friendly back then, but with a serious edge. Those rosettes affected the price you got. Joe had walked round behind one of the livestock trailers and caught Eric bent over a Swale with a pair of tweezers.

'Now that is truly pathetic,' Joe'd said.

'Ah now man, don't say owt,' said Eric. 'I've seen you do the same. Just a couple of grey hairs –'

Then Eric had stood back, admiring his ewe. 'She doesn't need any help, this one. She's nigh-on perfect.'

But Joe had won top prize and Eric had taken it with his usual good grace. Perhaps you were dealt the hand you could best cope with, Joe thinks now. Eric had got out of farming not long after – in 2001, after the foot-and-mouth culls, like Ron. But while Ron was driven out, for Eric, it was the assault on his feelings that he couldn't take. Seeing those pyres had finished him off. 'I admire you, Joe. Restocking, carrying on,' he'd said. And Joe had put an arm round him, saying, 'Could be the stupidest thing I ever do.' Now Eric was rich as Croesus, the smile all over his face. And with smart new shoes.

'How are your boys, Joe?' says Ron, interrupting his thoughts.

'Not so bad,' says Joe. 'Bartholomew's garden centre's going great guns by all accounts. And you've heard about the baby.'

'Smashing news,' says Eric.

'It'll be nice to have a little one around the place again,' says Joe. He sees Eric's face go slack, the darkness come over it like a shadow. The son Eric and Lauren had lost. Joe kicks himself for bringing Eric's lost child into the room. Say something, he thinks, but Eric's face is re-animating already, the sad lines stretching over another tight smile.

'Have you been down to Bartholomew's place then?' asks Ron.

'Not me, no. Ann's visited. She's says it's a nice place he's got down there. But the south's not my thing – too crowded. I'd sooner stay up here and hear about it on the telephone. Anyway, Bartholomew's none too keen on my advice, no matter how I give it.'

'Ah, they never are Joe, they never are,' says Eric. 'My Sylvie's marrying the biggest layabout this side of the Pennines, but she'll not hear a word about it from me. And Lauren shuts me up before I try.'

'You're best off without them, Ron,' says Joe. 'Nothing but worry.'

There is an awkward silence until Ron says: 'So Max'll be taking over the farm then, I hear.'

'Do you now?' says Joe. 'It's early days.'

'Only natural,' says Ron, 'if he's to have a little 'un.'

Joe flinches, hadn't realised how much this talk would rankle. 'He's a lot to learn. We'll do it gradual like.'

'Not too gradual I hope,' says Eric. 'Children are not known for their patience.'

'No, well, I'm not out of the picture just yet,' says Joe. 'Let's just see how he goes.'

Bartholomew straightens himself, his breathing heavy, and holds the brush's wooden handle with both hands. He's built up a sweat clearing the leaves and has taken off his fleece.Behind him is a whole avenue of plants which need potting; and everywhere a mess of dried stems which must be pruned off. Wonderful work, if only there was time. But in an hour the sun will plop below the horizon and the interminable winter evening will set in. Nothing depressed him more than 4 p.m. darkness. Even with floodlights or dragging plants into the warehouse, it was a struggle to keep the life of the garden centre ignited in the winter months.

He remembers a general slump which took over his family in the run-up to the clocks going back at the end of October, when all the jobs on the farm became a strain – the discomfort of cold, the dark mornings, the tripping up on unseen stones and the way the wet penetrated your bones. Even the laborious pulling-on of winter gear: waterproof trousers, hats, gloves that were stiff and scratchy, three pairs of socks inside heavy boots, so that you were tired before you'd even stepped out of the door. And then, in summer, the sloughing-off of this second skin. As early as March, they all began to breathe out, their bodies relaxing into lighter anoraks and wellingtons. And the physical lightness of stepping out in an ever-warming spring seemed to give the whole family an exuberance.

Not just the family. He remembers hearing it in the jovial conversations in the streets in Lipton or in the Fox of an evening. Everyone looking forward to lambing and then a warm May. And the smell of foliage straining forward and the grass so green it made your eyes water with happiness.

He starts sweeping again, aware that the light is fading. He stops and takes out his phone, switching it on. Three messages from Ruby, mostly pictures of food.

> Sturdy but too much salt. R.
> Winstanton in shock as soufflé rises. R.
> Mung beans actually not disgusting. Who knew? R.

He takes off one glove and texts her back.

> Running late. B.

'So that's a pot of tea for two. Anything to eat? I've got a lovely carrot cake. Come on ladies, you know you want to,' says Ruby. She feels her phone vibrate in her apron pocket. The two women look at each other, then hunch their shoulders in delight.

'Oooh go on then. We really shouldn't. One slice to share.'

'Right you are,' says Ruby.

The café has its usual smattering of teatime customers: the two ladies who will giggle and chat conspiratorially; the balding man who always takes the most secluded corner, setting out his laptop, looking up at Ruby often, as if in need of confirmation that his work – whatever it is he's writing – is important. There's a young woman at another table, texting on her phone. Next to her is a pram, entirely shrouded in a blanket and with a seeming exclusion zone around it, as if it's a bomb that could detonate at any moment. The woman texts with her arms close to her sides and she keeps on her coat. Ruby gives the pram a wide berth as she walks down the long room to the back kitchen.

She puts the kettle on and takes down a metal teapot from a high cupboard. She puts this and two cups and saucers onto a tray. She is facing into the room, working on a counter which forms part of an open serving hatch between the kitchen and the tea room. The café window is now an oblong of purplish blue, smeared with lights from the street outside. As she waits for the kettle to boil, she surveys the Christmas decorations she's been arranging in the window: several loops of flashing multicoloured fairy lights; a row of powdery snowmen figures in a row, each one smaller than the last; some spray snow at the corners of the window; a series of low-hanging golden paper lanterns (a bit torn, admittedly), which bob from the ceiling.

Needs something more, she thinks. Then she remembers the buzz from her apron pocket and takes out her phone.

Running late. B.

He was always keeping her waiting, always a flat hand up to her exuberance. She'd wanted to go with him to that Maguires thingy. No, I'd best go alone he'd said. She wanted them to move in together. We will do in time, he said. And now there was Christmas, hanging there like a big torn sodding lantern. Grown-up couples, she felt, spent Christmas together. They didn't act like they were still seventeen with pants in separate flats. She's exhausted, she realises looking at his text, with walking this tightrope with him. Hoping for more, that he'll come to it in time. Staying because she loves him. Trying to hold herself back but then boiling underneath with the feeling that she's disguising herself. And then back to the beginning again. Careful. Cautious. Because she wants him. She doesn't want to lose him.

She goes to the fridge and pulls out the carrot cake, its foil hat jostling against the others. She hurriedly takes the tea tray to the ladies and marches back to the kitchen, acknowledging the pram woman, who has raised her hand. That edge looks a bit messy, she says to herself, looking at the carrot cake. She cuts a slither and turns her back to the café room, tumbling crumbs into her upturned mouth.

Ruby had tried diets, but she found it hard to come to terms with restraint as a way of life. She wanted to finish the slab, lick the bowl, hoover up the crumbs, take it to the next layer. Dieting, she felt, was a bit like spending months learning a new and difficult language when you knew you were only going to visit the country for a couple of weeks; you were never going to live there. She couldn't *inhabit* the land of smaller portions.

She takes pram woman her bill, standing beside the table while the lady counts out her coins. She watches a half-socked foot, poking out from under the pram's blanket, begin to twitch.

'Ruby Dalton as I live and breathe!' says a voice in the doorway.

She sees a big man, buff, in a navy pea coat with gold buttons and charcoal wool scarf knotted at the neck. Well turned out. He is clean-shaven – a rather forgettable face – and hair slicked back with wet-look gel. Where does she know him from? Not one of those customers, she hopes, who couldn't take the hint.

Someone from her book club? Her mind is whirring, trying to place him. Yes.

It is Dave Garside, she realises, without much pleasure. Dave from school. Brave Dave (he was always rock-climbing or bungee-jumping or risking his life in one way or another). What was *he* doing down south?

'What brings you here?' she says as he bends towards her, putting his cheek to hers. The double. She hates kissing relative strangers. Always feels it like an invasion of her privacy. She doesn't want to smell people up close. What's Brave Dave doing air-kissing, any road? They never did that back in Leeds.

'Just moved here for work. I've been living in Guildford but the firm's moved me to the Winstanton office. I'm just getting my bearings.'

'Come in and have a brew,' says Ruby, injecting generosity into her voice.

Dave follows her down the long room, stooping to dodge the gold lanterns but hitting them anyway. He pulls up a stool on the café side of the hatch and Ruby puts the kettle on.

'This is a nice surprise. I'd never have put you down south,' he says. 'When did you move here?'

'About two years ago. I like it. It's small. Friendly too.'

She hands him his tea.

'So this is your headquarters,' Dave says, looking around the café room. Ruby can see him taking in the worn carpets and scratched tables. 'Very impressive.'

''Scuse us,' she says, and goes to attend to the two ladies who are preparing to leave.

The café is emptying as the clock ticks towards closing time, but Dave shows no sign of hopping it. She wants to pull out the Hoover and cash up but he's sitting there, on his high stool,

73

looking down at a folded newspaper that someone has discarded. He's taken her pen from the corner of the hatch.

'Seven letters,' he says. 'I'm tremendously keen to dissipate fat and I can.' She sucks in her stomach and tugs on the back of her skirt. 'No idea, Dave,' she says. She bends to fill the dishwasher, still holding in her tummy, the crumbs mingling with slurries of strawberry sauce.

'Fan-at-ic,' he says, filling it in with her pen. 'Fanatic.'

He was always like this at school. Superior.

'So whereabouts are you living?' he asks.

'Theobald Road. It's just along the river from here. I've got a little flat. And my boyfriend lives in the same street.' She throws it in, airily.

'Nice. You're all set up then. Are you going home for Christmas? Or spending it with your fella?'

She flinches. 'Oh no, god no, it's early days. Haven't really decided.'

'I can't wait to go back,' says Dave.

'You got a girlfriend?'

'No,' he says. 'Haven't met the right girl yet.' And he winks at her, then goes back to his crossword. He really is very muscly.

'Brazilian music, Ruby. "The Girl from Ipanema".'

Ruby turns from the dishwasher and starts to sing, sashaying and smiling. 'Tall and tan and da-da-da something, the girl from Ipanema goes walking.'

Dave is drinking her in.

'Do you know,' she says, glittering a bit under his gaze. 'I think that's bossa nova. Would that fit?'

74

Bartholomew props his bicycle against the wall outside the café. He is covered in a sheen of sweat, having pedalled hard from the garden centre on the outskirts of town, past the castle and through the abbey gardens to the centre – Market Street, where her café is. It's a shabby place – the sort that serves toasted cheese sandwiches with shavings of carrot on the side. A waste of her talents, he always thinks. Ruby's cooking is so much better than that: monkfish with pancetta, risottos and soufflés, steamed asparagus topped with perfect poached eggs. All of it tried out on him at home. She's the sort of cook who stoops over the plate.

It is fully dark now and Ruby's fairy lights trip out their coloured rhythm, doggedly. He can see her dancing in the back kitchen, a man sat on a high stool. His very broad back. He seems to be writing something. He sees them laugh together.

Bartholomew pushes open the door.

'Hello,' she says, kissing him on the cheek. 'Come and meet Dave. Bartholomew Hartle, Dave Garside. Dave Garside, Bartholomew Hartle.'

'Bartholomew,' says broad-backed Dave. 'That's an unusual name. Bit of a mouthful.'

Fuck off, thinks Bartholomew. 'You're from the north, too,' he says.

'Ruby and I were at school together. This is my new local,' says Dave. 'I didn't realise the food was so good.'

'Ruby's a good cook.'

'You're lucky.'

'I am, yes. Shall we go, Rube?'

'I have to lock up.'

'Don't mind me,' says Dave. 'I'm off. See you soon, Ruby – tomorrow probably.'

Bartholomew watches his huge outline disappear out of the door.

'He's buff,' he says.

'He works out,' says Ruby, absently, pulling a fistful of keys from her bag.

Bartholomew wheels his bicycle slowly along the smooth tarmac of the riverside path. The air is tinkling now with a light drizzle which pinks and plocks onto the surface of the river and patters through the tall trees. Ruby is walking on his left, the hood of her pea-green coat up so that all he can see is one shiny red cheek and the way her hair has curled with the moisture in the air. Every now and then she sniffs as a drip gathers at the end of her nose.

He has to wheel unnaturally slowly to keep pace with her and she sometimes, during this regular walk home together, remarks on how awkward it is. 'Makes me feel you'd rather be off freewheeling,' she'll say. This evening she is talking animatedly about her day.

'Do you have any idea how many people are mad?' she says. 'It's like 78 per cent.'

'Is that a statistical fact, or something you made up?'

'It's a statistical fact.' He raises his eyebrows at her. 'Which I just made up. I read this brilliant thing today in my magazine. It was by an agony aunt. She said she'd printed a letter from a man who could only, you know, climax if someone stuck Sellotape to 'im and ripped it off really fast.'

'You're kidding.'

'But the funniest thing about it was that six other readers wrote in to say, "Thank goodness. I thought I was the only one."'

Bartholomew laughs. She laughs too.

'Had some news today,' he says.

She looks at him.

'Max and Primrose are having a baby.'

He thinks he can detect something nervous – a flinch – but she just smiles, a thin, tight smile.

'Mum and dad are right excited,' he says.

'I'll bet. What about you?'

'Aye, I think it's nice. Primrose though. She's a funny one.'

'You don't think she'll be a good mother?'

'It's not that. She's just not that . . . open, I s'pose.'

'D'ye think they're ready?' she says.

'When is anyone ready?' he says. 'You just have to get on and do it, don't you?'

She looks at him now and her smile is full and open. He can feel all her natural warmth emanate towards him.

They clatter into the communal hallway outside Bartholomew's flat. She makes her way to his kitchen at the rear – a cold, hard room she's always thought, with faux-wooden units lit by a sixty-watt bulb. He's never made any attempt to prettify his home – no lamps or flowers or rugs. It half appals her and half seems an opportunity for her to provide something at some later date. She knows that part of him feels more comfortable at her cosy flat than he does here, even though he won't let go of it.

'Dave was askin' me about Christmas,' she shouts to the hall-way, where he is taking off his cycling gear. She's been em-boldened by the baby comment. Perhaps he is coming round. 'And my mum asked about it, too. Wants to know what I'm doing.'

There is no reply. Ruby stops. She is squatting beside the fridge, wondering how this is going to go and whether she'd be better off steering clear. She curses herself, as she does when she knows she's sent too many text messages.

He has come in and is sitting at the kitchen table, still in his cagoule. He fingers some takeaway flyers which lie on the table top among unopened post. She is searching through his tiny fridge and filling her arms with minced beef, celery and mushrooms.

'This is past its sell-by date but I'm sure it's fine,' she says, looking at the beef. She gets up and takes a knife from the drawer, slitting open the packaging to smell the contents.

'Smells fine,' she says, and she pushes it under his nose for a second opinion. He nods.

'If you don't want to come to Leeds,' she says, 'I could come and spend it with your family.' She has her back to him now, her whole body tense, but she keeps moving, taking out a chopping board and starting on an onion, not looking at him.

'It's a bit short notice,' he says.

'It's November.'

'There's not much room at ours. The house is a bit cramped.'

'I don't mind.'

'Let's not talk about it now.'

She closes her eyes, presses the heel of her hand into one eyelid, still clutching the knife, and sucks in through her teeth.

'Bloody onions,' she says.

Joe stands under the cathedral-like rafters of his hay barn, in the far corner of a quadrangle of outbuildings. The air is dusty –

November is turning out that dry. It is making the dogs sneeze as they snuffle about the base of the bales. He must check they're nice and dry, the bales, and the additional pellets he's bought in that have cost him so dear. His winter feed. If the hay's musty, or just doesn't smell right, the ewes could turn their noses up and they need their feed from now and for the four months till lambing. He'll need to increase their nutrition as their time gets near: lots of good home-made hay and silage, then cereal cake and ewe rolls when they're big with pregnancy. He'll be feeding them twice a day up on the fell, when the lambs start to press on their stomachs so they can't take in so much bulk. Especially those carrying twins – they'll need food that's small and rich with molasses.

The bales are stacked, perhaps forty feet, bathed in a weak, pastel light. He hears a crow's caw, giving an abrupt measure of the height and volume of the sky. The low-slung sun sends a burnished outline onto the beams inside the barn. There are gaps in the rafters, patch-worked with corrugated plastic, which cast golden squares onto the straw. Here you could find God, thinks Joe, taking in the sheer scale of the place as if for the first time, if you were looking for Him.

Joe begins running his hand along the hay bales to feel for patches of damp. He is clambering now, among the bales, sliding his hand between the tight rows. Too tight, perhaps, but the yield had been good at baling last June, when the hedgerows had been thick with cow parsley and elder, the uncut grass at the roadside swaying, soft as fur. He marvels that summer goodness can be stored like this – baled for the lean times, when the fell was covered in snow and pickings were slim.

He feels the hay blades prick into his skin. It is hard to feel the damp when the air is cold. He begins to forget what he's feeling for. And hay always feels warm to the touch. He looks up at the rafters and recalls Eric's suggestion, just after baling, to get a professional re-roofing job done while the beams were dry. Typical Eric. He'd been that sort of farmer, too – a great one for hiring in labour. Liked to keep his shoes clean. Hoovering his Nissan Micra. Getting Dennis Lunn to paint his windows.

'You're playing with fire there,' Eric had said, squinting up at the barn, rocking on his heels.

Joe had slapped Eric on the back, saying, 'Jeez man, you were always work-shy. That's nothing I can't handle myself.'

And he'd struggled up a ladder alone with those squares of plastic and a too-heavy hammer to repair the gaps as he spotted them. And Max, he'd been at the bottom, holding the ladder steady and looking up at Joe.

His right hand is becoming chapped with the cold and the scratching of hay. The winter light is fading, the barn now dim and eerie. A bairn, he thinks. A bairn will sort out Max, make a man of him. They changed everything, children. Made you who you were supposed to be. He looks out through the vast open mouth of the barn, to where the tractor is parked: dirty, rusted green, with high, wide wheels whose imprint is all over his farm. Quiet now, and silhouetted, it looks like a museum piece, which it soon would be. He'd started the application to the bank for a loan last night, after Ann had gone to bed. It'd take a while – probably come through some time in January. By that time, she'd see how fat the ewes were, how well they were going to do at lambing. And how long could the market stay so bad, with nobody wanting British meat? No, it'd have to change soon.

He's fed up of thinking on it. He's tired of feeling cold and stiff about the fingers. He wants to get warm by the Rayburn and drink his tea.

'You're about dry,' he says to his bales, and he whistles to the dogs to follow him in.

He walks in through the back door into the kitchen and the dogs clatter in behind him and find their padded baskets, which are matted with dog hairs. They each turn around twice on the spot, and lie down in the warmth of the Rayburn.

Joe hangs his coat on a hook by the back door and prises off his work boots. They are unusually clean because of the dry. He sees the surfaces wiped by Ann, the cloth resting where the sweep of her hand has last left it. Her faint voice drifts in from the hallway, louder now as he opens the kitchen door and approaches her.

'Yes, we have a family of sheep,' Ann is saying, her finger twisting around the tight coils of the telephone cord. 'Well, more than a family really – five hundred odd, sometimes more. They keep us and we keep them. Quite biblical, isn't it?'

She looks down at her slippers, blinking. Chap at the other end of the line is asking something about sheep breeds but she is distracted by Joe coming down the corridor towards her.

'No, they're Swaledales. Black faces, with a white nose. Curly horns, yes, that's it. Make marvellous mothers, Swales. They'll lamb in all weathers. Thrivers, they are. No, we tried with the Rough Fells, but it didn't work out. You don't find Rough Fells up here any more really.'

Joe walks past her in the hallway, about to climb the stairs when the doorbell goes. He and Ann look at each other. She shrugs, then motions to him to answer the door.

'Lost about two hundred in the culls in 2001. Devastated we were. We've restocked now though.'

Joe opens the door and there is Primrose. Ann waves to her, saying into the phone, 'Are you sure that's all you need? Well, call back if there's anything else.'

She puts the receiver down, flustered at this collision of events. 'Hiya love,' she says. 'This is unexpected.'

'How's that grandchild of mine?' asks Joe, ushering Primrose in with a hand on her back. Ann can see him beaming.

'Nothing wrong is there?' she asks. 'Everything alright with the baby?'

'Yes fine, I just wanted to ask you something,' says Primrose. Not like her, thinks Ann. Perhaps this is the shape of things to come. Mothers together.

'Come in, come in,' says Ann, and then to Joe, 'That was the chap from the *Dalesman*. Asking about sheep breeds.'

'Oh, hark at her,' says Joe. 'When's that out then?'

'I don't know actually. I forgot to ask 'im,' says Ann.

They troop down the narrow hallway to the kitchen, where Joe and Primrose take seats at the table and Ann goes to the kettle.

'Where's Max?' she asks, with her back to Primrose.

'At the Fox.'

'Tea alright?' asks Ann.

'Yes thanks. And some biscuits if you've got any. Got to keep me strength up.'

'Course you do. How about a fig roll?'

'Lovely.'

'What did you want to ask?' says Joe.

'Don't rush her,' says Ann, 'she'll come to it in her own time.'

'I wondered if you'd mind if I fitted a video entryphone on your cottage.'

'I'm sorry love, a what?' says Ann.

'A video entryphone. One of them cameras, by the front door.

And a monitor. I'd give you a release mechanism for the latch, so you could open the front door from upstairs.'

'Why would we want to do that?' says Ann.

'I don't know, you might be in the bath.'

Joe and Ann look at each other.

'It would mean I could try chasing in the coaxial wire and fitting the camera unit. It's the next project in my *Reader's Digest* book and I can't fit one at our house because . . . there's nothing to look out on – only fields – whereas here you could see the village. I could point the camera on the green and you'd have a proper picture on your monitor.'

'Has Max said no?' asks Ann.

'I haven't asked him,' says Primrose. 'I only thought of it today and I came straight here. I know Max wouldn't say yes. He's had enough of me rewiring at ours. He gets right fed up with it.'

Primrose takes a second fig roll.

'How long would it take?' asks Joe.

'Only an afternoon. I'd re-plaster wherever I'd had to chisel anything out, and I'd repaint it too.'

'Is that wise, in your condition?' asks Ann.

'It's fine. I'd like to get to the end of the basic course before the baby comes.'

'And I'd see the whole of the village, you say, from my landing?' says Joe.

Ann narrows her eyes at him. 'Joe . . .'

'If she wants to do it, let her do it,' he says.

'Joe,' says Ann, more insistently. Primrose takes a third fig roll.

'She wants to finish her course,' says Joe.

'We don't need a video entryphone,' hisses Ann.

'You go ahead, love,' says Joe. '*Mi casa, es tu casa.*'

'What?' says Primrose.

DECEMBER

— Let them eat cake —

Primrose lies in the bath, lifting and plunging. Her body is like a relief model of the dale, its valleys and swelling hills more pronounced these days. One hand glides over her pink chest, her nipples dark as mulberry. Her breasts are full and tingling, as if they too are charged with electricity, and the blue veins which eddy down them are like the blue wires she snips and positions with such ease, even with Joe crowding her.

He had watched every phase, standing inside the doorway as she dismantled the latch and fitted the release mechanism; pretending to tend to the front garden while she was up the ladder with the camera unit.

'How high d'you want it?' she'd asked. Her words emerged in puffs in the cold air.

'I don't know,' said Joe. 'Wherever you think.'

'Well, high up you'll get the village and the green, lower down you'll get your own front doorstep.'

'I'd put it high then,' he'd said.

She'd set it in on the brick, in between the bare stems of Ann's cottage rose.

He'd followed her, too, as she shut off the electricity supply and she'd struggled with him at her back while she chiselled out a channel just above the skirting board in the hallway so she could chase in twenty feet of coaxial wire.

'Cup of tea would be nice,' she'd said, just to get rid of him, so

84

that she could run the cable inside its chalky trench, up the left hand of the staircase to a point on the upstairs landing. Then Ann had come home and tripped on some of her tools which were lying just inside the front door.

'Flamin' heck,' she'd cursed, lifting her feet high. 'What a bloody mess.' And then she'd followed the trail of plaster and dust up the stairs and seen Primrose on the landing. 'Hiya love,' Ann had sing-songed, cheery like.

And then she could hear Ann and Joe arguing in the kitchen, but she'd just focused on installing the monitor and telephone handset. It sat beside Ann's mirror, above a white painted chest of drawers.

When Joe had stood behind her on the landing, holding her tea, she'd said, 'Right, shall we give it a try?'

She'd lifted the handset and they had both watched as a grainy green picture of Marpleton began to form out of disparate particles.

'Ann! Ann! Come and look at this!' Joe had shouted.

'Give over,' came Ann's muffled reply from the kitchen.

They had grinned at one another, she and Joe. She felt the satisfaction of a job well done. It couldn't have gone better, in fact.

Primrose looks at her thighs, lifting and plunging, feeling their buoyancy in the water. She takes her toe out of the faucet and wraps her foot around the tap, turning it. A stream of intense heat travels up her legs, spreading its warmth around her. She closes her eyes.

☊

A chair has become a permanent feature on the hallway landing ever since the video entryphone was installed and he knows how much it annoys Ann, because she trips over it every time she comes out of the bathroom.

She's in the bathroom now, and Joe casts a look at the door as he gingerly pulls the chair out from its sentry position against the wall. He's anxious for it not to clatter or scrape and he keeps an eye on the bathroom door while he sets it in front of the video entryphone, his knees knocking awkwardly against the chest of drawers. He can hear the water in Ann's bath and feels a vague heat through the bathroom door as it hits the arctic microclimate of the Hartle landing.

Initially, the video entryphone had been nothing more than a bit of fun for Joe and Ann. Well, less for Ann, more for Joe, who found it amusing to loiter at the top of the stairs when the doorbell rang and wait for Ann to be within outstretched arms' reach of the front door. He would then pick up the phone and press the buzzer, releasing the door mechanism. Something in the lie of the land and the looseness of the latch caused the door to swing out in front of Ann's startled face and her to exclaim 'For God's sake Joe, grow up.'

Ann got some pleasure from it though. That first weekend they'd had it, the winter sun had streamed into their bedroom. She'd sat up in bed with the tea Joe had brought her, the bedroom door flung wide and him on his rickety chair, reporting on the comings and goings of the village.

'Alan Tench has moved his van.'

'At last!' she'd said, sipping her tea.

'Here comes Daredevil Dawson.'

'Lord help us. Clear the roads!' Ann said.

'Looks like the Hardakers 'ave gone on holiday. Gate's shut.'

'Ooh, I wonder where. Must ask Lauren.'

He hears her now, turning the handle on the bathroom door.

He silently dashes to the back bedroom where he pretends to be flicking through some paperwork. He hears Ann cursing as she knocks into the chair – 'blasted thing'. She is hopping and shivering through the cold, racing to the bedroom where she closes the door to get ready for her pottery class with Lauren. Joe re-emerges from the back bedroom, back to his chair now enveloped in warm, lavender-scented steam from the bathroom.

Joe had begun to nip upstairs of a lunchtime for a quick peek at the green-glowing miniature picture of Marpleton. And then in the evening, if Ann was at darts or flower-arranging or some such with the WI, he allowed himself a rich, unfettered evening's closed-circuit observation. Marpleton at 8 p.m., 9 p.m., 10 p.m., lit by the lights of the Fox and Feathers – five of them, which hung over its sign like seasick passengers. (Lights that caused no end of village tutting when Sheryl and Tony Crowther first installed them. 'So vulgar,' Ann had said.)

He was grateful to those lights now – they cast a glow that pooled across half the green and illuminated the footpath. They allowed him to see Eric Blakely walking his dog; the late crowd spilling out of the Fox; Dennis Lunn stumbling past his front door on his way home – always the last.

Ann emerges from the bedroom. She's wearing her navy trousers and a blouse with a polo neck underneath, tight-fitting. She is curvy – wide-hipped and a little rotund after the children. Lively and homely at the same time. She has on a streak of lipstick, which is unusual for her. It is a bright red colour and it animates her whole face. Her skin is still glowing from her bath.

She gives him a suspicious look. 'Don't spend all evening on that blasted thing.'

'I'm not,' he says. 'I've plenty to do.'

'Right, well, I'm not taking the car – Lauren's giving me a lift. Won't be late.'

She kisses him on the cheek.

'You look nice,' he says, and he's made jealous by it.

'Well, you have to make an effort for pottery!'

She's at the bottom of the stairs now, putting on her coat. 'I got an email from Bartholomew by the way. He's booked his ticket. He's coming on Christmas Eve.'

'Not bringing Ruby?' asks Joe.

'No.'

'Everything alright between them?'

'How would I know?' she says, up the stairwell. 'I did invite her. Maybe she's got family to go to.'

'Be nice to have him home,' says Joe.

'Yes. Well, bye then, love.'

'Bye.'

The door closes behind her. Joe swivels his body around on the chair, now able to scrape and rattle as loudly as he likes. He lifts the handset in time to see Ann close their garden gate and cross the road onto the village green. She finds the footpath that bisects the grass and he watches her walk away from him, getting smaller. Another figure steps into the pool of green light from the left, someone in a long heavy overcoat. Eric and Ann fall into step beside each other on the path. He sees Eric's dog run into the lighted patch, helter-skelter as if it might overturn with its speed. The dog leaps up on Eric's legs. He thinks he can see Ann and Eric laughing, though they have their backs to him. He thinks he can see her hunch her shoulders and pull her coat more tightly around her and then he sees Eric place a gloved hand on Ann's back. He is squinting, following them up the screen. As they reach the far side of the light, Ann stops and removes Eric's hand from her back, making of his arm a loop so that she can put hers through it. And they step out, arm in arm, into the endless dark. Invisible to him.

☌

The room is over-warmed by a crackling fire which has dried out the air. Max looks up to see a group of walkers enter the bar, their waterproof trousers tucked into their socks. 'Ooh lovely, an open fire,' says one as they rustle and disrobe, talking to each other about which real ale to try. Behind the bar, and half obscured by a pillar which is wound with green tinsel, is Sheryl. Sheryl Crowther, landlady of the Fox and Feathers, forty-five if she's a day and still considered a newcomer despite five years in Marpleton. Maybe it's the accent – flat and hard, still full of Billericay. Grim-faced Sheryl, his mother always called her. Max watches her twist a tea towel inside a glass.

'Taken the sheep back up the fell yet?' asks Tal.

Max's focus returns to the table he is sharing with Tal and Jake. He's known them for ever, from the days they played football on that freezing grass pitch under Hambleton escarpment. Both of them labourers, working farm to farm, wherever the jobs are. Jake – he was bitter, always bitter, whether working or not. But Tal was a softer sort. He had dogs that were skilled at driving flocks down off the fell and he'd often helped with the Hartle Swaledales.

'Not yet,' Max says to Tal. 'Got to take the tups off first. Easier when they're down on the in-bye. They'll go up next week.'

'Aye, well, give us a call when you want them driving down off ridge for lambing,' says Tal, raising his pint to Max. 'There's no nicer work, when the trees are in leaf and everywhere's greened up again.'

'I'll be spending this week walling,' says Jake. 'Bloody awful. Freezing me tits off over at Talbot's place.'

Jake has the brightest blue eyes in a face otherwise red with the Yorkshire weather and the drink. He loves a rant and Max knows he can set him off like a rat up a drain. He just has to turn the conversation to the state of North Yorkshire farming and Jake will spit out his loathing for the local Labour MP, Colin Furslake, who's been giving out leaflets on 'diversification' and lecturing them that the future lay in 'agri-commodities'; that ministers wanted to make hill farmers 'custodians of the environment'.

'Talbot's the only one as can afford it,' says Max. 'Must be raking it in with the new fuel crops. That's where the subsidies are heading.'

'I don't know about you, but I'm not a fucking park-keeper,' Jake says.

Max is glancing at Sheryl, pulling down her pink top so it's tighter over her breasts. She returns Max's gaze, and fingers the gold pendant which rests on the swell of her cleavage. 'They can get themselves bloody gardeners for that,' Jake continues. 'I'm not going to tend a flamin' hedgerow. You can fucking forget it.'

Max drains his glass. 'I'll get another round in.'

He goes to the bar, leaning both elbows on it and raising one foot on the sturdy rail along the bar's base. Sheryl has pulled her top down again and when she turns to him, he sees that the low V-neck has exposed some red lace on her bra. Even on the other side of the bar, he can smell her perfume, mixing with the cigarette smoke in the room, sweet and heavy.

'Alright big fella?' she says. 'What can I getcha?'

'Two pints of Marston Moor, Sheryl,' says Max. 'And a half of Stella for Tal, who's bein' a poof.'

She smiles, tilts her hips as she pulls the lever towards her, the muscles in her arm tensing, one breast swelled upwards. Her collar-bones are protruding. She's not in bad shape, slim for her age. But then, she's never had kids.

'Primrose alright?' she says.

'Aye, grand,' says Max, looking away.

'Where's she tonight, then?'

'Dunno. At home. Doing her electrics probably,' says Max, still avoiding Sheryl's eye. Something about Sheryl talking about Primrose doesn't feel right.

'Hello Max!' says Tony Crowther, slapping him on the shoulder. He's on Max's side of the bar, carrying a bucket full of cigarette stubs and ash. Tony's face is open and benign, his voice like some friendly cockney policeman.

'Hello Tony,' says Max.

'I'm organising the Christmas quiz,' says Tony, straightening the mats on the bar. 'Set to be a corker.'

Max glances at Sheryl, saying: 'That'll get the village muttering. There were complaints after the last one. Dennis Lunn sang all the way home.'

'People hate to see others havin' a good time,' she says. 'I love a party. I'm going to really let me hair down.' She winks at Max.

'I don't think people'll begrudge us a spot of festive cheer,' says Tony. 'Anyway, I'd a thought the quiz has a special place in your heart, it being where you met your lady wife.'

Max remembers Tony's crackling, wheezing, high-pitched squeaking microphone; the way he tapped it, wearing one of his apologetic smiles, with a slight bow and a cough and said, 'Evening Marpleton!' And the team called the Co-op at the next table, and how he and Tal and Jake had started acting up in front of them. A distant country, that. Some of the excitement of those early days – a sense of life moving along at a tilt – had come back with the news of the bairn. All that approval from Joe had been like a shot in the arm for him, but it had waned, even though Max brought up the baby at every possible turn, looking to his father for another pat on the back. Like he needed it more now, was addicted to it. He can feel himself on the hunt for something – another boost.

'Not really,' he says to Tony. 'It were too long ago.'

'Aaah,' says Sheryl, twinkling at him, pinching his cheek. 'All the romance died has it?'

Max pulls his face away.

'You've got to keep the flame alive,' says Tony. 'Isn't that right, Princess?'

'If you say so,' says Sheryl.

'I think romance is overrated,' says Max.

'Me too,' she says. They linger on each other for longer than is seemly.

'Oh you two, honestly!' says Tony laughing. 'It's all about the small touches – the things that show the other person that you care.' Sheryl is taking Max's money as he says this, then counting out his change from the till. 'Only last week, I got her a teddy – di'n't I, Princess?' Sheryl gives him a hard stare. 'She loves a teddy that one. Show her I was thinkin' of her.'

'I'll make a note of that,' says Max.

Maureen Pettiford's voice has taken on an officious tone and Lauren sighs loudly. Maureen's chin is raised and she directs her words over all their heads, into the echoey rafters of Lipton Hall. 'Your aim is to keep a steady hand. Now, I know there aren't enough wheels for everyone, so those that can't get to one can practise turning their pots by hand. Plenty of water. Don't worry about the mess. Pottery is all about mess.'

'God, she's loving this,' whispers Lauren, and Ann smiles.

'—and I will fire your efforts in the oven over the weekend. You can pick them up at the next class.'

Maureen concludes her speech and there is a general clattering while the class settles down to their work. Lauren and Ann share a trestle table and are sat side by side on stools. Their table is already grey with rivulets of clay water and their hands thick with it as if made out of the stuff.

'Yours is already better than mine,' says Ann, leaning into Lauren while holding her hands out in front of her.

'Shurrup,' says Lauren, concentrating.

The room smells like school.

In the quiet of moulding soft wet gloop with her hands, Ann begins to run over the preparations she must make for Christmas – just three weeks to go which Joe would say was an age and why couldn't they begin on Christmas Eve which is when he'd rush into Lipton for something half-cocked to wrap for her. But it wasn't enough time at all. The pudding was done, yes, early autumn she'd done that, but there were sausage rolls to make and put in the freezer, the bird to order from Alan, cranberry sauce from scratch, chocolate cake for Boxing Day, toad in the hole – a meal-planning marathon it was. She decides to buy chocolates for after dinner. (Put that in your pipe and smoke it, Barry Jordan!) Peppermint creams or jellied fruits. Coopers is awash with festive boxes which send her into an excited spin at the very thought.

'I've still got a million things to get,' she says, still moulding and looking intently at her hands. The clay is cold and slippery. She feels an almost childish pleasure, squishing it through her fingers: delight and disgust at the same time.

'Oh god, me too,' says Lauren. 'Shall we go together? We could get everything in York – make a day of it.'

'Oooh yes. I'll drive if you like.'

'My car's nicer 'an yours,' says Lauren.

'Fair point.'

Maureen Pettiford's imperious voice rises over their heads from behind them. 'Less talking, more moulding ladies please!' And Lauren makes a face.

After a time, Lauren says, 'I'd like to get Primrose something – for the little one. Is there something they're in need of?'

'That's really nice.'

'It's nothing,' says Lauren.

'No it isn't,' says Ann.

He was always there, Lauren's lost boy, Jack. Meningitis at the age of five. Thirty years ago this January. She remembers standing in the street with Lauren all those years back, when Max and Jack were two or three or thereabouts, playing around their legs, and Brenda had stopped to chat. And she remembers Brenda saying to Lauren, 'He's a little heartbreaker, that one,' and nodding at Jack. 'A dreamboat.' And then Brenda had hastily added, 'And your Max too,' but Ann knew she hadn't meant it. And she'd felt stupidly jealous, because she knew Jack was a proper looker.

The shame. Begrudging her friend that moment. Begrudging that beautiful, beautiful boy . . . Ann knew it'd been hard for Lauren, to watch Max growing up. She'd loved Ann's boys as if they were her own, buying them presents at birthdays (Lauren never forgot a birthday) and at Christmas. Football-themed aftershave when they were teenagers. Wallace and Gromit socks. Toffees that were still going hard in the wardrobe of the back bedroom.

They'd never got mean with it, Lauren and Eric. Her and Joe, they would have got mean with it. Bitter against life. They'd never have survived it. She knows that. But Lauren and Eric, they seemed both to hold on to their boy – talk about him and remember – and to let it go. Oh, she shakes her head, she's not making any sense. All she knows is, she's never admired anything so much in all her life. Admired and envied it. And how could you envy a thing like that? But she does. Because she doesn't trust herself and Joe to survive in the same way, even against lesser odds.

'One of those baby gyms, I was thinking,' Lauren is saying. 'You know, they lie under it and stuff hangs down over 'em, to look at.'

'Now ladies,' says Maureen Pettiford, 'I want you to think about form.' She is wandering between the tables like she's Margot Fonteyn, banging her stick on the floor. 'Think about a smooth line. You want to echo the curves of the human body. Use your hands to ... That's right, Glynnis.' Maureen has stopped at a table and stooped low, dropping her voice. 'A bit less water.'

'God, where does she get off?' says Lauren.

'She's not that bad. She is there to teach,' says Ann. 'Mine's not echoing the human body. More an alien life-form.'

'She works in the bloody newsagent,' hisses Lauren. 'She's hardly Barbara Hepworth.'

'Oh for god's sake. You could never take instruction. It's a wonder you sign us up for so many classes.'

They simultaneously crane their necks back to look at their work, clay-wet hands in the air.

'Ruby coming to yours for Christmas?' says Lauren.

'No, she's not. I don't know what's going on between those two. Just us, the boys. And Primrose of course.'

'You'll need to get extra food in then,' says Lauren. 'She'll be eating for three.'

After a spell of moulding and considering and moulding, Lauren says, 'What d'you suppose Joe and Eric will get for us this year?'

'Oh, whatever riches Malton garage forecourt has to offer.'

'Go on,' says Lauren. 'What are your top five worst Christmas presents?'

'Joe gave me a hydraulic top link once,' says Ann, her head to one side.

'You're kidding. For a tractor?'

Ann nods, maintaining her gaze on her work. 'Trussed up in a bow it was. Bought it on eBay.'

'Eric has strayed into Tupperware in the past.'

'Well that's sackable.'

Lauren nods.

'Thing is, sometimes it's worse when they get it almost right, you know? Like bad earrings,' says Ann.

'Or really nasty jumpers.'

'Yes, always too small.'

'Or in Eric's case, too demure. D'ye not remember that polo neck he bought me? I looked like a toilet-roll tube made out of wool.'

'What're you two getting Sylvie?'

'We want to buy her a new car.'

'Goodness!' says Ann. She feels the urge to pat her collarbones but stops herself in time.

'I know, I know,' says Lauren, putting up a lead-coloured

hand, 'she won't be the least bit grateful. But she's our only one, Ann. She's all we've got.'

෧

Bartholomew's kitchen is flat and still without her.

He rests a hand on the over-shiny beech table and looks at the nasty wood units, the magnolia walls. It is all washed in a kind of rental beige under the strip light. There are no decorative touches – no paper chains or painted bowls or fairy lights. These things don't occur to him, even though he feels their absence.

Ruby's flat is another story – full of rich, dark corners; cluttered and soft; festooned now with pin lights and tinsel. Like Santa's grotto.

He hears her key in the door.

'How was it?' he shouts to the hallway. He can feel the pleasure seep into him. He watches her take her coat off.

'It was brilliant,' she says. Bright, shining. She brings all the energy of the day into his flat kitchen: her apple cheeks, her hair frizzing in the warm. 'They had these potato cakes,' she is saying, breathless. She is taking out her mobile phone and scrolling through the images. She has photographed the potato cakes, to show him. 'I think they had dill in them. They were amazing. With a poached egg on top.'

'Sounds very haute cuisine for a book club,' he says.

'Yeah well, Sheila's into it.'

'You should go into business together.'

'Elaine did a bean salad, which was nice. She'd cut chives into it. But the dressing was a bit sharp.'

He looks at her. He loves that the book is of secondary

97

importance to the food. He loves that she photographs food. He loves that she brings into his flat all this life and warmth and joy.

And then he feels something inside him contract again. Is it the force of his feelings or the force of hers, which makes him shrink back? And then the pressure comes – pressure from he doesn't know where, laden with obligation: to his parents, to the farm; the burden of that lease on the garden centre and the money he's poured into it. Most of all, obligation to Ruby, who is backing him into a corner. Closing down his options.

'How are you, anyway?' she says, coming over to where he sits and cupping his face in both her hands. Kissing his cheek. 'How was your day, my lovely?'

'It was good thanks.'

She yawns and stretches. 'I might turn in. All that murder and intrigue has done me in.'

'What are you reading next?'

'*Tess of the D'Urbervilles*. Can't wait. Freya chose it. She always chooses good ones.'

She's walking out of the room when he says, 'I've booked my ticket by the way. For Christmas.'

'Oh right,' she says, not looking back at him. 'When are you going?'

'Christmas Eve.' He can only see the back of her in the hallway.

'You'll have a good time, I'm sure.'

'When are you going up?'

'Haven't decided.' She turns and leans her body against the kitchen door frame. Brittle and bright. 'Dave Garside has joined our book club.' She smiles a mean smile, right at him. 'I invited him. Thought it might help him to settle in.'

A frosty fortnight later, Bartholomew bends to pick up a tray from where it is propped on the floor against one of the kitchen units. The room is cheerless as ever, even in daylight. You'd never know it was Christmas Eve. He's barefoot and wearing a faded towelling dressing gown which is falling open, causing a draught to whip inside his boxer shorts and T-shirt. He hops about on the lino, freezing, but determined not to put the heating on. The bills have been extortionate this winter – more than he can afford – and anyway, he's catching the train to Yorkshire in a few hours, so he considers it profligate to heat the flat. Ruby has complained about the cold more than once, and a couple of nights ago slept in her bobble hat as a form of protest.

He has set the tray with breakfast in bed for her. Tea. Toast with honey. Orange juice. And then he bends to retrieve her Christmas present from the cupboard where it's hidden behind a stack of telephone directories. He looks down at the crinkled paper covered in rosy-cheeked Santas. It's that slippery wrapping that's extra thin – extra cheap. He has packed the rest of the roll to take home with him.

He'd done several circuits of Blue Cross Shopping Centre, footsore and with a headache from its harsh lighting and the crush of festive shoppers, shuffling against each other, swearing and tense. He'd walked and walked, searching for something for her. And stopped, several times, outside the over-lit sparkle of Michael Roberts jewellers. But the prices were eye-watering and anyway, he'd never seen her wear delicate, dingly-dangly stuff like that. Ruby wore huge costume jewellery – stones which covered half her finger in turquoise, squatting in a thick silver setting. They were like boulders weighing on her hand as she cooked. And he was frightened for another reason. He felt this type of jewellery was as loaded as a gun. It sent a message and he wasn't at all sure which message he wanted to deliver. So he'd walked, more and more. Until he ached more than he ever ached after a day's labour at the garden centre. And in the final hour, he'd panicked.

He carries the tray down the corridor to the bedroom, his feet relieved to be off that freezing lino. When he enters the bedroom, she's just sitting up, her hair flattened against her head on one side and sticking out on the other.

His half-packed bag is open against the wall. They've been tense this past fortnight, with the run-up to Christmas and the looming time apart. At times he could see how disappointed she was and felt wretched for being the cause of it. But defiance would quickly push all that away and he'd find himself thinking: 'Why shouldn't I spend time with my family at Christmas? Why does she have to go making things difficult?' And he'd bank it as further evidence that life with Ruby – well, maybe it was just too complicated.

'What's this in aid of?' she says.

'Festive breakfast,' he says. 'I wanted to give you your present, as we won't be together on the day.'

'Ooh goodie,' she says and leans out of the bed so that she is upside down, feeling for something underneath. 'Here's yours,' she says, heaving herself up and presenting him with a small wrapped box.

She watches him begin to unwrap it. 'I'm really sorry, Bartholomew, for being so arsey – about Christmas. I was just a bit hurt, that's all. But I do understand, about you going home on your own. I'm sorry I've been a cow.' And she lays a hand on his forearm and he stops unwrapping and kisses her on the cheek.

'That's alright, lovely. I am going to miss you, you know. You'll have to send me lots of pictures of what you're eating.'

He lifts a white box from the wrapping and eases it open against a stiff hinge. Inside is a bed of black velvet and resting there, a watch. White face, roman numerals and a black leather strap. Classy. Minimal. He is taken aback, and then a kind of cold fear grips him. 'Wow, Ruby, I didn't expect. Golly, this is very generous. Yours,' he glances at her parcel, still unopened, 'yours isn't your main present. That's to come. It's a stocking-filler really.'

'Do you like it?' she says, clapping her hands together. 'Put it on. It's waterproof, so it doesn't matter if it gets knocked about when the sprinklers are on.' She is tearing at her present absently, but looking at his watch and saying, 'I thought it was classy. And you really shouldn't be wearing that old digital thing at your age. Ah, very Sean Connery. It looks lovely. Really suits you.'

She is lifting her present from its wrapping, holding it in the air between them.

'A scarf!' she says, bewildered, and he can see her trying to fashion her face into an expression which both hides her disappointment and also appears grateful. 'Ooh, it looks warm,' and she tries to sort of snuggle into it with vigour. The label is dangling down and she turns it. 'Angora, lovely. And . . . reduced.' He grabs it and pulls the tag roughly from the scarf but not before she says sadly, 'You got a bargain there.'

Then she forcibly brightens. 'Thank you darling.' And she kisses him. 'I shall wear it all day.'

Bartholomew has slept for the bulk of the train journey and now looks out at snowy countryside: black-silhouetted trees, their branches blown permanently one way – a row of melancholy dancers behind a veil of falling flakes. You'd normally see the slow crawl of ploughs across these fields, like bottom feeders tickling along the ocean floor. The snow has stopped them in their tracks. The soil will be hard as steel and Bartholomew knows the work on the farm will have slackened its pace with the short winter days. Lots of feeding up on the fell. He knows this without having to summon it. Nothing pretty about snow on a farm, much as it might look like a Christmas card. Winter is a battle.

He looks at the time on his shiny new wristwatch and tries to push away thoughts of Ruby. Nothing sits right inside him – neither his generous impulses, nor his withholding ones. And the more magnanimous she is about it – she'd given him an affectionate goodbye, wearing her scarf, with its yellow fur frothing about her mouth – the more discomfort he feels. Perhaps it's just not right, he thinks now: her and me. He shifts his body to try to find a position in his train seat which doesn't ache or crush his knees. Maybe when it is right, I won't feel like this. And he begins to settle into this position, feeling its comfort, the way it holds him: this possibility that the problem lies with her, well, with their 'fit' and not at his door at all. He just needs to wait for the right one, the perfect fit, and then his inabilities, so visible to them both, will evaporate like an early summer mist burnt off by the sun.

The train slows under the magnificent steel and glass arches of the station. He stands, half bent, in the tiny gap between his seat and the table, and reaches up to the luggage rack for his bag and the unwieldy bulk of his coat, which tumbles onto him as he tugs it.

Joe watches the snow falling on the village green. Big floating flakes, which meander down like feathers from an eiderdown. He looks at his watch. Bartholomew will be driving now through the snow. He'd insisted on hiring a car on the station platform, said they had a cut-price offer on, even though Joe had offered to pick him up in the Land Rover. 'Don't be daft, dad. Mad to come all that way when snow's so thick.' And Joe had felt grateful, that his son seemed to have some inkling of his exhaustion. He'll be able to tell Bartholomew, or let him know, that he's getting old – that all hands should be on deck under his tutelage. And Bartholomew will step up. He'll come to the rescue. Joe realises that his fantasy, if he's honest, is to have Bartholomew return to the farm. Devote his life, with Max, to its survival. Hartle men together, like it used to be.

He shakes his head. No, he must be careful, he tells himself. Make sure it doesn't go like last Christmas. He has to keep it buttoned. Ann has told him. No, he won't let that happen again.

'Your little project.' How he regretted saying it that way. He saw how wounded Bartholomew had looked but for some reason, he'd pressed on. 'You could do so much more, son. There's nothing wrong wi' it – nothing wrong in ladies tending pansies in hanging baskets. But it's not a living for a man.'

Bartholomew had glowered. He'd kept his eyes lowered but Joe could sense his whole body shaking as he picked up his keys and left the house. He hadn't come back – had driven straight home in that car of Leonard's. And then they hadn't spoken for weeks, though Joe had called saying, 'Come on son, don't be offended' into Bartholomew's answer machine. Ann had been livid with him. 'You and your big flaming mouth,' she'd shouted. 'You don't even know what he does down there. It's beautiful and you won't even go and see it.'

And then Bartholomew had called. Joe had felt so relieved, just to hear his voice, it was like a month of heartburn had disappeared with that call. 'Ruby said I should call,' Bartholomew said, reluctant. Cold. And still, even after all that, Joe felt he had to get his message through – that Bartholomew and Max, they were everything, every bit of potential that existed. Unspoiled. That's what Joe had felt when his boys were little. With their smooth skin and red lips and perfect bodies and no possibility closed to them. Then they grew up to be ordinary. Hairy and fat about the middle and limited, like everyone was. But Joe, he can't accept it. It was only human, wasn't it, to expect some progress? To expect them to do more than you did? He can't resist the urge to drive them on, like his dogs harrying the sheep to push them up onto higher ground.

He sees a shiny black VW Golf park in front of his garden gate and hurries to the doorway, watching Bartholomew get out. Is that really my little boy? A man, wearing a bright-red padded jacket which makes him look as if he's been inflated with a bicycle pump. A five o'clock shadow. A face beaten by the weather. But still a fine head of curls.

'Ann!' Joe shouts down the hallway as Bartholomew opens the front gate. 'He's here!'

Bartholomew can see Joe open the front door and lean his body on the door frame, hands in the pockets of his trousers, waiting for him. The greyness of his father's hair is a surprise to him, though it's not new. Silvery straight and thin it is. His face is oval and ruddy. The roundness of it makes him appear fatter than he is, when in fact he is whippet-thin. Bartholomew has the same roundness in his face, though he's taller, like Ann's brother. He is taken with an urgent burst of love for his father, all fresh to him after six months' absence. He sees Joe shout something down the hallway.

Bartholomew looks up at the house as he walks up the snowy front path. The daylight has been all but sucked away and the snow glows blue in the dusk, making the atmosphere moon-like. He can see a camera pointing out from the farmhouse façade like some alien probe.

'What on earth is that?' he says.

'That, my boy, is our new video entryphone,' says Joe, ushering Bartholomew into the house, one hand on his shoulder. He is beaming. 'Come on, I'll show you. You can see the whole village on the little monitor on the upstairs landing.'

'Surely you can see the whole village if you look out of the window,' says Bartholomew.

'You've got a point son, you've got a point.'

They smile at each other.

'Have you seen the video entryphone?' says his mother, waddling down the hallway and receiving his kiss while wiping her hands on a tea towel. The smell of cooking – her homemade sausage rolls, always served with mashed potato and Branston pickle for Christmas Eve tea – drifts down to them from the kitchen's open door.

'I have. Very high-tech.'

'Very pointless more like. Your father's becoming obsessed.'

'I am not. I'm just keeping up with modern technology.'

'Is that your bag?' says Ann. 'Set it down there for now. Looks heavy – full of expensive gifts is it?'

'Actually, I thought I'd make you something, mum,' he says, putting his arm around her and giving her a squeeze. 'Out of toilet rolls.' She is like a Weeble toy and the jingle from his child-hood pops into his head. 'Weebles wobble but they don't fall down.'

'That won't wash now you're in your thirties,' she says. They clatter down to the kitchen together. 'I want material evidence of love,' she says as she walks ahead of him. 'Or summat from Coopers.'

'Right you are.'

In the kitchen, Joe stands over the hotplate of the big green Rayburn, where a kettle is coming to the boil. Ann has her whole body in the larder, so that only her ample bottom is visible.

'Fruit cake alright, Bartholomew?' comes her muffled voice from inside the cupboard.

'Lovely.'

Joe has one hand on the kettle's horizontal handle, which is wrapped in a coarse oatmeal cloth. The cloth, it seems, has al-ways been wrapped around the handle and has taken on its shape. The cloth never moves. Like so many things in the Hartle household, it is so embedded in its role that it has long ceased to be separate from the kettle. It is something Bartholomew used to like about his childhood home – the permanence of things. In the same way, the dogs' baskets have always had their po-sition next to the Rayburn and are embedded with the dogs' imprint. When Lily and Robbie stepped in, they always circled two or three times before lying down. They seemed to settle in the same position, their backs moulded into the brown cush-ions, lightened by a mesh of dog hairs. Of course it isn't Lily and Robbie these days, but their successors – Tess and another working dog, whose name escapes him.

He watches his father fill two brown mugs with boiling

water. Still wearing his green cords, thinks Bartholomew – another thing that carried the imprint of its role in life – and the cardigan Joe puts on every day when he comes in from the field.

'How's the garden centre doing?' asks Joe, dunking the tea bags.

'Fine. It's fine. Tons to do, and Leonard's not much use. There's new stock to get in – that's an outlay and a half. But I want it properly ready for the spring season, not like the last couple of years. Money's tight.'

'I know that feeling,' says Joe, walking to the fridge for milk. 'But it's coming on alright – you think you'll make a success of it?'

'I don't know. I hope so.'

'You could always go back to that place – what was it? The Garden Store?' says Ann. She is gathering plates and cutlery for the table. 'I'm sure they'd have you back. Didn't they say you were a good little worker?'

'They probably would, mum.' He and Joe roll their eyes at one another. 'But that's not really what I want.'

'Don't be daft, woman. He's his own man,' says Joe. 'A man o' business. Wants to be his own boss and good on him.'

'Well,' she says, bringing the fruit cake to the table. 'I just think a steady job and a reliable income and not having to worry about the overheads – it shouldn't be sniffed at. But pardon me for breathing.'

'No, you're right, mum,' says Bartholomew. 'There's a lot to be said for it. But it's the right time to make my own way. It's getting through the winter – god it's hard.'

'Tell me about it,' says Joe.

'You don't want to end up in our shoes,' says Ann. 'Barry

Jordan says there's no getting out. We'd make a loss, selling the flock at current prices.'

'Arh, we don't want out,' says Joe. 'I wanted to tell ye, Bartholomew, we both did.' Joe looks to Ann but she has begun busying herself excessively with the cooking. Draining the boiled potatoes over the sink so that plumes of steam rise into the room. 'Now that Max is having a baby, well, we think it's time the farm should go over to him.'

Bartholomew feels all the blood drain from his face. 'What, straight away?'

'Naaooh,' says Joe, over-loud. 'Gradual like. I want to build it up for 'im. So that he's got a livelihood.'

'I see. And what about me?'

'What about you?' says Ann. 'You've got your garden centre.'

'No one gave me that. I'm up to my ears in loans.' Bartholomew wants to walk out, to get the train back to Winstanton.

'Max needs our help more 'an you do,' says Joe. 'He's not, he's not so . . .'

'How's he going to run a farm then?'

'Well, hang on a minute,' says Ann, 'he's not incompetent. He works very hard with your dad.'

'Come on,' says Joe. 'You knew this were coming. You never wanted the place. Never wanted to stay.'

His mother and father begin covering up the moment, Joe telling Ann how good the sausage rolls look.

'Any road,' says Joe. 'How is Ruby? Are things alright between you?'

'I don't know, dad,' say Bartholomew. If he tells them things are fine, well wouldn't it just confirm their view? Bartholomew all set up and doing well for himself. And anyway, things were not fine, they were far from fine. He wants to spill out his theory, about the 'fit' not being right and he wants Joe to confirm to him (while gazing into Ann's eyes) that when you meet the love of your life, everything falls into place. 'I'm not sure we're right for each other,' he says.

He sees Ann and Joe throw a glance at each other.

Bartholomew presses on. 'She's a bit keen.'

He is startled to see his mother swing round, her face as sharp as a wasp's sting. 'Good god Bartholomew, you're not that much of a catch.'

'Ann, calm down,' Joe says. He is cowering too, Bartholomew notices.

'Thanks very much, mum.'

'I'm just saying. It's not all hearts and flowers, a relationship.'

'I'm not saying it is. I just think you need to be sure that you've found the right person. For it to work.' He can see he's not winning himself any favours, pursuing this course, though he's unclear why not. The air is too charged for him to think it through.

'Well,' says Ann, visibly rearranging her face. She is wiping her hands on a tea towel which she then folds with considerable force. 'It's none of my business.' And she leaves the room.

Joe and Bartholomew sit at the table together.

'When are you seeing your brother?'

'Tonight. We're going for our traditional Christmas Eve pint at the Fox.'

Max and Bartholomew's boots crunch in the fresh powder. Beyond the pool of light cast by the pub, the village is virtually black. Like falling off the edge of the earth, thinks Bartholomew.

Max pushes open the Fox's outer door. 'After you,' he says, and Bartholomew steps inside, where it is warm and dark. Its sounds – the fruit machine, the fire, the music from the jukebox – so familiar to him.

'The Hartle boys!' says Tony Crowther. 'Welcome home, Bartholomew. What can I getchya?'

'I'll have a pint of Marston Moor. And one for Max. You still drinking Marston, Max?'

'Aye, that'll do.' Max has taken his coat off, lain it on a banquette and has sat down, chatting to Tal and Jake, who are one table along. Bartholomew brings their drinks to the table.

'The wanderer returns,' says Jake.

'How's things, Bartholomew?' asks Tal.

'Fine thanks. Happy Christmas.' He raises his pint to them and sits down on a stool opposite Max.

'Brass monkeys out there,' says Jake.

'It is,' says Bartholomew.

'How's life down south?' asks Jake. 'Garden centre going well?'

He is smoking a roll-up. A snaking coil drifts up from its tip and he squints as it hits his eye.

'OK,' says Bartholomew. 'Not bad. Make a living.'

'Business-wise, though. Is it a good earner?' Jake asks.

Bartholomew can feel Max's gaze on him.

'Hard to say. It's so seasonal. If you have a good spring, then you're OK, but the winters are a bit hardgoing. Quiet.'

'What would you say, though, per year?' Jake asks.

God, he's relentless, thinks Bartholomew. 'Why do you want to know, Jake? You thinking of branching out?'

'Not me. Farming's bad enough.'

'How bad?' Bartholomew says, looking at Max. He has been

silent, watching Bartholomew's answers; sipping his pint and glancing over to the bar where Sheryl is serving. She is wearing a skin-tight leopard-print top. She's looking old, Bartholomew thinks. Her make-up sits thickly over a leathery face.

'Bad,' says Max. 'Worst I've seen it. Stores going for less than twenty pound. Mule gimmers getting little over sixty pound. And feed is dear. Just 'ave to see if we can make it through till lambing.'

'If?'

Max glances again at Sheryl. Not at her face, Bartholomew notices.

Tal has put another song on the jukebox.

'The Streets,' Bartholomew says as the song comes on. 'Good choice.'

'Aye, well, "Rockin' Around the Christmas Tree" was doing my head in,' says Tal.

'You heard about Talbot – he's experimenting w' all sorts of new fuel crops,' says Max. He has half an eye on Jake. 'Willow's his latest thing. Burn it for heating. He's got some government grant to grow it instead of set-aside. Supposed to be an alternative to fossil fuels. It's carbon-neutral.'

'Sounds like a good idea,' says Bartholomew.

'Yeah but no one's got wood-fired heating, have they?' says Jake. His voice is quick, his face red. 'Plus, they need a bloody great lorry to shift it anywhere.'

'Still,' says Bartholomew, 'surely it beats being paid tuppence for a lamb. Is that what you were thinking – growing fuel?'

'S' up to dad. He wants to carry on with sheep for now,' says Max.

'Yes, but if you're taking it over –'

'Dad knows what to do.'

'You could take it in a new direction.'

'We're alright as we are,' says Max, his gaze still on the bar. 'Don't you worry. Here, how old d'ye think bairn'll be before dad has him driving the John Deere?'

'Six or seven months at least,' says Bartholomew. 'There's health and safety to think on. Course, he'll let him play with power tools in the barn.'

'And a ewe roll to suck on, 'stead of a rusk,' says Max.

They chink their pints.

'He's buying a new tractor – getting a loan. Don't tell mum. I'm sworn to secrecy,' says Max.

Bartholomew frowns. Max is leaning too hard. 'Can they afford that?' he says.

'Says he wants to build the farm up, for when I take it over.'

'Maybe it's you who should be doing that,' says Bartholomew. 'Build it up yourself once it's yours. Get your own loans.'

'Dad's happy to do it.'

'I don't think that's the point, is it?' says Bartholomew.

'And what would you know about it?' says Max.

'I've got me own loans. I'm not living off my father age thirty-five.'

'You're not helping him either,' says Max.

'Go easy lads,' says Tal.

'I'll get another round,' Max says.

Bartholomew watches him lean both elbows on the bar, his broad back sloping up towards Sheryl. He has one foot on the bar's skirting rail. He can see Sheryl laughing, fingering the gold pendant around her neck. Max is smiling, murmuring, though Bartholomew cannot hear what he is saying.

Eventually, Max returns to their table.

'You want to watch yourself there,' says Bartholomew.

Max smiles at him, raises his pint and drinks half of it down without drawing a breath.

Bartholomew sits down heavily on one of the kitchen chairs. He can feel his head swim with the pints he has consumed at the Fox. His mother has her back to him, scooping wet piles of potato peelings into the composting bucket. On the side are several pans and various bowls draped with tea towels. Joe is watching television next door and the muffled sounds of clapping periodically drift in to them.

A marshy gas hits Bartholomew's nostrils. 'Oof, Tess, that's revolting,' he says to one of the dogs, who is asleep in her basket.

'She's getting on a bit,' says Ann. She is wiping the kitchen surfaces now. 'Happens to us all.'

'Not the flatulence I hope.'

They hear Joe turn off the television and the creak of the stairs as he climbs them. They hear the scrape of the landing chair being pulled away from the wall. They are looking at each other. Ann rolls her eyes.

'Has it all been finalised yet?' asks Bartholomew.

'About Max and the farm?' says Ann. 'I don't know, love. You'll have to ask your father about that.'

'D'ye think he's ready to take it over? Why does he even want it? No one's taking over farms these days.'

'Did it ever occur to you,' says Ann, 'that it might be nice for us, that he's taking it over? Nice for us to have 'im around?' She is cross again. He always seems to make her cross. 'No? Well, shurrup then.'

He is silent, not wanting to irritate her any more than he has already. A coldness seizes his heart. He wants to leave Yorkshire, now, this instant. He wonders if he could catch a train this evening, after his parents have gone to bed. Then remembers it's Christmas Eve and he must sit it out.

'Do you want me to help you bring down the presents?' he asks.

'I did it while you were out,' she says. 'Right, well I think I'll turn in. Switch off the lights before you come up.' She stops in the doorway. 'Are you going to ring Ruby?'

'I don't know.'

'Well, maybe you should. Be nice to wish her a happy Christmas.'

Bartholomew is left alone in the kitchen, where the tired light shines on neat surfaces and washed crockery on the draining board. He can hear the murmuring of his parents on the landing and a door close. In the absence of people, the house begins its amplified ticking – the uneasy creaking as it shifts and settles, the hum of fridge and boiler. Bartholomew sits, unable to begin his slow journey up to bed.

Poupff.

Tess lets out another sulphurous wet guff. He notices, as he sits there, how shabby the room is. The paint on the skirting boards is flaking. The armchair next to the Rayburn has frayed fabric on its arms. The yellow walls have a greasy sheen. They haven't decorated the place in more than fourteen years. But he also notices the precision in all the hooks Joe has put up for Ann – little tacks banged in for spare keys; larger ones for her pans; the short shelf by the sink for her scourer and single hook beneath it for her washing-up brush; the coat rail next to the back door. And the neat square of newspaper on which are lined up various working shoes, hardened and muddy. He is touched by this thrifty DIY orderliness. It speaks to him of collaboration. He and Ruby haven't built up any systems for living. It doesn't seem as if they can.

He switches the lights off and walks down the hallway, stopping at the open door to the living room, which is dark except for the rich multicoloured glow of the Christmas tree lights and the sheen they cast onto the wrapped presents below. He can smell the fresh spruce needles and the generalised wood-smoked air of the house and it brings up a surging childish thrill, except now he knows he can walk past the presents without rattling them, and that he will be able to get to sleep.

Reaching into his pocket for his mobile phone, he presses 'Names' and 'R' for Ruby. Looks at the little screen whose illumination gradually fades out. He switches the phone off.

Bartholomew stands holding his book in one hand, a glass of water in the other, gazing down at the narrow single bed in his parents' back bedroom. Staring back at him is a superhero dressed as a banana, the faded corners of the duvet tucked in tightly, smoothed by his mother's house-proud hand. At the end of the bed is a fraying hand towel, folded to a square.

He pulls back a corner of the duvet and gets in, inching his way down, wondering if single beds were always this narrow. He breathes in the washing-powder smell of the pillowcase, its fabric thin and cold like a compress. The feeling of being back at the farm has brought back his childhood frustrations, especially the teenage ones when he'd have to work with Joe and Max through the interminable school holidays – cutting and baling the grass (smelt like human sick once it started to ferment, if you asked him, which nobody did); returning strays to neighbouring farms (Max did all the heavy lifting. Bartholomew bolted the ramps); checking those on the in-bye for foot rot (Bartholomew seemed mostly to open and shut gates). He'd wanted, those summers, to be left alone to eat cheese-and-pickle sandwiches, think about Claire from Form Three and listen to the Fine Young Cannibals, nursing the way he felt apart from them, his family.

He remembers sitting on the fence, which looked out on the field where the fattening lambs were grazing, Lily snuffing around the mud and straw behind him in the yard.

'Everything alright, Bartholomew?' his father had said, coming to lean on the fence.

'Yep.'

'Why've you got a face like a wet weekend then?'

Bartholomew didn't answer. They had been separating off the weak lambs earlier in the day and he'd watched as Joe pulled the tiller gate towards him to take off the smallest of the lot, had heard the cries from its mother and its healthier twin as they were forced the other way. Panicked bleating. The weak lamb, not fine enough for breeding, would be fattened on the in-bye and sold for meat.

'What you listening to?' Joe had said at his side.

'Fine Young Cannibals.'

Joe crouched then to stroke Lily.

'Would you send Lily to the slaughterhouse?' asked Bartholomew.

'Make a nice Sunday cut that,' Joe had said, running his hand down the back of Lily's haunch, then patting her hard.

'I don't know how you do it.'

'Come on, don't be so dramatic.'

'Because you know them. You know who they are. What they feel – like when you take the lambs off at weaning and they cry out all night.'

Joe had stared at the ground. For a moment, he'd seemed bewildered. All Bartholomew had wanted, he thinks now with his arms behind his head on the pillow, was for Joe to say that he felt it. Really felt it – what he was doing to those animals, year in, year out. Tending and killing. Working so hard to keep lambs with their mothers only to tear them away from them come September, when their cries would echo all night across the farm and the family, they'd lie in their beds listening to it.

ᖆ

Christmas morning and Ann sits in her apron on a dining chair, which has been brought into the living room. She has set it close by the door, so that she's got easy access to the kitchen. She holds a glass of fizz in one hand, put there by Joe, and the fizz is going straight to her head because she's not used to drinking at 11 a.m. And she feels woozy, too, from being up so early and so frantic.

When she'd woken at seven, Joe had rolled over and placed a heavy arm over her body. 'Give us a cuddle,' he'd said drowsily but she was up and out of bed like a whippet out of the traps. 'Give over. I've far too much to do.'

Downstairs in her dressing gown, she'd pulled the bird from the cold store (it was too big for the fridge). Her hands, now, are swollen and chapped with all the washing and forcing them un- der the cold skin of the bird, peeling it gradually from the flesh so she could push the parsley butter in between.

She takes a sip and looks at Bartholomew who is sat forward on his armchair, his elbows on his knees and his hands clasped together; that intense look he often has on his face, watching Max turn the CD in his hand. Bartholomew leans further for- ward still, saying, 'It's a good album. One of my favourites. Anyway, I thought you'd enjoy it.'

Come on you miserable beggar, she thinks. Give him

something back.

'Right,' says Max. 'Thanks.'

And her heart sinks when she sees him set the CD down on the floor by his feet, where it becomes part of the pile of gifts that she has bought him – the pile which is identical to Bartholomew's (socks, underpants, wash bag, shave foam, nail clippers) because even now – and honestly, they're grown men – she is anxious not to throw petrol on to that flame.

'Bartholomew,' she says. 'This one's from me and your dad.' In her peripheral vision she can see Max alert, watching. Calm down, she thinks, for heaven's sake. It's only fudge.

She blows out into her cheeks, gazing at them. It was a myth that fierce motherly love blinded you from seeing your children clearly.

She remembers the simplicity of her feelings when they were small – how physical her love was then: lifting them out of the cot after a sleep, holding them pressed against her body, their hot bread-loaf legs circling her waist; how she would sink her face into the skin at the nape of their necks and breathe in very deeply and it was as if they were a drug and she could feel this tingling sensation right up into the follicles of her hair. Fierce pockets of protectiveness – a primal thing. Knowing you'd throw yourself in front of a car ahead of them.

But by god they were annoying.

She looks at them now, Bartholomew full of these high ideas as if the ordinary stuff of life were beneath him. She watches him take another handful of bacon bites from the bowl on the side table. And Max, visibly doing an audit of Bartholomew's present pile. Always counting up.

'This is from me,' says Joe. He is handing her a small parcel. 'More fizz anyone?' he says to the room.

'Thanks, love,' she murmurs and begins absently unwrapping it on her knees but her eyes are still on the general hubbub and the rustling pile of paper which is growing mountainous in the centre of the room. Joe is trying on the cardigan she has bought him and saying, 'It's very nice, love, but I'm not sure it's better than the one I've got.'

'You mean the one with holes in it?' she says.

Bartholomew has turned away from Max and is saying to Primrose, 'What did Santa bring you, Prim?'

'Pans,' says Primrose, pouring peanuts into her mouth. 'But they're not from Santa. They're from Max.'

'Romance not dead then,' says Bartholomew.

'How d'you mean?' says Primrose.

'Never mind,' says Bartholomew. Ann watches him lean back in his armchair and take out his phone from his pocket. Fiddle with it. Then she looks down at the present on her knee.

'My god Joe, we can't afford this,' she gasps, holding up a necklace. Beautiful it is, little lilac stones and diamante. Old-fashioned. Glittering.

'Yes we can,' says Joe, stepping over the paper mountain and raising her up from her chair and taking her, still bewildered, in his arms. 'Nothing's too good for the woman I love.'

And she doesn't know whether to give in to the feeling she has of being ever so touched or whether to give more to the sense of anger rising, at his being irresponsible with money. And when he was always telling her to tighten her belt. There is a third feeling, that she bats away, about the necklace being not . . . well, totally to her taste (though it's lovely, she can see that). Just not quite the sort of thing she wears. And if they were going to splash out, she'd rather have halogen down-lighters in the kitchen, like Lauren's. But marriage has taught her to receive gifts for the meaning. The little things, you had to let go of. She turns while he fastens the necklace around her neck. She pats it and she feels it sit there, the cost.

꩜

The kitchen is all movement as everyone idles in. Ann is removing the bird from the oven and its juices are spitting noisily in the pan. The room seems briefly packed with unusually large adults, though Primrose hangs back, patting the dog in the doorway. Tess's tail thuds against Primrose's leg.

Bartholomew notices the care Ann has taken over the table. There are crackers on each of the plates, red paper napkins and a holly wreath at the centre of the table. Joe is filling the glasses with more wine. He and Ann are growing garrulous with it.

'Sit down everyone,' Ann shouts, bringing a bowl of roast potatoes to the table. 'Joe, I need you to carve now.'

'Right you are.'

'Shame Ruby's not here,' says Max, and Bartholomew feels himself bristle. 'Not ashamed of us are you?' Max is looking at Ann and Joe as he speaks, though they are too busy with the food to notice. 'Not joining the ranks of old married couples any time soon?'

'Well, I . . .' Bartholomew begins.

'Here girl,' says Max to the dog, bending under the table to stroke her as she slinks past, 'where are you going? Dad, I've heard of a tractor that's coming up for sale over Malton way: a good one, apparently. Five years old. I could go up there next week, take a look.'

'Sounds good,' says Joe.

'If you two think you're going tractor-shopping any time

soon, you've got another think coming,' says Ann, bringing over the carrots and the sprouts. Steam rises up to her face from the bowl. Her complexion is red with the heat and the wine. Knobs of butter slide over the vegetables. 'There's no money and you know it.'

Bartholomew sees Max smile at Joe and Joe return with a wink.

Bartholomew feels his phone vibrate in his pocket. He takes it out and opens the message from Ruby. It is a photograph of another festive table, groaning with turkey, potatoes, parsnips, sprouts and various other bowls too blurry to identify. Her text says:

Veg boiled for two hours. No vitamins have survived.

When he looks up, Primrose is pointing a Christmas cracker in his face. 'Will you pull mine?' she says, without smile or frown.

Lunch is eaten too hastily, he thinks. The Hartles eat with a Neanderthal urgency, as if they might never eat again. Joe and Ann's faces are flushed and bloated. They all wear paper hats from their crackers and as he looks around the table, Bartholomew thinks it makes them resemble in-patients in a mental institution or a retirement home.

His phone vibrates again.

If only there was more lard. Rx

'Ruby at home with her folks?' says his mother.

'Yes. In Leeds.'

'Might you go and see her?'

'Oh, I don't know,' he says, leaning back in his chair. 'We see enough of each other at home.' He is surprised to hear himself call Winstanton home.

'I could never live down south,' says Max. 'Too crowded.'

Joe has his head down, pushing food urgently onto his fork.

Ann snorts. 'You could barely leave Marpleton. We thought you were going to stop at home till you were fifty. Terrified we were. Thank god for Primrose is all I can say,' and she pats Primrose's knee.

'I think if Max and Primrose are to have a child, then she ought to know about the trike incident,' says Bartholomew.

'Ooh yes,' says Ann, rolling with it, taking another slug, 'we must tell you that one. Chuh, the shame of it. D'ye remember, Joe?'

Max colours up. 'Don't, mum,' he says.

'Yes, go on,' says Bartholomew. 'Tell her.'

'Well, Max was at nursery,' says Ann, 'must've been three or four at the time, and all the kiddies were fighting over the tricycles. There were only five of them and Max had bagsed one and he were riding around, crowing like. And all the other kiddies were waiting for a turn. Anyway, he needed a poo – this is what the teacher told me. And rather than give up his trike, he just stood up astride it and pooed right there in his pants.'

Joe is cackling. Primrose giggles into her napkin. Bartholomew smiles. Max's face is like thunder.

Ann is laughing, saying, 'And I said to him, "You daft apeth, you bought yourself, what, three minutes, tops?" He was that desperate not to give up his place.'

Max stands up and throws his napkin down onto his chair and walks out of the room. They all look at each other, hearing Max climb the stairs and then bolt the bathroom door.

'Are there seconds?' asks Primrose.

'Of course, love,' says Ann. 'What would you like?'

'Everything,' says Primrose. She watches Ann fill her plate.

'And another potato,' she says quietly.

'How are Eric and Lauren?' asks Bartholomew. 'Are they coming over later?'

'Eric'll be too busy polishing his Nissan Micra,' says Joe.

'They're well,' says Ann. 'Having their kitchen done. That's dragging on, driving Lauren nuts. Goodness, it'll be beautiful though. They've got these little spotlights in the ceiling and they give off this sparkly pinkish light, like in a hotel.'

'Not good for your electricity bill, halogens,' says Primrose, with a full mouth.

'We don't need spotlights,' says Joe.

'No,' says Ann, 'we probably don't. But I wouldn't mind painting this room. It's looking very tired. Hey ho. Things are just too tight.'

Joe has got up from the table and is clearing some plates.

Bartholomew feels his phone vibrate again. Two messages. The first is a picture of a white bowl containing brown sponge submerged in a lake of cream.

Mum's yule log. Heart attack in a bowl.

The second says,

Have exploded. Just scraping self off ceiling.

He decides to turn his phone off.

'Right,' says Ann. 'Who's for Christmas pud with brandy butter and rum sauce? Just a slither, Bartholomew?'

He is used to hearing his mother tell him he needs feeding and pushing food at him but now he notices her adjust the lie of her knife.

'OK, thanks mum. Can anyone smell burning?'

Bartholomew gets up and pushes his chair out with the backs

of his legs. He wanders about the room sniffing – towards the oven, then through the kitchen door to the hallway, the dogs following him to where the air is cool. But the smell recedes in this direction, so he returns to the kitchen. The others have now stood, raised by a vague curiosity.

'Your mother will have left something on the stove again,' says Joe, investigating.

'I have not,' says Ann. 'P'raps it's next door's dinner.'

Bartholomew walks around the table to the back door and opens it tentatively and the noise hits his ears, even before the smell. Smoke is pouring from the black mouth of the hay barn, on the opposite side of the yard. He takes several broad steps towards it until a wall of heat stops him. The snap and pop of flames on the bales can be heard over the engulfing roar.

'Dad!' Bartholomew tries to shout but no sound emerges. Joe is already at his elbow, straining forward. Everything seems to Bartholomew to be in slow motion. Joe is stumbling towards the barn.

Bartholomew runs forward after him, hoping to grab Joe. Needles are pricking the edges of his eyeballs; he squints into the drifts of grey and black smoke. Joe is shouting but he can't hear what he's saying, so Bartholomew goes further in. When his hand finally reaches Joe's back in the darkness, he finds his father beating something, his whole body flailing onto the bales. Bartholomew pulls at him, first his cardigan, then his whole body, dragging him backwards.

'What the hell are you doing?' he shouts. 'Come out, dad!' He forces Joe towards the doorway. 'Max! Get some help!'

He and Joe are bent double, coughing. He notices Joe's hand, where the skin is puckering and bubbling, strange lines appearing as if threads were being pulled taut.

Max has been standing, rooted, but now he runs inside.

'I can't look,' says Joe and he leans his forehead against Bartholomew's shoulder. Bartholomew holds him, looking at the smoke billowing out of the mouth of the barn and at the white plastic sacks of ewe rolls, leaning against the nearest barn pole, which are now melting onto the floor.

Ann stands at the open back door, her arms folded across her chest against the arctic air. The yard is still milling with firemen, though two engines have pulled out of Marpleton and driven away. Four firemen still have their hoses pointed at the barn. The stripes on their enormous rubber coats flash as they move. Two firemen are reeling in their equipment, another is inside the engine, speaking on a radio handset. The eighth, who seems to be in charge, stands beside the engine writing on a clipboard.

She looks at the barn. She can hardly believe it. There it is, in all its inglorious wetness. The black struts and arching roof are presiding over its charred interior like some impervious mother. Smoke is still drifting out from its mouth and she can see the bales – sodden and black – like a smoking dung heap, but worth less money.

The fireman with the clipboard walks towards her.

'What a mess,' she says.

'You've been lucky,' he says. He is a kind-looking man with a doughy, open face and ginger eyebrows.

'How's that?'

'Well, for a start there's no wind today. If there'd been a wind the surrounding buildings might have gone up – your farm-house, for example. And second, your livestock are penned away from the barn, so no loss of life. That's the main thing.'

'I s'pose. I've never seen anything like it.'

'Commonest thing there is – hay-barn fires.'

'Oh yes, of course I know that,' she says. 'It's just never happened to us, that's all. And in December. I mean, you expect it in June or September, after baling, but in the snows? I didn't think it were possible.'

'Aye but November were that dry, d'you remember?' He seems enthusiastic now, the puzzle-solver. 'And then, two weeks ago, the snows came. I'd put money on there being a leak in that roof. Wetness got in, seeped through to the centre of the bales and set off the decomposition process. That's what made them heat up. Once they get to 160 degrees – whoosh. Up it goes.'

'How can it get so hot though, when it's so flaming cold out?'

'Well, bales might've been too tightly stacked. Don't forget, once you're in the centre of a stack, it's well insulated. Toasty it is, in there. I could be wrong. But that'd be my guess.' He steps away from her and looks around the corner of the farmhouse, towards the gate to the village. 'The stack is a bit too hidden from the road to be arson. And it's not the time of year for it. Kids do that in summer.'

They stand for a minute, watching the firemen.

'Why are they still hosing? Doesn't look like the barn could get any wetter.'

'We have to make sure there's no heat left. We don't want to leave and find there's a patch still smouldering somewhere, which could then catch on to your other buildings.'

'Would your lads like some tea?'

'Now you're talking.'

'And some Christmas cake? Oh I do feel bad, getting you all out on Christmas Day.'

'That's what we're here for, love. Mind if I come in?'

He steps into the kitchen and removes his yellow hat. He seems impossibly big, stood there next to her sink in his creaking yellow trousers and boots as big as U-boats.

'Your insurance will cover it,' he is saying. 'There's just some paperwork to fill out.'

She keeps her back to him, gathering plates and knives and taking the foil cover off the cake.

He fills the silence. 'Still, looks like you'll have to buy in your winter feed. What was that lot worth? About ten thousand pounds?'

'About that, yes,' she says quietly.

The boys have come home from the hospital with Joe, who sits at the kitchen table holding his bandaged hand as if it belongs to another person. His nostrils are black with soot.

The chief fire officer – Ken, as Ann has come to call him – is still in the kitchen, standing with his bottom leaning against the counter. He is drinking his third cup of tea. He sets it down, saying 'Do you mind if I use your bathroom?' and she says 'Of course, up the stairs and it's straight ahead of you,' and they can all hear him creaking as he climbs them, two at a time.

Bartholomew, Max and Primrose are sitting at the table with Joe. Primrose is eating a slice of Christmas cake. Bartholomew is reading a leaflet that Ken has handed out. They hear the flush from the landing.

Ken reappears.

'We have testing kits you can use,' he says, taking up his tea and his position against the counter. 'It's a free service.'

Ann has been looking out of the kitchen window at the fire-

127

men clearing up but now she shuts her eyes for a minute, over-whelmed by tiredness, as if her body has been revved up by a strong electric current all afternoon and someone has just shut the power down.

Lauren had called, hours ago, not long after the sirens had blasted through the silence of the village. She'd rushed to the phone, thinking it might be the boys from the hospital. Ann had stood in the hallway, the handset to her ear, looking in through the lounge doorway. The flashing lights from the en-gines parked in front of the farmhouse did a three-second sweep of her living room, like a blue searchlight picking out the aban-doned wine glasses, the scrunched wrapping paper on the floor, and the tottering little towers of presents at the foot of the arm-chairs and sofa.

'Oh no, not the hay barn. Oh Ann!'

'I really can't talk now, Lauren.'

'No, of course you can't. I'll call round later. Let me know if there's anything I can do.'

A few from the village had gathered to watch, though they were kept back by the crews. Dennis Lunn staggered over from the Fox. A couple of toddlers stood and pointed at the nee-naws, as if they'd been laid on as a festive treat.

Ken is saying: 'It's basically a probe with a thermometer at-tached. You push it into the centre of the bales and it tells you whether they are heating up or not. 100–140 degrees and you're getting into the danger zone and the bales need separating and ventilating so they cool down. 160 degrees and she's likely to go up.'

'So it's possible that it happened because the bales weren't stacked properly,' Bartholomew says.

Here we go, thinks Ann.

'We stacked them as we always stack them,' says Max.

'I wouldn't say it was a cause, more a contributing factor,' says Ken.

He's been on a communications course, thinks Ann.

'But if they'd been stacked more loosely . . .' Bartholomew is saying.

Joe is slumped. He looks tiny, his face furrowed and darkened with the soot. He is in a world of his own.

Bartholomew and Max have their voices raised.

'You need to take responsibility,' says Bartholomew. 'Look at him. He's taking on too much. He can't cope.'

'Boys,' Ann hisses. 'Now is not the time.'

A blast of cold air enters the kitchen as one of the firemen pops his head round the back door. 'All done here, chief,' he says to Ken.

'Right you are,' says Ken. 'Right, we're going to leave you to it. Any other problems, give us a call. We'll come and do a proper site investigation next week and then your report will be complete and you can use it for your insurance claim.'

Everyone is silent, looking at their cups or the table. Ann pushes her fingers into her closed eyes. 'Well, thanks for everything, Ken,' she says. 'It's been, well, a bit of a shock.'

'Worst's over,' he says. He waves as he steps out of the door. 'We'll make sure we close the gate after us.'

The door shuts.

A suspicion is seeping into her. 'The insurance, Joe,' she says. 'There is insurance, isn't there? You did renew it, didn't you?'

'I was saving the pennies,' he says. 'I was keeping summat back. Waiting till we were a bit more flush. There's never fires in December. They happen in summer. I thought it could wait.'

She raises her eyes to the ceiling. She can feel the rage start to pop in her head and the tears prick in her eyes and all this bile rise up in her throat.

'I could kill you right now,' she says. 'That were ten thousand went up in that fire. How are we going to feed the sheep?'

'I'll find a way, I'll sort it,' he says.

'You won't sort it, you stupid man. You'll make a mess of it, just like you make a mess of everything. Just like you'd never get that roof fixed. You scrimped on it, as usual. And it leaked. This is your fault, you stupid, stupid, stupid man.'

She storms out of the kitchen and down the hallway.

JANUARY

— *Frozen ground* —

'Joe?' she calls. 'Joe, love?'

Ann steps out of the back door into the yard. She zips up her fleece as the frozen air whips about her neck. A fog has rolled down off the moor and is swirling about the farmyard, like more of the smoke that has only stopped rising off the hay barn in the last day or two. She sees Joe over on the other side of the yard, his back to her, looking up at it. He is tiny against the charred mouth of the barn. Its metal pole struts are rigid while the interior is a collapsed carbonised mess.

'Why do bad things keep happening?' he says as she approaches his back.

'Now come on,' she says, as she fortifies the capable person inside her, like she'd had to, to get over the business of the insurance, because she could have nursed that one. Oh she could. 'You're not the first person this has happened to.'

'I'm probably the first that wasn't insured. What'll we do?'

She is caught. She can sense an opportunity, while he is sad and wrung open with it, to direct him gently. Let's gear it up for selling. Let's get out of this game, she thinks, though she knows he's not the only impediment. The economics are against them, now more than ever, and there's still Max to think of, though she wouldn't wish this mess on her worst enemy, let alone her son. But she can see now how reduced Joe would be by the failure of it. Joe without a farm. Be careful what you wish for.

'We're going to clean the place up, that's what we'll do,' she says, putting an arm through the loop of his. To their right, the bales at the edge have burnt right through and are precarious towers of ash. Ghosts of themselves, she thinks.

'We're going to clean it up,' she says, gathering up the burnt-out fragments of her kindness. 'And somehow, we're going to get through to lambing. I don't know how. But no one got hurt in this, Joe. It's just hay. And the blessed ewe rolls. I wish we hadn't stored the sacks in there.'

He puts his arms around her, pushing his cheek next to her cheek and she can feel his gratitude – that she's not still harbouring a grudge about the insurance – and so she's encouraged in her kindness. She says into his ear, 'And lambing always cheers us up.'

She kisses his cheek – papery in the cold.

'What would I do without you, Annie?'

'Don't be daft,' she says, still with her face against his.

'There's something I need to tell ye,' he says and she pulls away.

'What?' she says, her heart starting to beat harder. 'What, Joe?'

'It's nothing that bad.'

'Can you just tell me?'

'I've bought a tractor.'

'What?'

'Well I didn't know this was going to happen, did I?'

'Jesus, Joe,' she shouts and begins pacing the yard, her breath coming out in white puffs. All the care, the delicacy, she's taken in dealing with the situation and with his feelings, well, that's all over. 'Did you not think renewing the insurance should ha' come first?'

'We needed a new one. The John Deere was on its last legs.'

'How much, Joe?'

'Seven thousand.'

'How much, Joe?' she says more forcefully.

'Eight and a half.'

'Jesus! What were you thinking? And you bought it on the never-never, I take it. Well, you'll just have to send it back.'

'I can't. I've taken out a bank loan. I can't undo it.'

'And of course it didn't occur to you to talk to me before taking out a loan, did it? Christ, Joe. When does the loan come through?'

'This month.'

'Right, and you've bid for the tractor on farmautotrader?'

'And won the bidding,' he says. 'It's a beauty, Ann – nearly new. A real bargain I got.'

'Right, well, you'll not go through with the purchase,' she says. 'And that loan – the eight thou. That'll buy in our winter feed. You'll have to go and see Granville Harris. See if you can get a deal on some hay. And the ewe rolls we've lost – they'll need replacing. It's still not enough, but it's something. I'm going in for a brew.'

She can't help treating him like the impossible toddler who's spilt the paints. Even though it's a blessing – this loan he's got. It's the manner of it she can't forgive, not so soon after forgiving him for the other thing.

'You coming?' she says.

'In a minute,' he says.

Joe has taken his mug of tea back outside and is standing once more in front of the hay barn. It's cold out, but not half as frosty as it is in his kitchen. And why should she be so sore when the timing couldn't be better? He regrets having to duck out of buying that tractor – especially as he'd emailed the chap who owned it over in Tibberthwaite Fell, with such excitement. But Ann was right, they needed the money to buy in the winter feed. Negotiating with Granville Harris, he wasn't going to enjoy that, but they could still get through to lambing. That was the main thing.

He looks into the barn, as if looking helps him gain some sort of mastery over the mess within. Hell of a job that, more than a job for one man and there was no hiring anyone in, not with things as they were. They'd have to store the bought-in feed in the other outbuildings, then repair the pole barn in summer. He hears the tramp of boots on the track and turns to see Eric Blakely entering the yard.

'What the bloody hell are you wearing?' Joe says.

'My overalls,' says Eric, looking down at his legs, which are billowing with an excess of thick navy cotton. 'They're new.'

'Very smart. Did ye come to show 'em off to me?'

'Look, I'm ready to work, aren't I? Where d'ye keep your brooms and such? Ron Chappell's on his way over.'

Joe then sees Dennis Lunn walking round the corner into the yard, his hands in his pockets. Dennis nods at Joe. Nonchalant. As if he's at the bar in the Fox and there's nothing out of the ordinary.

'Where's a spare broom then?' says Dennis. 'Tal and Jake are on their way over – Max's gone to fetch 'em.' Then Dennis turns to Eric. 'Keith Tindall says he'll join us in an hour.'

'Jolly good,' says Eric.

'Ah, look lads, I can't afford . . .' says Joe.

'Don't be daft, man,' says Eric. 'Take us no time if we all pitch in.'

Joe watches his friends head to one of his outbuildings, where the tools are kept, cracking a joke to each other. Max, Tal and Jake arrive and they all get to work, shovelling debris into the truck that Max has backed towards the mouth of the barn and parked there. Sweeping, shovelling, laughing together, then shedding their jackets as their bodies warm up with the exertion and the sweat gathering on their foreheads. Only Eric keeps his coat on – one of those country coats from Fairbrothers, with crisscross padding and a brown corduroy collar. Joe looks at Eric's broad back. He's fat, and out of puff with the sweeping. The most generous man Joe has ever met – large with it. Then he remembers Ann's admiration, the way she twinkles whenever Eric's near.

Joe sees Ann in the doorway of the house with her arms folded against the cold and against him too, probably. She's watching them work. He smiles at her, hoping she can see his gratitude. But she looks away. Still frosty.

'How do I look?' shouts Eric, doing a backwards moonwalk-with-broom across the yard towards her.

'Quite the little worker,' says Ann. 'You'll need feeding after all that graft.'

'Ah, now you're talking,' says Eric. 'Might you have a bacon butty or six for me?'

'I might,' she says, and Joe sees them smile at each other, Eric's sheer good humour overcoming his protruding belly and balding head to make him seem quite the catch. He can see her taking in his smart Barbour coat, which gives him the air of landed gentry. And here's me, Joe thinks, shabby and injured – he looks down at his bandaged hand – relying on charity for help with a burnt-out barn. Can't even buy her her own house. Why would she want me when there's men like Eric in the world?

'Have you got through to Bartholomew?' Joe says to her, as he edges past her into the kitchen.

'No, no reply. I've left another message.'

Then she brightens for the other men. 'Right, who's for a bacon butty then?'

From: ann.hartle@cooperative.coop
To: b_hartle@hotmail.com
Subject: Dad
7 January 2006, 10.43 a.m.

Just a note to see how you're getting on son – you must be too busy with the garden centre to return my calls. I hope you're not upset with us.

We've begun clearing up the hay barn – everyone came to help and I think your dad was quite moved by it, the way they all showed up and took it on without any asking.

Oh but we still don't know where the winter feed's coming from. Joe went to see Granville Harris (odious little man – Granville, not your father) and they had a right set to. Joe says Granville quoted him through the roof and they had a shouting match, with Joe accusing Granville of kicking a man when he's down and of trying to humiliate him by making him barter and beg. (Joe's temper is short, but to be fair to him, Granville is a mean beggar.) Any road, Joe came home with nothing. We've a few ewe rolls and some roots that were kept in the other outbuildings – but it won't last past next week and the ewes can't go without, not with so many carrying twins.

Bandage'll come off your dad's hand in a couple of days. He's rather quiet, I've noticed. Sits on his chair on the landing, looking into the video entryphone (god I wish Primrose had never installed that blasted thing).

Try to keep in touch son. I know Christmas was, well, a bit of a disaster. I'm sorry for it, but there's no need to cut yourself off.

Mum

Max bounces on the quad bike as it climbs the fell. One of the dogs runs beside him, playing, knowing she doesn't have to work today. He has loaded the bike with the last of the winter feed. There's no more. Dad'll have to do a deal with Granville Harris, like it or not.

Max's eyes are sore. It was another heavy one in the Fox last night with Tal and Jake, Max showing his appreciation for their work on the hay barn with round after round of Marston Moor until both Tal and Jake put their palms up to him and he found himself drinking them single-handed.

His painful eyes are being sandblasted by frozen air, caustic with hail which drives into his skin as he revs the quad bike, up the steep incline of the fell to where the flock could be found grazing. This is their coarsest land – the heathers springy and purple with patches of grass between the grey, craggy rocks. He looks around him. It's vast – that's the thing Joe says he loves most about the fell. Like there was no arguing with it. Said it made every human struggle look like a child's tantrum. But Max can't see it, can't feel it. He's been waiting for some of that wisdom to come: for his purpose to take hold of him as his baby grows in Primrose's belly. But it hasn't. Nothing's taken hold of him except a vague gloom about the hay-barn fire and a sense of wounded disappointment that he'll not be getting that new tractor after all.

He parks the bike and drags the sacks of food off it across the grass, into a metal feeding trough. The sheep begin to gather restively, knowing what he's brought. The sky is flat and white and thankless, like the news of the bairn, which has dulled. All the praise and the announcement he was to be given the farm and the sense that his inheritance was upon him, it had all stalled. He tries to focus on the future, feeling some of the ewes as they feed – checking their swollen bellies. There would be lambing and warmer times ahead. The farm would seem more of a going concern come spring. And everyone would gather round when the baby came, shower them with gifts. They'd not need to buy anything. By next auction time, he'd be a proper farmer – a family man with his own place – and that sense of purpose would come to him, like Joe said it would.

Out of a corner of his eye he spots a ewe that hasn't come to feed. She's out on a limb, lying in the shelter of a rocky crag. He walks over to her.

'Whas up w' you?' he says. She is panting. He decides to take her down to the farm for checking over. They'll be bringing the others down off the fells end of March anyway – to lamb on the milder in-bye early April – so this one'll just come down early. He lifts her gently and she submits to him, which makes him more certain she's not right. Sheep should struggle away on scratchy legs. Fight you a bit. He ties her to the front of the quad bike. The dog jumps onto the back of the bike.

'Lazy beggar,' Max says to the dog behind him.
He carries them both down the escarpment to the farm.

From: ann.hartle@cooperative.coop
To: b_hartle@hotmail.com
Subject: everything alright????
15 January 2006, 1.17 p.m.

I do wish you'd get in touch love, if only to let me know you're alright. I've tried calling the garden centre, but your assistant (is it Leonard?) is rather short with me. Says you've not been around half so much lately, which makes me worry.

There's been a turn-up for the books on the winter feed. Out of the blue, Granville Harris called and offered us two months' worth at a knock-down price – quite the lowest price I've heard of round here. Joe was suspicious but Granville said he had more of a surplus than he'd first thought and it'd go to waste if we didn't take it. Joe agreed, thank goodness, but I have my suspicion that Eric Blakely went to see Granville and had a word in his ear. I don't know if any money changed hands, but Lauren was very strange about it when I saw her at the WI – she seemed to know the story before I told it.

So I think we might actually get through to lambing in one piece. I must say, Eric is marvellous – so generous. He doesn't fall out with folk like your father. I daren't tell Joe my suspicions about the feed – he seems sensitive all of a sudden to charity and Eric's help in particular, though there was never a better friend. He's bruised by it all, even though the barn's been cleared and the replacement feed is in. Just sits on that landing, every minute he gets, watching the village. I hear him in the night, too, picking up the receiver, sitting there – as if he's going to discover something on Marpleton village green at 2 a.m.

So that's the latest Hartle insanity. I'd best sign off – Lauren is on her way over to take me to the WI meeting in Lipton. It's Geology night, a history of Ribblehead Quarry. The excitement! I can barely contain myself. Irony is of course, your father would have been riveted back in the day (he always loved his rocks). Please call Bartholomew.

Mum

Primrose sees Lauren's watery form behind the mottled glass front door. The door opens and the warm air of Lauren's immaculate home hits her face – furniture polish and the scent of the new, unmuddied. Lauren's pearl-stud earrings are bright beneath her short, textured hairdo.

'Primrose!' says Lauren, full of that generous pleasure that Primrose has always liked so much. 'What a nice surprise.'

'I wanted to say thank you for the baby gym.'

'Come in, love. Got time for a brew?'

Primrose steps into the thickly carpeted hallway with its polished dark-wood table with a mirror above. Lauren leads the way into the kitchen, which looks to Primrose as if it has slid off the page of a glossy magazine. Primrose is taking off her coat and Lauren stops making the tea and looks at her belly.

'Oh look at you. Can I touch the bump?'

Primrose nods, feeling the pleasure of Lauren's excitement, almost as keen as her own.

'What a miracle it is,' Lauren is saying, placing a hand on the little swollen roundness of Primrose's lower belly. Primrose thinks she sees then a flicker of something – a shadow of pain across Lauren's face. But then she goes back to her tea-making, saying briskly, 'How are you feeling?'

'I'm well,' says Primrose and she sits on a high stool at the central island.

'Max excited?'

'Ye . . . es,' says Primrose. 'I think he were happy that Joe was so happy.'

'Joe always loved bairns, I remember,' says Lauren. 'And of course, a farm goes with this one.'

'Yes, Max were right pleased all that's happening. More pleased about that than about anything. Says he's arrived.'

'Does he now?' says Lauren, placing a cup of tea in front of Primrose. 'Biscuit?'

'Please.' Primrose is happy to see Lauren bring out a posh packet – the kind of biscuits that are individually wrapped in foil. Thick chocolate, flavoured orange or mint. She feels a seeping pleasure to be here, in this warm, snazzy house with the posh biscuits, talking to Lauren who's so motherly, and without that faint whiff of disapproval she always gets off Ann.

'Always comes first, the farm,' Lauren is saying. 'I remember with Eric, I were last in the pecking order behind a thousand Herdwicks.'

Primrose laughs.

'How are you in yourself, love?' Lauren asks.

Primrose takes another biscuit. Lauren isn't eating them, she notices.

'OK I s'pose. A bit . . .' Primrose coughs, puts the biscuit down by her cup. She can feel Lauren's eyes on her. 'Maureen Pettiford came into the Co-op the other day. She was being kind, congratulating me on the baby, you know.' She can hear her voice – the drag on it. She plays with the foil-wrapped biscuit, turning it over. 'She was being really nice, I know she was. Said being pregnant was the best time in her life, the happiest time.'

'Oh bully for her,' says Lauren, snorting. 'Give the woman a medal.'

'Only I don't feel . . .'

'Bursting with joy at every second of it?'

'No,' says Primrose.

'Course you don't. And I'll bet Maureen Pettiford didn't either. It's like anything else in life – it's got all shades to it. I remember I found it an agony of waiting. Everything's all up in the air.'

'Yes, p'raps it's that. I think . . . I think I won't be much good at it.'

'Yes, ye will,' Lauren says. 'You'll have to learn it, just like you'd learn anything – darts or knitting. And you get good at it, gradual like. By the time you have another one, you're a pro.'

Primrose unwraps her waiting biscuit and takes a bite, putting a hand up to catch the crumbs that fall from the side of her mouth.

'Max'll help,' says Lauren.

Primrose looks at her, her mouth full, and raises her eyebrows.

'P'raps not,' says Lauren. 'Ann then. Ann'll help. And you'll not prise the thing off Joe. He'll be driving the tractor with the baby in a sling at his chest.'

'Wonder if I'll get a look in,' Primrose says.

From: ann.hartle@cooperative.coop
To: b_hartle@hotmail.com
Subject: Hello????
20 January 2006, 10.51 p.m.

I'm really worried now Bartholomew. Please drop us a line. I just
need to know you're alright love, that things are going OK, with
Ruby and the garden centre. I know you're a grown man etc. etc.,
but it doesn't stop me worrying.

Things here are ticking along – you know what a dreary time
winter is. Feeding and feeding and feeding some more. In
between, your dad spends most of his time on the blessed video
entryphone. He's up there when he comes home for his lunch,
and again before tea and after it. I talked to Max about it but he
said dad was fine, just a bit tired. The ewes are fat, some with
twins, so that's good. Do get in touch, son.

Mum

Ruby is in the back kitchen. She looks out through the hatch and
makes slow circular motions on the counter with a cloth.

She is hypnotised by the rain, which slides down the window
like dishwater. The light is dusk-like even though it's just noon,
and the café is miserably empty. The early lot have shuffled away
after their breakfast toasts or mid-morning pastries.

She walks out into the aquarium room where the rain is
throwing patterns onto the smoky glass. She switches on a

standard lamp and it casts a circle of orange in one corner of a blue sea.

Sunk, she thinks. Her body feels slow, as if her sadness is a physical leaden thing and she can barely carry it. And hollow too. She feels hollow from not eating. 'Make the most of it!' her mother had said on the phone. 'The heartbreak diet. Always works a treat.'

As she turns back towards the kitchen, a low beam of sunlight breaks through the rain and illuminates Dave Garside's broad back where he sits on his usual stool at the hatch counter. Most days he sits there, so he can talk to her while she's working in the back kitchen.

'Seven letters,' says Dave. 'Tragic lover married, for example, all for nothing.'

'No idea, Dave,' she says quietly, coming back into the kitchen.

She looks at him, head down over his crossword. She notices the mousse in his hair, which has made it stiff, like whipped egg whites. Brave Dave. Well, Gay Dave, as it turns out. Who'd have thought it, after all that macho stuff at school – all the skateboarding and the go-kart racing. (His T-shirts were quite tight, mind.)

Dave the gay estate agent. He sits in her café to escape the over-gelled, shiny-suited 'banter' at his office (Dave always does enlarged quotation marks in the air when he mentions it), which generally centres on his sexuality.

'Gary and Wayne,' he'd said a week ago, sitting at the counter as usual, eating one of Ruby's speciality omelettes for his lunch. 'God, where did they mislay their communal brain cell? You'd think Winstanton would be more evolved, wouldn't you? I mean, we're only a couple of hours out of London. But it's like they've never come across a gay man before. They just can't leave it alone.'

'Maybe Gary and Wayne have a bit of a thing for each other,' she'd said, getting the teapots down.

'Now there's an idea,' said Dave, looking into the middle distance. 'Friends of Dorothy but so deeply in the closet that even their brain cell doesn't know.'

She'd laughed. And then she'd started to cry.

'Oh god Ruby, what's happened?'

'I think it's over. With Bartholomew.' She could feel her face dissolving into tears.

'Oh dear, sweetie. Come on, group hug.'

Bartholomew hadn't been in touch at all over Christmas – no replies to her avalanche of texts; to her snapshots of food; no affectionate late-night calls to say goodnight. That scarf should have told her something. Horrible thing, over-fluffy and custard-yellow, like something Big Bird would wear.

She thought of him in Marpleton – a place she'd visited only once. She pictured him in that warm house where the bedding smelled of starch, where his mother baked bread, where the banisters gave off breaths of polish. She thought of the armchairs – their lovely faded pink and the neat antimacassars. He'd kept her apart from it. He'd guarded it to his chest like a mistress. She thought of him laughing in the pub with his brother.

After a week of his silence and just before she was due to catch the train back to Winstanton, with her bag packed next to the front door, she'd talked to her mother about it.

'Oh lovey,' her mother said. 'I am sorry. I thought you seemed quiet.'

And Ruby knew then why she hadn't wanted to talk about it earlier. She didn't want the patient pronounced dead at the scene. If she didn't talk about it, she could tell herself he was just being a typical rubbish bloke. Uncommunicative. Or that somehow it would all come right.

'I think every person has a temperature,' her mother had said, after Ruby had told her everything. 'And you need to find someone who's the same temperature as you. I know a couple – Alan and Hilary – and they spend most of their time apart. She works away, they take separate holidays. And it works. Don't ask me how. They're just both built that way. Kind of chilly, if you ask me. Now me and your father, we could never do that. Would be torture. We'd argue all the time. It's bad enough when he goes on his golf weekend once a year. We're just not built for it.'

Ruby had started to sob, the snot trailing down her upper lip and her mother had walked over and scooped her up, cupping her head into her shoulder and saying, 'I'm so sorry, love, you were so happy. And he seemed such a nice chap.'

'What if,' Ruby had juddered between sobs, 'what if he seemed like my temperature, at the beginning, but now all of a sudden he's not?' And she'd juddered again and her mother had kissed the top of her head where it lay.

'Lovey, you can't make him into something he's not. You can't do anything about the way he is. You just have to accept it, and maybe look for someone who is more at your setting.'

'I'll never find anyone,' she'd wailed into her mother's perfumed chest. 'No one wants me. I'm too full-on.'

'I want you,' her mother had soothed, and she had taken her face in both her hands, pushing her wet cheeks together, so that she thought she probably resembled a goldfish. Her mother looked at her eyeball to eyeball. 'And you're not too full-on.

You're just full of life, my darling. And if he doesn't want that then he needs his head examined.'

Back in Winstanton, she'd walked up Theobald Road carrying her bag and as she did so she noticed how much of this world was one they'd built up together. Fetching the paper from Mr Shah on Saturday mornings; walking home along the river together after work; Bartholomew sitting at the kitchen table reading out from the television guide while she cooked. What would she have left, without him? Her job at the café, her little flat, her book club and Sheila, who's into cooking. They called each other about new recipes, but there was no one she could talk to about this.

She'd looked up and seen a light on in his flat and it came to her that it had all been a silly mistake. He'd been busy, or his phone had got lost or there were things on his mind but nothing so catastrophic as the things she'd been imagining, nothing to provoke such a flood of tears as she'd given way to. She'd rung his bell. And suddenly there he was, standing in front of her. Real. Alive.

'Ruby . . . hi,' he said. He'd used her name as if she were an acquaintance. As if she disturbed him. He was wiping his palms on the back of his jeans and he stepped backwards in the hallway saying, 'Come in'. She didn't know what on earth she was stepping into.

'How have you been?' he said.

'Why haven't you called me?' she asked.

'Oh god Rube, I'm really sorry. It was just really hectic at home. I didn't get a chance.'

And for a minute she'd thought it was all going to be alright.

'How was your Christmas?' he asked, and it struck her that this was the kind of thing you asked a colleague, or someone in a shop. 'D'you want something to eat? I'm just making something.'

She'd set her bag down in the hallway and came to sit in his kitchen but she kept on her coat and the ugly scarf, only removing her woollen hat for the purposes of dignity. He busied himself at the stove – something he never usually did – and she realised that the very texture of the air was different.

'Is everything alright, Bartholomew?' she said. She felt small and she stayed still, as if trying not to dislodge anything. No sudden moves.

'Yes, fine. I'm just tired. It's been a long week. And it's going to be very busy at the garden centre. I'm bracing myself.'

She had nodded slowly. 'Perhaps I should brace myself too,' she'd said quietly. He hadn't responded. She said, 'I think I'll just drop my bag back home and then I'll pop back.'

'Right you are,' he said.

She had walked slowly to her flat, unable to work out what was different but knowing that nothing was the same. Her mind was a complete fog. At the flat, she plumped up her hair and put on some lipstick and a spray of perfume, then walked back down the stairs with the feeling of being condemned.

She doesn't remember what they talked about that evening. How the conversation went – the babble on the surface. All she remembers is his coldness beneath. It had surprised her with its force. It was as if he was smiling at her from the very surface of himself and yet she could detect some malevolent force or an undercurrent of cruelty at his core.

She had debased herself by staying the night. Perhaps some part of her thought she could thaw him out in the intimacy of the bed, but they didn't touch as if they both understood that touching was prohibited in this new frozen landscape. The duvet covered his shoulder like snow on a mountainside. She'd turned over in the bed, her back to his back. And tears had run down her cheeks. She must stop crying, she thinks now, as the tears prick up again in the back kitchen. She's crying all the time.

Two solid weeks of it, as if her whole being were liquid and only held in by a weak membrane which gives way too easily: on the walk to work, in the toilets, but most of all in the evening in her flat, where she sobs on her bed. Moments of reprieve come, like when Dave tells her about a couple he knows (Brian and Steve) who split up lots of times before ending up together ('God, it was the most boring saga in the world – no offence, Rube – they're happy as anything now.'). She grasps it as concrete evidence that all is not lost, though she knows it is. She reads old text messages, lying there among the tissues at night. Sends new ones.

I miss you

How did this happen?

Where is the love train? Are there leaves on the line?

But she never receives a reply. He might as well have died.

'I have to move,' she says. She wipes her eyes with a tea towel. She can feel how puffy her face is beneath the fabric. A bruised thing. 'I've got to get out of Theobald Road. It's doing my head in.'

'Actually, I've got a place – it's coming onto the books next week,' says Dave. 'Landlord wants it tenanted because it's falling to pieces. Old lady died there apparently. Any road, he told me he'd rent it for next-to-nothing if someone was willing to clean the place up a bit. You'd have to see if you think it's too grim.'

'No, no,' she says, 'I'm in. My lease on the flat comes to an end this month and they're asking if I'm staying and I just can't sign for another six months. There's no way.'

She puts both palms over her face and throws her head back. 'Urgh. I hate this. Please get it for me, Dave. I've got to get out of Theobald Road. Anyway,' she looks at him, 'I've always fancied doing a place up.'

'Slow down. You need to take a look. I'm telling you, the place really stinks. But it's enormous – much bigger than your flat. Think this old bird used to piss her pants while she watched telly.'

'Urgh, more information than I needed,' she says.

'Right, well,' he says, 'you get out that walnut cake and I'll make a few calls.'

She gets out the cake and cuts a complimentary slice for Dave but none for herself. It is as if food's gravitational pull – its position as the planet around which she orbited – has been switched off. She looks down at the cake as an inanimate object, dirty almost. She resents handling it. She has become irritated by the need to eat in order to function – those times when she must force something down because a dizzying weakness is getting in the way of working or sleeping. 'Hold the fort will you, Dave?' she says, feeling in her apron pocket. 'I'm just going out back for a ciggie.'

Joe stands holding the petrol-pump nozzle into the tank, scanning across the garage shop, its frontage set with buckets of pink and white flowers and trays of tabloids. He looks out through the sheltered forecourt to the car park beyond, where the rain bounces off car roofs – one of the cars red, like the cheerful red and white awning of the Little Chef. It is then that he sees them.

They are talking over the roof of Ann's car, cowed a little by the rain. Eric is holding a newspaper over his head. Ann holds a bunch of the garage flowers. Joe watches them talk, then they both get into Ann's car. Eric's red Nissan Micra, which had drawn his eye, is parked in the adjacent bay. They sit in the front seats of Ann's car. Every now and then he sees Eric turn his head to look at Ann. Why are they together? A coincidence, probably. No, he shakes his head. Looks again. Something about the intimacy of sitting together in those front seats – like a couple . . . He starts to quiver. Why would she want me, when there's men like Eric in the world? There's so much to admire in him – his good humour, his largesse, his big house and posh carpets. She'll come home and say, 'He's done well for himself, has Eric, getting out when he did.'

Gusts of wind blow the spray even to where Joe is standing in the sheltered forecourt. The pump's nozzle has clicked a while ago, and he shakes off the drips and returns it to the pump. He sees Eric climb out of the car, stoop to say something through the open door, then return to his Micra.

The flowers stand awkwardly in Ann's lap. The stems poke into her knees while the stinking blooms are too close to her chin, radiating upwards. Chrysanthemums. Garish pink. Nothing natural, that would flower at this time of year. But it's not a time of year for flowers at all. Everything is hunkered down or frozen solid. Waiting it out. The cellophane around the flowers is wet and it's soaking her trousers. She turns and lays them on the back seat.

'They're for Lauren,' she says. 'I'm going to see her later.'

Eric nods.

'How are you holding up?' she says.

'Ahhh,' he sighs and closes his eyes. His face, usually garrulous and tight, has gone slack. 'Difficult day.'

She lays a hand on his hand, which rests on his leg. 'I know love,' she says. 'He was a smashing lad.' And she immediately regrets trotting out this cliché, so insufficient.

'How's Joe doing?' Eric asks.

'His usual ray of sunshine,' Ann says. 'We wouldn't be able to carry on without, what you did, with Granville.'

'Nasty little man, that,' says Eric. 'Don't tell Joe it were me. He's got enough to deal with.'

'You've noticed – how sensitive he is, all of a sudden.'

'Ah,' says Eric. 'It's not easy for 'im, with prices so bad and the fire. Under a lot of pressure.'

'Any road, he doesn't have a clue,' she says. And she is brought up short by an image of herself, sitting in the car with Eric, deceiving Joe even though they'd only bumped into each other by chance and she'd wanted to take her time with Eric, talking gentle to him on this of all days. But she thinks of how it would seem to Joe and she looks down at her lap.

Eric says, 'You look after him. He needs lookin' after, and bring those lambs out with the daffodils and I'll be happy.' He pats her hand. 'I'm going back to my car. Lauren's best not left alone today.'

'I'll see you later, chuck,' she says through the open car door. He slams it shut and she starts the engine.

A couple of hours and some errands later, Ann stands under the thin shelter of the door lintel and rings the bell. While she waits, she looks in through Lauren's gleaming front window, past the doily and the rearing porcelain horse to the sitting room. The cream carpet is immaculate. The ivory leather sofas (three-seater, two-seater and matching armchair – what you'd call a proper three-piece suite) have a soft shell-like sheen, good as new. On a small coffee table is the *Radio Times*. It is precisely aligned with the table's edge, and on it a remote control (at an angle but not, Ann thinks, a random one). There's no mud or dust. She always finds Lauren's house almost excessive in its comfort. Like a pale marshmallow, big enough to envelop the whole body in its spongy embrace.

Lauren appears behind the rippled glass of the front door. When she opens it, Ann notices she has dispensed with her usual care about her appearance. Her hair is flattened as if she's just woken up, rather than in its rigid, highlighted waves. She has a balled tissue in her hand which she pushes up into one nostril. She is wearing a purple velour tracksuit and slippers.

'Difficult day?' says Ann, pushing forward her flowers.

'The worst. Thanks for remembering, love.'

'I've been thinking of you.'

'Come through,' says Lauren and she leads the way, pushing her feet forwards in her slippers and throwing the balled tissue in the hallway bin as she passes it.

Ann follows her into the kitchen.

'Here,' Ann says, 'this looks well.'

It's all been finished off since she last saw it. The pinkish light glitters down and bounces off the impossibly white stone work-tops. Ann runs a hand over it. Cold and smooth. Lauren is at the sink (a sink which sparkles as if straight from Hollywood, set with a very tall swan-like tap). She is running water into a vase for the chrysanthemums. Ghastly things, Ann thinks, ashamed.

Should have taken the time, driven to Helmsley and that posh place where they have proper lilies and things. Not been so mean.

'I can't believe it's thirty years ago,' Lauren says, sniffing, pushing back the (is that porcelain?) lever of the tap. 'When I think of it,' Lauren shuffles over to a box of tissues, 'honest to god, Ann, it hurts as if it happened yesterday.'

Ann goes over to her friend and hugs her. Over her shoulder she takes in the under-cupboard lighting which makes the white tiles shine like river stones under the surface of water. Give anything for tiling like that.

'It's always a difficult day, this,' says Ann. 'You've got to expect it.'

'Cup of tea?' says Lauren, pulling away.

'Smashing,' says Ann and she takes off her coat. She walks out to the hallway and hangs it on the stair banister. When she returns to the kitchen, she pulls out one of the high stools (cream leather with stainless-steel legs) from under the central island. Lauren sets her tea down in front of her.

'Come on then, what's your news? Take my mind off it,' Lauren says.

'Well,' says Ann, 'The really big news – and I don't want to sock you with too much excitement, not today of all days – but Ivy Dawson's had a caution.'

Lauren's eyes bulge. 'What, from the coppers? Has she lost her licence?'

'Don't think you need a licence for a mobility scooter. But when I drove past yesterday she was pulled over on the side of the road – this was just outside the village on the Lipton Road – both hands gripping the handlebars with Plod stood next to her writing in a pad.'

'Oh that is too good.'

'I know, and then I talked to Dennis Lunn and he said the police had pulled her over and warned her about driving without due care and attention.'

'Oh please,' says Lauren. 'Is it driving? Really? Only in the loosest sense of the word. I'd say it's more pressing forward with hope in her heart.'

'My guess,' says Ann sipping her tea, 'is that the woman can't see two yards ahead of her.'

Lauren nods. She dabs at her eyes with her tissue. Ann pats her arm, then rubs it a little.

'How's Joe?' asks Lauren.

'At what point can you get your spouse locked up under the Mental Health Act?'

'Still the video entryphone? I'm amazed you allowed Primrose to fit that thing.'

'I didn't. Joe did.'

'Is he still on it every hour of the day?'

'Morning noon and night. It's so boring, Lauren. He's just staring and staring and there's nothing there to see. And when he looks up, it's like he doesn't know how to live in the world.'

'Marriage,' says Lauren.

Ann nods. They sit for a minute, sipping.

'How's the snoring?' asks Ann. 'Have you tried those foam earplugs I told you about? I've not looked back.'

'Didn't even make a dent,' says Lauren. 'Sweet Jesus, Ann, you'd think he had workmen up there, breaking up the tarmac.'

'What's so funny?' says Eric, over their laugher. He is padding in, also in his slippers and setting down his newspaper.

'Nothing, dear,' says Lauren.

'I'd best get back,' says Ann. 'I've a stew to make.'

'I've got to take Sandy out,' says Eric. 'Give me a minute to get my shoes on and I'll walk you across the green.'

'Alright,' says Ann. Eric pads out. She hears his slippers schlumping on the thick stair carpet. Everything in this house is insulated.

'We're so grateful, Lauren. Well,' Ann looks down, '*I'm* so grateful. What you did, it were above and beyond.'

'No it weren't,' says Lauren. 'We talked about it, me and Eric. We wanted to do it. You're our friends, Ann. My best friend. Anyway, life's too short. Our Jack taught us that.'

Ann looks at the garish chrysanthemums, arranged in Lauren's white vase. 'Right, well. Bye, love,' she says. 'Well done for getting through it. Today I mean.'

Eric is standing by the door holding Sandy's lead. The brown springer spaniel – as glossy as everything else in the house – leaps and springs at his feet. It pants, while Ann puts her coat on.

As they find the path, and with Sandy crossing their legs this way and that, Eric says, 'It's not that bad, you know.'

'What's not?' says Ann.

'Getting out. Selling. The sky doesn't fall in.'

'God, Eric,' she says, 'd'you not think I'd get out tomorrow? It's not that easy. It were different for you – you owned your land. We'd have nowhere to live.'

'P'raps. But the longer you prop him up, keep balancing the books, the longer he'll hold on,' he says. She feels annoyed, that he's glossing over the numbers involved. Only the rich do that.

She loops her arm through his. 'I'm not the only one propping him up, am I?' she says.

'Ahhh,' he says, at the base of his throat, 'No, you've got a point there. Maybe we're all a bit terrified. He would come to terms though – eventually. And I'd happen you'd both feel relieved.'

He sits on his hard little seat. It is 2 a.m. and he can hear Ann's faint snoring from the bedroom. He looks at the video entryphone's monitor and the handset squared up alongside it, lifts it and the screen blinks on. Its green is over-bright at first, then the grains form themselves into images. It takes a few seconds to make out the grass of the village green and its bisecting path. It has a wet sheen under the lights from the Fox. The black mound of a bench. Alan Tench's white van. The picture itself seems to throb, as if Marpleton has a pulse or the same shallow breathing as a sleeping body. Joe's lungs fill up. For all his exhaustion, it's a relief, this little picture. He can face it, live in it, this domestic view to the front. It offers him relief from the farm, where the pressure is becoming unbearable and why was that, when the barn was tidied up and the replacement feed was in? Was it age, making his feelings so unbridled?

When he thinks of the flock out there on the fell, the wind so cold and blowing their fleeces into rosettes on their backs, he almost can't stand it. They seem so dependent on him. But they always were, so why does it hurt him to think on it now? Losses were to be expected, of course. They were part of the farmer's lot. It was a business – they weren't pets. He tells himself this over and over. Some sheep drown in the burn, some die of exposure or old age. Foot rot is common, after all. Sometimes they get caught in snowdrifts or stuck on their backs. He can feel a tear rising, pricking the back of his eye. Ordinary losses, man. There's no avoiding it. But the flock, for him – it's not just a business. You care for them like they're family. It was your duty to look after them right and when you didn't, well you didn't feel good in yourself. More and more these days, Joe feels the task might be beyond him. He thinks of Bartholomew's teenage face all those years ago, full of righteousness. 'You know them. You know who they are and you won't stop it.'

'What d'ye think about this one?' Max had said the week before, untying a ewe that he'd brought down off the fell and lifting her off the quad bike.

'She's got twins,' Joe had said, with more confidence than he felt. He always had to take the lead with Max. He was always looking to Joe for the answers. That had begun to exhaust him, too. 'Twins is always early,' he'd said. 'We'll put her in the old cow shed till it's her time.'

He is bent forward on his chair. His face is right up against the monitor. He wishes there were people in his picture. The village has bedded down into the valley floor for the night and will remain immobile for another few hours at least. Joe replaces the handset. The screen blinks back to grey. He waits. Closes his eyes. He sees Eric and Ann sat in that car, secret like. Talking about what? About him? They were always full of each other, like that time they went to the Fox to do the new quiz that Tony Crowther had organised (cramping Max's style) and she was all dolled up in lipstick. She and Eric knew more of the answers than him and Lauren. Showing off all their interests, they were – history, geography, the news – like it made them better people. He'd sat back, gone silent, feeling smaller and meaner next to Eric's largesse and hating the way Ann tittered like a schoolgirl, saying, 'Here, isn't he well read? You should go on *Mastermind* Eric.'

When they got home, he'd gone straight to the lounge and switched on the telly.

'Who's pissed on your chips?' she'd demanded, following him into the room.

'You're full of it aren't you,' he'd muttered. 'And Eric, too.'

'Full of what?'

'Full of yourselves – your mutual appreciation society.'

'Well at least he's got a flaming sense of humour,' she shouted and slammed the door and stomped upstairs to bed.

He opens his eyes and lifts the receiver again.

'What are you doing coming with me?' says Ann irritably the following morning, as the bell rings over the chemist door. Joe is too close. He is bunching up behind her as they shuffle into the shop.

'I need some Lemsip,' he says and he is too much, she thinks, in this carpeted, over-shelved room. They bump down the aisle, the two of them. Ann looks over and sees Karen Marshall behind the counter, looking back at them. The Lipton bush telegraph. That's all I need.

'Well go on then,' she hisses to Joe. He's been fussing around her all morning, worse than a teething toddler. 'Go and get your Lemsip and leave me alone.'

She is looking at the bubble baths.

'What are you getting?' Joe says. He is too close again. He is at her back, looking over her shoulder.

'Will you please give me some space?' she whispers. She casts a glance at Karen and meets her eye. Karen hastily looks away. 'What do you care what I'm getting from the chemist anyway?'

'Make-up?' he says. 'Perfume?'

'Joe, what is wrong with you?'

'Something for Eric?' says Joe. He's not whispering. Ann casts another anxious glance at Karen. She's all ears.

'Shut up, Joe,' Ann hisses. 'Stop being ridiculous. Go and get your Lemsip.'

'You're full of sparkle for each other,' says Joe.

'I beg your pardon?'

'Oooh, Eric, what a smart coat!'

'Oh shut up,' she says, trying to edge past him.

'You and he . . .'

She interrupts him. 'I'm not listening to this. I've put up with enough from you. I'm not putting up with this Eric rubbish as well. Not after he's helped you so much.'

'Bit o' sweeping,' Joe snorts. 'Hardly deserves a medal.'

'Not just that actually,' she says, wanting to teach him a lesson. Silence him. 'Granville Harris. The feed. You don't think he dropped his price out of the goodness of his heart, do you?'

Joe stops. He looks at her, bewildered, and she feels the slow seep of regret.

'He did it out of friendship,' she says. 'Eric and Lauren, they wanted to help us through a difficult time.' She glances again at Karen, who is not even making a pretence of not listening. She is gazing at them as if intimately part of the conversation. 'Just getting some Radox!' Ann says loudly, waving a box of bath salts as if Karen were deaf or stupid. Chance would be a fine thing.

Joe is stood there, looking down now at the bottle-green cord carpet. Rubbing his face with one hand.

Ann shuffles past him. She edges around the end of the aisle, where nappies and baby wipes are stacked in claustrophobic towers. She approaches the counter and hands Karen the box of

Radox 'Muscle Relax' salts. Ann smiles at her with a rigid jaw.

'Just this please, love,' she says.

'How's Primrose?' says Karen. 'Baby must be getting big.'

Max is parking when he sees them come out of the chemist. His mother is marching ahead with a face like thunder.

Max feels the moments lap away when he could wave to them or hoot his horn or leap out of the car. Instead, he waits for them to drive away. Then he gets out of his Land Rover and crosses the road to the Co-op to pick up something to eat. He is undecided between a Melton Mowbray pork pie and a cheese slice but if it's to be a cheese slice then he'd be better off going across the way to Greggs, where they're warm at least. By the time this occurs to him, though, he's standing in front of the Co-op chiller cabinet, a place to kill off even the mightiest appetite in a man. He is surveying the limp sandwiches spewing anaemic lettuce and the processed meats, when Tracy Hardaker shouts over from the till, 'Here, Max, what happened to Primrose this morning? She's left us short-staffed. I can't go on my break because Claire can't cover both ends of the shop.'

He looks across at Tracy. Face like a slapped arse. He hadn't even scanned the room for Primrose, he realises.

'What?' he says. 'She were up when I left. Didn't she call in?'

'Nope. Downright inconsiderate if you ask me.'

Claire has walked over from the storeroom and says to him, over-gentle, 'I tried calling her because I was worried. It's not like her not to show up. But there's no answer. She hasn't rung you at all?'

'Nope,' says Max.

He scans the shelves again, stopping at the Ginsters pasties. (But the chiller cabinet makes them stick to the roof of your mouth – the fat gets congealed in the cold.) Claire has put a light hand on his elbow and says, 'Maybe you should check on her, Max? It could be something to do with the baby.'

He is irritated by Claire's nearness. Like it's any of her business. So he leaves the Co-op empty-handed but not before Tracy says to his back, 'Tell her she owes us a day.'

He crosses the high street again to Greggs where he picks up a cheese slice, warm and stringy, and a bag of crisps, and he sits in his car eating them in peace with the Greggs paper bag surrounded by crumbs on his lap and the crisps open behind the handbrake.

The side of the bath is cold against the base of Primrose's back. We've run out of toilet roll, she thinks.

She is sitting on the bathroom floor with her knees up. Under her bottom is one of the peach towels folded into a square. Between Primrose's legs is a maroon blotch – like ink on blotting paper. It is pooling, imperceptibly. Close to her body is a ball of something black. A kind of sac, like a tea bag. And around it streaks of very dark gloopy snot. She has her head down, almost between her knees, and her elbows propped on them. She is looking at the bobbles on the peach towel. Shouldn't have used the peach. It would have barely shown up on the navy. But she'll never get it out now, not with a whole pot of Vanish. She'll have to scoop it all into a bin liner and put it out back and hope Ann doesn't ask about them – about the peach towel set she'd bought for them. Bath sheet, hand towel and flannel (that matching flannel, it's somewhere), tied up like a present with lilac ribbon. It won't be a set now because she's gone and ruined the bath sheet. And Ann might ask about it because she was like that – always chasing up after the things she'd bought them (like the china, that floral set, when she came over and said, 'You're not using that floral boxed set I bought you, Primrose?'). She'll wonder what happened to it and ask why Primrose didn't take better care of it.

She was getting ready for work when it began. She was stood at the sink when she bowed her head down almost into the bowl and leant both hands on the sides and felt this creaking in her belly. She'd felt these things before, milder – a kind of menstrual shifting about down there. She'd walked back to the bedroom and got back into the bed. She was lying on her back and she pulled the covers back over her. But it wasn't where she wanted to be. So she got up and went back to the bathroom. She could feel the wetness between her legs by then. That was when she pulled a towel (any towel) from the airing cupboard and positioned herself against the bath, like the ewes she'd seen so often, taking themselves off to a particular place when it was their time.

By the time she hears Max's key in the door she has showered. She is wearing her dressing gown and slippers and a big brick of a sanitary towel between her legs. She stops on the stairs, one hand on the banister.

'Why are you not at work? Tracy Hardaker's got a face on her.'

Primrose says nothing. She shakes her head. She can feel herself about to cry, now that he's here. She's unable to speak – to say it.

'What is it, love?' he says. He is looking up at her from the bottom of the stairs, one hand on the finial, and she wonders why he can't tell what's happened. Surely it's obvious. 'What's happened?' he says.

'I lost the baby,' she says in a great heaving sob and the language of it – the blame that seems to carry in those words – makes her tears come thick. She comes down the last steps. He is bewildered. He puts his arms around her shoulders but they lie, light and bloodless, like damp leaves.

'When did it happen?' he says.

'This morning, as I was getting ready for work.'

'Where . . . where is it?' he says. He sounds dazed, like his mind's occupied taking it in.

'In the bins outside.'

She feels his chest heave at this – a sharp intake. She's never seen him cry. She pulls away and looks up at him, almost out of curiosity. His eyes are dry.

'I'm sorry,' she says. And she's crying again, because it's like everything about the two of them together has failed. 'I'm so sorry, Max.'

The lantern light swings in the rafters of the small outhouse, no bigger than a stable, where Joe has brought the ewe. She is panting where she lies on her bed of straw. She had stood earlier and cried out, as her waters broke onto the straw, and even her cries were stoic. He will stay with her for as long as it takes.

So Eric had helped him. Why would he do that if not to make himself the giver of riches? Eric was lining them alongside each other before Ann and coming off the bigger man.

She is close, he thinks. He looks at her eye and sees patience

– or is it stupidity – which makes her submit, even when he pushes his hand inside her to feel for the first lamb. Warm and slippery, that mammalian smell – sweet and yeasty – hits his nostrils. 'Nearly there, girl. Nearly there.'

His arm is inside her up to the elbow now, and she shifts in the straw. She bleats loud, meeeh, meeeeh, as if taking umbrage at his intrusion. He is feeling around the unborn lamb, its sliding body hard to his touch. An everyday miracle. He makes sure the hooves are forward then pulls the head, easing it out through flesh which stretches pink like rubber. Slowly, slowly. And then out it comes in a rush. It is yellow and sticky and cellophaned in its sac. Strands of the straw stick to it. He wipes the lamb's nose and eases open the mouth for it to take its first breath. He lifts it, a slippy fish, and places it onto the straw in front of the ewe's face where she begins to lick it, doggedly. The lamb is small. Even for twins.

Joe steps back. She knows him, this ewe, and he knows her. He had breathed into her mouth when she was born, to help her take her first breath. Bartholomew was right about that. 'You know them, dad, each one of them. And they know you. How can you do it?' And he wonders now, watching the ewe licking her lamb. For a moment, Joe wonders if he can take any more of it.

He pushes a hand back inside her, this time up to his shoulder, to feel for the second. This one doesn't feel right. It is hard and still. He pulls it towards him and eases it out, head first, the body following quickly. It lies on the straw. Dead. Eyes closed. Legs ahead of it like the galloping horses on a merry-go-round. Its hooves are dainty. Its skin is waxy and yellow like a human cadaver.

He steps back and looks down at it and then over at the

ewe still patiently licking her first-born clean. But this one, too, should have raised its head by now. And he knows it won't last the night.

'I'm sorry,' he says to her. He wonders what it is. Chlamydia or vibrio or bad luck. And he knows he was right to isolate this one from the rest of the flock. Ordinary losses. The rest can still come right.

Max sits on a high stool at the bar of the Fox and Feathers.

'You're quiet, big fella,' says Sheryl from the other side. She is tilting her hips, pushing out her tits, asking for attention and he can't be bothered to give it.

'Am I?' he says. His focus is hazy, she swims in front of him. He drains his glass and holds it up for her to refill. He deserves it after what has happened to him, the loss he'd suffered. He deserved to lose himself in the drink, because life had dealt him a bitter blow and where was the fairness in that? It was supposed to be his time, supposed to be all coming together for him.

'Blimey, you're thirsty,' she says. 'Shouldn't you slow down a bit?'

'I've got the money, ha'nt I?' he says, hanging his head low between his shoulder blades like a lead weight. There's only so much a man can take and Primrose, she couldn't expect more from him. He'd looked after her – made her a tea, put her to bed. But the need for a pint was starting to pull at him hard, so he told her he was popping out.

'Something on your mind, darlin'?' Sheryl says. Scraggy old Sheryl, pouting and winking. As if he was interested in that. She's leaning over the bar and her pendant hangs in the air.

He watches it through glassy eyes. 'Anything you'd like to talk about? No? Well, you just sit there and think things over nice and quiet.'

The bar empties at closing. Sheryl invites him to stay for a lock-in. It's not so much that he says yes, more that he can't move for the pints swilling inside him. Through a fog, he hears her tell Tony to get himself off to bed – she'll close up and if she needs help with the barrels, she's sure Max will lend a hand.

'So how's married life?' she says to him, still glittering in the face of so little encouragement. Christ, he thinks, she's desperate.

It's just the two of them in the semi-darkness.

'Blissful,' says Max. The word comes out slowly, like a record player on the wrong setting. He's hardly spoken all evening.

'You'll be a family soon,' she says.

'If you say so,' says Max, staring into his glass. Then he looks up at her. 'You and Tony, you never had kids.'

Her face darkens. She fingers her pendant. 'No, well, it doesn't suit everyone.'

She gathers the dirty glasses from the bar and puts them in the dishwasher. Then she walks round to his side, up close to him.

'It doesn't mean the end of your life, you know,' she whispers in his ear. 'A baby.'

He stays hunched on the bar but turns his head to her.

'Everyone's a free agent,' she says and she runs a hand across his shoulders. He barely feels it. 'Marriage doesn't put a stop to that. What are you supposed to do if you're not happy? It's not your fault.' She kisses the back of his neck and he feels something bubbling up inside him. 'Sometimes things just happen.'

He turns and pushes her backwards against a pillar, where the horse brasses judder behind her head. She is smiling at him but he can't look at her. He pushes up her skirt, wanting to go at it hard, to lose himself in the dirt of it. If he looks at her, things will go slack. He closes his eyes, willing it all to stay disconnected. So he keeps going, frantic, his eyes shut, trying to disappear in the abyss of the drink and the dark. The hard wooden pillar, the feeling of blood draining down his body, the drink making his head swim, the arousal in the nerve endings of his body so long as he doesn't open his eyes and see what he's doing. Yes, this is it, this is it, this is it, this is it.

He steps back and she hoicks her skirt down, straightens her top. She plumps up her hair as she walks back round to the other side of the bar.

'I'd best be off,' he says and he makes for the door, still not wanting to see her. He unbolts it and falls out into the freezing January night.

FEBRUARY

— *Putting on fresh growth* —

Bartholomew opens his eyes. Blinks a few times. Lies there on the pillow. He brings his fists up to his face and rubs the sockets then rolls over, punching the pillow as he goes, to look at his clock radio. 9.37 a.m. Should've been in work an hour ago. The alarm went off two hours before, but as is his habit these days, he'd thumped down on the snooze button until it gave up all hope of rousing him.

Ruby is the first thing he thinks of as he looks around the room – the emptiness of the place without her clothes thrown on the chair or her grapefruit shower gel coming out with the steam from the bathroom. He's no right to complain of course – it was his decision. And just because he feels it, just because she's the first person he thinks of in the morning and just because she appears sometimes in his dreams and just because he looks up to her window in the street, doesn't mean it wasn't the right decision.

He sits up and bends over the side of the bed to where his jeans are two rumpled leg holes, like casts. He feels in the pocket for his mobile phone and looks at the screen. Nothing. The phone has become inert since they broke up, when before it was always haranguing him. Silly to check it – an old habit.

He lies back down in the bed, unable to generate the required energy to shower, have breakfast and go to work. He'd been like this throughout January – in at ten, away by four, his efforts lacklustre. It was as if a careless co-pilot had taken control of the plane, ever since Christmas.

He'd offered to stay after the fire, but Joe had said no, you get home, son, home to your business. And Max had chimed in: 'We'll manage. We always do.' And he'd felt he was being ushered out, to the train station. When he'd looked back from the end of the path, Joe was standing in the doorway, holding his bandaged hand in his other, and a gust of rude wind blew at his hair so it stood up in a lick on his head. He'd never seen his father look so vulnerable. Max had stood next to him, towering over him. Taking them for everything they have, Bartholomew had thought as he ducked into his hire car, except there was nothing to take. He had driven away from the acrid barn smoke that'd made his snot go black and the worn warmth of the farmhouse and the crow's cawing that were so visceral to him. And it was like an awful claustrophobia lifted. All the things he couldn't bear, they were receding, and he seemed to exhale as the train sped down the country, fast and warm and civilised. He'd got back to his own life.

He swings his legs round forty-five degrees so his feet plant on the floor, but he stops there, staring down at them. Back to his own life. He couldn't help his parents, not from so far away, and if they were giving it all to Max, well, let him deal with it then. His heart had hardened and he'd felt pleasure in it.

Back on Theobald Road, he'd walked straight past Ruby's door to his own. He wasn't going to deal with any of that pressure either – the scarf guilt, the failure to return her texts, the spectre of her questioning face asking what the matter was. It's not like he owed her anything, not like they were beholden to one another. He stays there, his elbows on his knees, staring at his cold feet. Yes, life was a lot simpler now.

'Afternoon,' Leonard says, tapping his watch. 'Nice lie-in?'

'Sod off, Leonard,' says Bartholomew. He bends down to chain his bicycle to a pipe at the side of the building.

'I'm just finishing off the pruning and then I thought I'd start re-potting some of those hellebores,' says Leonard, jabbing a thumb over his shoulder.

Christ, thinks Bartholomew, it's like he's been on assertive-ness training.

'They're a bit pot-bound some of them,' Leonard is saying. His body is quick with new energy. 'And then I'll top-dress the rest, I think. Gorgeous day, isn't it?' He claps his hands together, rubbing them rapidly and squinting into the sun.

Bartholomew says nothing. Ever since he returned from Yorkshire, all these weeks when he's expressed no real interest in the work, there's been a creeping sea change: Leonard keeps coming up with ideas. Taking the initiative. He's working longer hours, hasn't taken a day off since Christmas. Driving him nuts. Why can't they both just kick back? Make a brew and sell some fishing gnomes and head home to watch telly?

'Also, I'm going through the tool shed,' Leonard is saying. 'I'm going to chuck some of the really rusted spades if it's alright by you. Most of the secateurs will come up with sharpening. Nearly spring, Bartholomew. We have to be ready.'

'You knock yourself out, Leonard,' says Bartholomew.

'I'm making tea,' says Leonard. 'D'you want one?'

Inside, he peels off his cycling gear while Leonard fills the kettle. The faucet squeaks in the roof as Bartholomew walks over to the counter and begins flicking through a laminated catalogue from one of the wholesalers. He's already tired. Already sick of the day.

'The quinces have flowered on the bottom trellis,' Leonard is saying, over the growing rumble of the kettle. 'Have you seen them? "Phyllis Moore". Just glorious. The colour of lobster.'

Bartholomew keeps staring at the laminated catalogue.

Leonard presses on. 'What are we doing with that long trough to the left of the hydrangeas? Last summer you talked about having a section of tall meadow plants – you know, your Baltic parsleys and your angelicas, valerians.'

'Didn't know you were listening.'

'Only I'll need to start them off in the greenhouse.'

'D'you know what? Fuck it,' says Bartholomew. 'I'm going to order a ton of these,' and he's tapping the page in the catalogue, the page showing plastic toadstools and butterflies on metal poles. 'This shit sells.'

'But the plants for that trough –'

'Nope,' says Bartholomew, and he's hard, hard on the inside. 'We're going to clear that trough and fill it with plastic shit that makes money.' It's like he's drunk on carelessness.

'Have you seen the paper anywhere?' Leonard asks.

'Here you go,' says Bartholomew, handing it rolled.

Leonard takes it and his tea in the other hand and says, 'Well . . . I . . .' and half his body is pointing down the corridor.

'Off you go,' says Bartholomew. 'Far be it for me to interrupt the call of nature.'

Leonard laughs.

'What's so funny?' Bartholomew asks.

'No, it's just, you sounded just like me, then.'

'My life is complete,' says Bartholomew.

They are outside in the impossible warmth. February sometimes threw out days like this, full of false promise, and then

March would come in bitter as anything. Both have taken off their fleeces as they work in the shimmering sun, which slants across the land. Bartholomew sees a whole trough full of 'Harmony' dwarf irises, electric-blue like peacock feathers against green stems, and for a moment he admires Leonard's work, which has gone on without him all these weeks.

'So, we're going more down the accessories line,' says Leonard and he tips a hellebore into his gloved hand. The white roots of the plant have formed a dense mesh, still holding the shape of the pot. Bartholomew sees how gently Leonard teases them out.

'I don't know what I'm going to do yet,' he says. 'I might sell up.' He throws it out like a hand grenade. 'Haven't decided.'

'Sell up? When?'

'Dunno, summer maybe.'

'What will I do?'

'You'll live. Get a job at Maguire's.'

'I gave up a job at Maguire's to work for you.'

'Yeah, well, like I say, I haven't decided.'

'This is my livelihood.'

'Oh back off, Leonard.'

'When d'you think you'll know? Only, I have to renew my lease on my flat but if I'm not going to have a job . . .'

'I'm not your mother, Leonard.'

'No, you're my employer.'

'Oh god, look, forget I mentioned it. I'm sick of being responsible for everything, alright? This place, you, Ruby – we all just have to do what's best for ourselves, individually, that's all. You live your life, I'll live mine.'

He knows he isn't telling the truth.

Leonard is frowning but he goes back to his work. Bartholomew takes his phone out and looks at the screen. Nothing. A crazy habit, but he sets no store by it, the way he still searches for her, though it's been six weeks now. He still slows on the street outside her door, looks up at her windows, can feel his heart quicken whenever her light is on. It's the habit of it and it will lessen with time, especially now that she's moved on.

About a week ago, he'd walked down Theobald Road and her door was open. He had slowed and heard footsteps tramping down the steps from her flat and all of a sudden there she was, on the street in front of him. She was carrying a box to an open car boot. Dave Garside came out after her, carrying another, then went back up the stairs.

'Hello,' Bartholomew had said, standing next to his bicycle. His whole body was pulsating with the strangeness of seeing her. He wished he wasn't wearing his helmet. She was thin – gaunt really – and so pretty with it. Her eyes looked bigger in her elfin face.

She looked at him, but said nothing.

'What's Dave doing here?' he'd said.

'He's helping me move.'

'Move? Why are you moving?'

'Isn't it obvious?' She placed the box in the car boot.

He was bewildered by the finality of it – that he had set something so irreversible in train.

'I didn't mean . . .' he started.

'What, Bartholomew? Didn't mean to shit on me from a great height?'

'There's no need for that. We can still be civil,' he'd said.

'I don't feel civil.'

'Where are you moving to?'

'Dave's got me a place.'

'Are you two . . . ?'

174

'None of your business. Now, if you don't mind, I've got a lot of boxes to bring down.'

And he'd heard her say 'twat' as she stomped up the stairs.

He watches Leonard walk away to the warehouse. Fast pigeon steps, the panic written all over his back. Bartholomew knows he'll not hear the end of it now.

Evening time and the dark surrounds Max, right down to his feet, and he is grateful for it. His heart is thudding and the sweat is drying off his face, cold and relieving. That had been a close call – the closest yet. He's thankful to be out of there, that hot bar, too many folk asking too many questions and her. He's relieved to be walking home across the moor on this uncommon mild night, back to Primrose. He's not done right by her. It's been two weeks since the baby was lost and he should have looked after her better but he forgives himself because he was under the weight of that sad thing and he'd lost control. But tonight, that was different. That was a narrow escape.

He'd been about to leave the Fox when Sheryl had nodded towards the hallway behind the bar where the stairs led up to her and Tony's living quarters and the crisps were stacked in boxes. He had gingerly followed her there, and she – she had pushed herself against him, licking his ear and his nostrils had filled with her over-sweet perfume. Sickly musk. She seemed excited by it – with the pub full and Tony pulling pints a few feet away. Max had looked nervously to the side, checking if anyone could see.

'Careful,' he'd said and he could hear how weak it sounded. 'I should get back. Sheryl, watch it. I really have to head, Prim's expecting me.'

'Wonder what people'd say,' Sheryl had breathed, rubbing up against him next to the crisps. 'Everyone round here – if they found out.'

'Aye, well, let's not chance it, eh,' he'd said, trying to edge out from under her.

'I wonder if anyone suspects,' Sheryl had whispered and she was clearly getting off on it. Nothing short of scary.

He'd escaped out through the bar and past the tables but not before Fat Mo Dorkin had met his eye, raising her pint and saying, 'Alright, Max? What were you doing back there with Sheryl, then?'

Never missed a trick, Mo.

'Just helping with a barrel,' he'd said and pulled the door open, grateful to the fresh air for hitting his face.

෨

Primrose has her legs curled under her. She is wearing her pink chenille dressing gown – thick and warm, if only it wouldn't give off those occasional electric shocks – and her fluffy slippers with the heart motif. She's on the sofa. The room is dark and the television is on, though she's not really taking in the programme, some game show or other. She has a limp hand on her lower belly, out of habit maybe, or perhaps because it's starting to ache a bit, the last day or two. She's hardly shifted from this position since it happened, hasn't changed her clothes. The only person she's told is Claire, to explain why she's not coming to work.

'Course you're not,' Claire had said. 'Don't give it a second thought. D'ye want a visit? Can I bring you owt?'

'No, you're alright.'

There's a little hardened bit in her lower belly and she doesn't feel right but the hardened bit might just be the sadness which is all over the room and all over the house. When she looks in the mirror, she sees she's very pale but it's as if she's looking at a stranger, or someone she doesn't care much about. So she goes back to the sofa and the flickering blue lights of the telly.

She hears Max's key in the door but doesn't move or respond to the sound. He's not been around much since it happened and when the bed heaves downwards when he gets into it in the early hours, she can smell the beer reeking off him and it makes her feel vaguely sick. But she doesn't really care about him, either, if truth be told.

He has sat down next to her in the dark. The blue lights of the telly illuminate his features, bright then dark. He pats her knee. She looks down at his hand on her leg. Then she shifts her body so her legs are curled to the other side.

'What'ye watching?' he says.

'Dunno, reruns of *Celebrity Squares* I think. Another night at the Fox?'

She says it without accusation – she doesn't care enough to accuse him. But it doesn't come out that way.

'Only a quick one after work. How're you feeling?'

'Fine,' she says.

She hears his mobile phone bleep in his pocket. He stretches his legs so he can reach into his jeans and looks at the screen, then gets up hastily and goes out of the room.

After a minute or two, she hears him shout from the kitchen. 'Jesus Prim, you could've cleaned the place up a bit.' He's agitated. She can hear it in his voice. True, the kitchen was a mess. She'd had no energy to wash the plates or clear the crumbs, the apple cores, the bits of toast. They mingled with her tools on the table, from earlier when she'd taken apart a lamp.

She can hear him clattering about in there, can hear he's cross from the way he's throwing crockery into the sink. But through the fog of her lethargy and the dull ache in her belly, she couldn't give a —

'Could ye not have washed up at least?' he says, behind her in the doorway.

She continues to watch the television.

He walks out again.

🎵

Joe steps outside and smells the air suddenly full of spring. It is so warm, the atmosphere appearing to carry currents from some tropical zone. The smell is of drying grass and plant sap rising.

He stands in the yard out back and takes a deep breath, his chest opening, and he feels some of the tension of winter begin to evaporate. His limbs, for the first time, do not feel cold or damp – he can move them freely. The barn is there, still a charred silhouette, but neat and swept up in its destitution at least.

'Fine day,' he says to Max, who is fixing a nut on one of the tractor attachments. Joe sees his reddened face and eyes, small and deep-set. He's smelt the drink on him, this last week, but doesn't like to mention it. Thinks it must be the pressure of the baby coming – all men feel it – and then the farm coming to him, and Joe thinks perhaps they should hold off on that last thing. Give it another year, until Max is more ready. But he doesn't say anything about this either, not yet.

'Let's move the stores over to some fresh grazing – they've stripped that field bare on the east side,' Joe says. They are fattening lambs on the in-bye, ready to sell at auction the following month: the males, the females not good enough for breeding and the draft ewes that have lost their teeth with age and so can't pull at the rougher upland turf.

'Right you are,' says Max, and he calls to the dogs.

'I'll get my stick,' says Joe.

They walk together across the in-bye – thirty acres that have emerged muddy green since the snows went. Joe looks forward to when they'll drive the ewes down off the ridge for lambing, end of the month or early next. He loves that job – the sense of anticipation of what the ewes might produce (because you never know, not until the lambs actually come), the fell dancing its different browns and the trees in leaf and if you've decent dogs and the job's done right, it's a skill to be proud of. His father would've been pleased to see him do it, with his son alongside him and the next generation on the way.

'Have you finished the fences like I asked ye?' Joe says to Max, who is tramping silently, the dogs running alongside him.

'Not altogether,' Max says. He doesn't meet Joe's eye.

What *is* wrong with the boy?

The sheep fill the lane like a white woollen river.

Max and Joe walk with them and with the dogs and they call out during their slow march. They keep the sheep moving and stop them from straying or nipping at the grass on the verge with strong mouths. Cars idle behind them and the sun flashes off their windscreens and when Joe finally nods them past, the drivers wave and Max can see how proud his father is to be seen doing this work.

Max's mind is fogged with sleep and worry. He's got to knock things on the head with Sheryl, but she's only becoming more insistent. Last night – that text – with Primrose in the room. That'd unsettled him. Like Sheryl had barged into his house.

You're a dirty boy

He frowns.

'Primrose must be getting a bump,' shouts Joe, over the wool. 'When are we going to see her?'

Max calls to the dogs. Pretends he hasn't heard. Walks up ahead planting his stick on the verge where the grasses are coming up new. The season's turning. Usually it gives him pleasure, but not this time. He's engulfed in shame – lying to his father about the baby because it was easier. If he tells him, that makes it true, and all the other things that went with it a lie. Max can't bear that. And he's been wanting a drink so badly that it eclipsed all other wants; and this ugly thing with Sheryl. His phone vibrates in his pocket.

Come and do that to me again dirty boy. Tonight. S.

'Did ye move the flock over alright?' Ann says to him as he takes off his Barbour in the kitchen. He is ruddy with the walking, his hair all blown about.

'Yes,' says Joe and he slumps down in a chair. 'Right warm it is.'

'I know. Tropical. You must be pooped. Bacon sandwich?'

'Oh yes, that's what I need.'

She begins rummaging in the pantry, which is usually frigid with its wire-meshed window to the outdoors. She finds the bacon on the sill, folded in a brown paper bag, some tomatoes in there too. She hears his voice in the room behind her, saying, 'Max looks bloody awful. Hasn't even started on the fences I asked him to do, would you believe it?'

'Really?' she says, and she keeps herself hidden in the pantry for a moment, trying to keep her voice light even with all the lying she's been doing this past fortnight, since Max had told her about the baby. He'd called the evening it happened. 'Primrose lost the baby,' he'd said and it reminded her of when he was little and he'd come running into the kitchen saying 'Barty broke my truck.'

'Oh love,' she'd said, but softly and with her hand cupping the receiver. Her eyes were on the door to the lounge where the sound of the television news was drifting out. Joe was in there. They hadn't discussed it explicitly, she and Max, but there grew a tacit understanding that it was best not to burden Joe with the loss of the baby. They each had their reasons, telling themselves it was for his good, though she sensed the truth of it was that telling Joe was the thing that made it real. As if telling him would somehow force up their own bad feelings, especially when it came to Primrose.

'Maybe he's tired,' she says now, backing out all blustery and breezy, saying into the clear room: 'No one likes February, do they? Boring old month.'

She sets the pan on the stove and the bacon in it, which starts sizzling quick enough, while Joe says, 'What's wrong with that boy, Ann? What's happened to him?' and she's jiggling the bacon but she can hear how bewildered he is by it. 'I can smell the drink on 'im. His face is all messed up with it. Why would he be drinking now, when there's so much to look forward to, with the baby? I'll tell you something, I'm not handing my farm to some good-for-nothing who's not responsible.'

She stops jiggling. 'Don't be hard on him, Joe,' she says.

'Well, it's not good enough, Ann. I've said I'll give him everything and this is how he answers it – with drinking and not doing the work.'

'There's more to it than that,' and she turns the heat off on the stove. She can't keep going with this. 'There's something I haven't told you,' she says. She is standing over him, clutching a tea towel in tight fists. She smooths his hair down.

'Joe, love,' she says. 'Primrose lost the baby.'

She looks at him and he closes his eyes.

'Ah no,' he says quietly. 'No.'

'Yes, love,' she says, sitting down beside him. 'A while ago now. I didn't like to tell you because . . .' Joe is not saying anything. But he has opened his eyes. She continues, 'Well, I didn't want you carrying more bad news, worrying more. I think that's why he's been drinking. You know Max. He's not one to talk about it.'

'Ah no,' says Joe and it's soft, like the saddest exhaling. 'No, no, no.'

She takes his hand on the table and they look at each other.

'Poor Max,' says Joe. 'Poor Primrose.'

She nods. Rubs his hand. Then he makes to get up but she grips his hand. She knew this would come – him wanting to fix it all for Max. Take it all over and make it good for him again.

'No you don't,' she says.

'I've got to go to him, Annie. Talk to him. He's gone up the fell on the quad bike all by himself. I didn't know . . .'

'He's a grown man, Joe. And look at you, you're exhausted. You've been working hard, Joe. Not now.'

Joe doesn't resist her too much. 'When did it happen?' he says.

'End o' January,' she says.

'Two weeks ago? A full two bloody weeks? All this time and nobody thought to tell me? Like I'm some idiot child – not you, not Max.'

'I didn't mean . . .' she starts.

'Anything else you're not telling me, Ann?' he says. 'Any other little secrets you're keeping?'

'Oh don't start,' she says. And she gets up to go back to the pan of bacon.

'Well it begs the question,' he is saying, loud now. 'If you kept something as big as that to yourself all this time, what else is there?'

'I didn't tell you because I didn't want you upsetting yourself. I was trying to protect you.'

'Like I'm some senile old fart! You had no business deciding for me, Ann. That was my bairn, as much as yours.'

'It wasn't either of ours,' she says. She hasn't relit the stove, doesn't want the sizzling over the top of all this noise. 'It were Max and Primrose's. It's their loss to get over, not ours, and we should give them the space to do it.'

'Oh aye, that's you all over – let them go hang,' Joe says.

'That's not fair.'

'You never want to help them. Didn't even want to give Max the farm.'

'What is there to give, Joe? A bunch of debts, some ewes that are worth next to nowt? A clapped-out tractor we can't afford to replace? What's this great gift you're giving him, Joe?'

'He wants it. He wants to stand among men, have a place in the world. I can give 'im that at least.'

'If that's what you want, Joe,' she says. 'If that's what would make you happy. But it gives me no pleasure to see Max hang on your every word and do everything to please you. It's like he's got no backbone.'

Joe sits quietly at the table, one elbow resting on it. She turns away and lights the gas under the frying pan and the bacon starts sizzling. The maple smell and the warming sound seem to relieve them both.

'Is Primrose alright?' Joe says.

'I've not seen her,' says Ann, and she keeps her face on the pan, not wanting him to examine her on it.

'What? All this time and you've not seen her? Why've ye not taken care of her? You know she's not got her own mother to rely on.'

She flares round fast and sudden. 'She doesn't want me, alright? I've tried and she doesn't want me.'

Primrose walks into the hallway and lifts her cagoule off the finial at the bottom of the stairs – the first time she's got dressed in a long time – then she stops and grips the banister, feeling her head swim. She is all tender and weak, but she pushes herself on. She puts the cagoule on, remembering, as she does it, all the bicycle rides across the moor with her little squatter, the friend in her belly, and the feeling she'd had of not being alone. And she remembers the way just the idea of the baby changed everything about the bicycle rides into Lipton because in her imagination she was a kangaroo with a bean in her pouch. And now she is empty of it and the bicycle ride is returned to what it was. Unspecial. She feels the elastic on the wrists of her coat scratching and even this reminds her of the body that failed.

She pushes hard across the moor and the wind pushes back

in an argument with her. The ache in her belly is powerful, like a stitch, as if bits inside are knitting together, but she pushes on, pedals hard. Punishing her body or showing it who's boss. Or showing it her hatred for the way it failed her. She's no sympathy for it now.

But she needs some help, she knows that, after all that time in the house. She doesn't want her mother – there were seven at home and her mother had made no secret of being pleased to be shot of Primrose. And she doesn't want Ann, with her critical face on, putting up with her out of the goodness of her heart but all the while blaming her for it, and why did she need that when she blamed herself anyway?

By the time she arrives at Lauren's door, the ache has become a sharp, stabbing pain. She props her bicycle and leans one hand high on the brick wall while she stoops to recover.

She rings the bell and the sing-songy chime is muffled within. She has her head bent low with the pain as she feels a warm gust from the door opening and the smell of polish. She hears Lauren gasp, 'Dear sweet girl, whatever's wrong with you? Come on love, get yourself inside,' and she is ushered into the maternal warmth of Lauren's house.

'I'm sorry,' Primrose says, out of breath with the cycling and with the pain, 'I didn't know where else to go.'

'Don't be daft,' says Lauren. 'Are you in pain? You look like you're in pain.'

Primrose is at once glad she has come. Lauren has a hand on her back and she is brisk and it seems to Primrose as if she might be alright. She bursts into tears.

'I lost the baby,' she says, between gulps, 'and now it hurts.'

'Come here,' says Lauren and she takes Primrose in her arms, though she is tiny and Primrose towers over her. Primrose rests her head awkwardly on Lauren's shoulder, against a hard string of pearls, and there's so much perfume there that it makes Primrose want to cough.

'You poor dear,' says Lauren. 'Rotten,' she says then, rubbing her back. 'Rotten, rotten, rotten.' And this makes Primrose cry some more. But it feels like a good sort of crying. 'Come on lovey, you need some sugary tea and a biscuit. Have you been seen by a doctor? We need to sort you out.'

In the kitchen, at a bar stool and with her cagoule off and a biscuit in hand, Primrose exhales and the pain subsides a little.

'So you haven't been to the doctors?'

'No,' she says.

'So you've not been checked over? It were two weeks ago, Primrose!' Lauren is mock-angry but it's full of affection and like she's going to take over, which is what Primrose wants. 'You might have an infection. Might need a D&C.' Lauren is looking down through half-moon glasses at an address book open on the worktop. 'I'll try my doctor but I'll happen I should get you over to Malton General sharpish.' She takes off her glasses and looks at Primrose. 'Is there still bleeding?'

'Yes, and it smells funny.'

'Right, well, you need checking,' Lauren says, brisk and kind, with her glasses back on like a schoolmistress. 'And you need rest. Why is Max not taking care of ye?'

'He seems to be mostly taking care of his bar bill. He's at the Fox all the time. Rolls in at 2 a.m. reeking. We've barely said a word to each other since it happened. I think he hates me, Lauren. For losing it.'

'Don't be daft,' says Lauren, uncertainly. 'Men don't deal with their feelings so well. Why have you not had it out with him?'

'Dunno,' says Primrose. 'I've not felt up to it.'

'Too upset yourself?' Lauren says, and Primrose nods.

'Did ye not want to go home to your mam when it happened?'

'She'd not have me.'

Lauren was right. She did need a D&C. And she'd sat alongside Primrose on those plastic chairs that are welded together. Waited for her. Carried her home in her warm car. Now they are back in Lauren's spangly kitchen. It is dusk outside.

'Well, you're stopping with me for now,' Lauren is saying, still with her coat on and putting the kettle on to boil again. 'Doctor says you're to rest and rest and rest. And then we'll get you that prescription in the morning, for the extra antibiotics. D'ye want me to ring Max now?'

It's the third time she's asked.

'No, you're alright. I'll ring him meself later,' Primrose says.

'Right,' says Lauren. 'I'll take you up to Sylvie's old room. Bed's made up. And I'll get you a guest towel.' She looks at her watch. 'Oh god, I've got the parochial committee meeting in half an hour. Will you be alright here by yourself? Eric's in Scarborough today, so he'll not be in until dinner. You can rest in bed, which is what you need. Are you'll sure you'll be alright? I can call the vicar – cancel.'

'I'll be alright,' says Primrose. 'I've got my Household Electrics book. It's in my bicycle pannier.'

Ann sits on a bench at the far end of the churchyard. The warmth is still swirling in the air like some sub-Saharan current, even in the gathering dusk. A watery blue light washes over the grasses and bare trees. The cemetery is all greys and blues and silvery sages. She can smell the last of the mahonia on the air, heady and sweet. She's amazed to be sitting on a bench at dusk and not to be stinging with the cold.

She stares ahead at the church where she sees the door open and members of some committee or other emerge. She can see Lauren's smart cream coat with the funnel collar, the one that brings out the shine in her pearl studs. Expensive, from Browns in York. Lauren was always beautifully turned out. She is milling in the group as they stop to chat in the church porch, thirty-odd yards away. Then Lauren's face turns towards her and Ann returns her gaze. And then, after that moment of staring at each other across the churchyard, Lauren returns to the group, shakes the hand of the vicar, then drifts away with the others down the path. Ann hears distant car doors slam and engines rumble into life.

So that's that then, she thinks. She's not speaking to me. It's only confirmation of what she knows already. Lauren is bruised by the talk, because of that stupid tiff in the chemist, which set Karen Marshall off (it didn't take much). It's not even that any-one believed any of the gossip, about her and Eric. But Ann knows Lauren, knows her better than anyone. She's a proud woman, proud and elegant. She likes things just so. She'll not want to talk about it, not want to dignify it with comment. But she's stopped offering Ann lifts to things. Barely returns her calls – just the stiff pleasantries, all from the surface.

She can see the trail of it now. Karen would've put her head to-gether with Fat Mo Dorkin, the two of them chewing on it like some bit of gristle on a lamb chop. Karen would've exaggerated – 'A right ding-dong it was. Ann Hartle and Eric Blakely, more 'an friends!' And Mo's eyes would have shined bright with a tale so tall (and her so short), across the counter of the newsagents to

Maureen Pettiford. And so it goes on and on. It was the very worst thing about living in a small place – the way every little thing got blown up, all your dirty washing aired for all to see.

She stays there in the lost dark. It's like everything's falling apart – all the bad things about her on view. Shaming it is. Her whole family on its uppers, and being talked about with grimacing mouths, false with pity. She and Joe – it's as if they're surrounded with failure, a couple born to incompetence, life's D-team. She has a capacity for this: lining themselves up alongside others so they came off worse, her own particular form of self-harm. End of their lives and nothing to show for it. Even her lump of a daughter-in-law refuses to see her. She's called and called but Primrose keeps putting her off. 'I just need to rest,' she keeps saying. 'I'll stop at home. Work've been fine about it.'

She is hurt by it, Prim not wanting to see her, as if all the things she'd told herself about her strange daughter-in-law, and all the doubt being on Ann's side but her being tolerant of Primrose, that pudding of a girl, well it wasn't the full picture. The feelings were mutual. In her hour of need, and even in the absence of her own mother, Primrose didn't want her.

She'd not talked about the baby with Max – that wasn't his scene, talking. Drowning himself in the drink instead and never mind who sees. And Bartholomew, he was his usual wall of silence. But worst of all was this – that the woman she most wanted to talk to about all of it – her best friend, had shaken her off like a bad lot.

'Uterine infection?' Karen Marshall whispers, over-mouthing the words with her head to one side and Primrose's prescription in one hand. She wrinkles her nose, as if she's actually holding Primrose's sanitary towel and sniffing it. Primrose has the urge to smack Karen in the face, but it's the day after the D&C and she's feeling weak. She clutches onto the counter and Karen says, 'There's a chair in the corner if you'd like to have a sit down. That was my idea – customer care.'

Karen hands the prescription up to the chemist in a booth above her head.

Primrose only just makes it to the plastic chair and is relieved to sit, though it's too close to the towers of nappies and baby wipes.

'Poor you,' says Karen. 'Max alright is he?'

Primrose nods, feeling too heavy for the chair.

'He's been down the Fox, drowning his sorrows, ha'n't he? That's what men are like I suppose.' Karen has come out in front of the counter and is unpacking a box of Yardley talcum powder: purple and green bottles with gold lettering.

The door of the chemist opens and Primrose peers above the shelves and sees Claire coming in. She walks around the end of the nappy aisle to where Primrose is sitting.

'Hello you,' Claire says. She stands beside her, stroking her shoulder and saying 'Feeling alright? You don't look too good,' but in a gentle way, without Primrose having to explain anything. She's always liked Claire. In fact, now she thinks on it, Claire is the one person who seems to talk *to* Primrose and not over her head, or with some double meaning that's intended for someone else in the room.

'I'm just waiting for my prescription,' Primrose says. She hasn't the energy to look upwards. Feels like she's eighty years old, sitting there. She can feel Claire above her, one hand on her shoulder, ever so kind.

'Missed you at work,' Claire says and then says quickly, 'I don't mean that in a naggy way – we're managing alright. Well, Tracy moans like anything, of course. But I mean it's dead boring without you.'

Primrose smiles up into the air with a cricked neck.

'I was just saying to Primrose,' Karen says, 'that Max has been in the Fox a lot. You must be worried about him.' And she crinkles her nose as if she's adorable, with her head to one side.

Claire doesn't say anything but Primrose can feel her hand moving on her shoulder, as if something might be taking place on Claire's face, in the direction of Karen.

Claire stoops and says, 'D'you want to come to mine for tea tomorrow Prim? I'll be home about six. I'm just off the high street. Literally, round the corner.'

As Primrose looks up to reply, Karen says, 'Yes, Jake said he's there most nights, like it's a second home.'

'Shut your mouth, Karen,' Claire says sharply.

'Do you know Sheryl?' says Karen. 'You must know Sheryl.'

'Yes, I know her,' Primrose says.

'Max and Sheryl. Funny friends!' Karen is saying. 'I wouldn't like it myself – if it were my fella. But you're very much your own person, aren't you Primrose? With your wiring an' everything. I've always admired that about you.'

'*What's going on in your house?*' asks the heading in bold type. Beneath it is a diagram showing a simple ring circuit with double and single sockets leading to a central fuse box.

Primrose reads under a cone of light, which shines down on the kitchen table. It is 4 a.m. She's back in her dressing gown, which carries the beddy smell of illness in it, and her furry heart slippers. A cold snap has shoved the warm spell away and laced the night with frost. Such a change from the last two days in Lauren's spongy, overheated home. Back here, the draughts blow under the back door and a chill sits resolutely in the stairwell and the floors are hard. She is reading Chapter Three of *Home Electrics* by Julian Bridgewater.

'*In the average house there are usually three basic electrical systems.*' Primrose knows all this of course. It is elementary. But she is looking for comfort and she reads it like a child returning to a familiar bedtime story. '*The power circuit, the lighting circuit and the dedicated circuit.*'

Lauren had pressed her to stay – had been waiting for her in her car outside the chemist. 'Stop another night with us, love. You still look awful pale.' But Primrose asked her to drive her home. She told her she needed to get back to her own bed, her own things. She wanted to spread out again into privacy. Dismantle things.

On the table in front of her is a fragmented lamp – a small blue ceramic base and next to it a dented shade. She has cut a length of new flex from the cardboard wheel at the far end of the table; undone the screws in the terminal inside the lamp and eased the old flex out. She has stripped back the lengths of insulation from both the plug end and the appliance end of her new flex and fitted the rubber grommet. Now she's ready to jimmy the new flex into the lamp's terminal but her fingers are *so* cold. She puts the lamp to one side. She thought it would warm her, like a soothing bath, but it's not doing its job.

Max had not been in the house when she'd put her key in the door, ever so quietly, and found the kitchen strewn with breakfast bowls and egg-smeared plates. The milk left out. And he wasn't there when she'd woken just now, alert and with a pounding heart. She doesn't know where he is or what he's doing, only that her existence from now on depends upon their paths not crossing. She pulls the book nearer again, turning away from the lamp.

'*Repairing appliances requires working through a process of elimination to pinpoint the exact nature of the problem. After all, most devices are extremely complicated and have hundreds of working parts.*' She bites her lip and pulls the flex towards her again, trying to jimmy the wires while reading at the same time. She is pushing and pulling at the three cores, yellow-green, blue and brown, but her fingers are too thick and too cold and too tired.

'*Look carefully at the cost of replacement and consider whether the appliance is economic to repair.*' She drops the flex as an inaudible growl spreads through her temples, heating up behind her eyes, and she sets her teeth, taking the lamp, the flex, and shade and hurling the lot against the wall where it clatters rather inconsequentially to the ground and lies beside the grubby skirting. The gentle hum of the house resumes.

Primrose sees a hammer lying on the counter on the other side of the kitchen table. She walks over to it, lifts it and bounces its weight a few times in her hand. Then Primrose raises the hammer above her head, bringing it down on all that's littering the table top – on the fuses, the twisting wires, on Julian Bridgewater and his stupid diagrams, where it only creases the page, on the side plate from which she'd eaten some toast, on her mug of tea. Primrose lets them have it: tea splatters the floor and chairs, shards of crockery fly towards the cooker; the table top begins to splinter. She growls and hisses. When there is nothing more to smash, Primrose stands, her mind feeling its way like hands in a dark hallway, over all the things she might destroy.

The following evening, she walks into Claire's bright living room, where there is a neat sofa and coffee table. There is a hatch through to the kitchen where Claire is making them tea. Primrose can hardly believe it. All this space to yourself and no one coming in unannounced and all your things, just where you left them. She thinks of the things left out in her kitchen – the shards and splatters from her hammer attack. But that kind of not putting things away, between her and Max, is different to this. Theirs was something like leaving dereliction out on the kitchen table for the other to see. This, this was being yourself, free and spread out.

Underneath Claire's kitchen hatch is a dining table and on it a half-finished puzzle. It shows a fragmented picture of an old steam train. The black metal of the train itself, from skirt to blast pipe, is all filled in but there are gaps where the steam billows up and meets with a white sky. Beside the puzzle is a jumble of pieces and to the other side, the lid of the box showing the finished photograph – a 1940s scene in 1970s colour.

'I'm addicted to puzzles,' says Claire through the hatch. 'Take your coat off, just throw it on the settee.'

She comes through, carrying their tea. 'That steam is a devil to fill in.'

Primrose takes a sip and looks around the room. 'This is a right nice place,' she says. 'What happened to your flatmate?'

'Moved out. Blessed relief actually. She was always humping her boyfriend really loudly, morning, noon and night. Was like living in a knocking shop. It's lovely being here by myself. Bit expensive though. Here, I've never been to your place. Is it big? Lots of animals?'

'No, not big. It's all smashed up, actually.'

Claire looks surprised.

'Well, not all smashed up. I got a bit angry. Got a hammer out. Made a bit of a mess.'

'Don't blame you,' says Claire.

'What Karen said . . .'

'Oh flaming Karen Marshall. Someone wants to gaffer-tape that woman's gob.'

'Yes, I know, but what she said.'

'Do you want the truth of it?' Claire says.

'I know what the rumours are. I want to know if they're true.'

'That Max 'as been knocking off Sheryl after closing? Yes Prim, I'd say they're true. Tal told me – not in a gossipy way, mind. More out of worry for 'im drinking so much.'

Claire says this without stumbling or looking away. Primrose shuts her eyes and leans back in her chair.

'Are you alright?'

Primrose doesn't reply.

'I'm so sorry Prim.'

'It's better to know. I'm just tired. Tired of all of it.'

They sit together for a time, their hands cupped around warm mugs of tea.

'I'll tell you one thing,' Primrose says eventually. 'Sheryl – she won't be having a good time. Take my word for it.'

Claire makes them dinner: chops with Co-op cauliflower cheese that's a day past its sell-by and frozen peas. They eat it at the dining table, absently working on the puzzle between mouthfuls and with the telly on, burbling out *Coronation Street*. When they have cleared away the plates (Claire washing, Primrose drying), Claire wipes her hands on the end of Primrose's tea towel and says, 'Why don't we go for a quick drink at the Crown? It's only round the corner.'

'I don't know,' says Primrose. She is loving Claire's flat, warm and cosy with the curtains drawn and the telly on.

'Oh go on,' says Claire and she goes through to the living room and switches the television off.

'I'm not looking my best,' says Primrose.

'When has that ever bothered you?' asked Claire.

'I just feel a bit . . .'

'Not up to it?'

Primrose nods.

'Fair enough,' says Claire.

'Right, so, the George's team is incomplete – they've lost two of their key players to the barn dance over at Kirkby Lonsdale,' says Elaine Henderson. She's filled out into her role of Mrs Iron-Knickers-in-Chief, thinks Ann. 'So we'll just play between ourselves shall we? Lauren, would you like to captain one side and I'll take the other?'

Ann looks over to where Lauren is standing – a couple of feet from her, with several ladies in between, including Fat Mo Dorkin and Smiling Pat Branning. Lauren has not met Ann's eye since they arrived in their separate cars at the George for darts night.

'I'll take Mo Dorkin,' says Lauren, and Mo gives a little dance, jabbing her elbow downwards with a 'Yessss'.

'I'll take Ann Hartle,' Elaine says.

'Good luck with that,' mutters Lauren. 'And Pat Branning,' she says louder, nodding to Pat. Pat shuffles towards Lauren.

The rest of the teams are selected, eight on each side, and during the process, Elaine places a hand around Ann's shoulder, and Ann has the impression this is all for Lauren's benefit but she submits to it. Then, once Lauren, Mo and Pat have taken their drinks to their usual banquette – the captain's work all but done – Elaine stoops to whisper in Ann's ear.

'I'll keep you in reserve if it's alright,' she says, and nods towards the door. 'Brenda Farley's just walked in.'

Ann stands at the bar, ordering a cider and black and thinking how little she's enjoying herself – you could cut the air with a knife – and whether it'd be bad form to leave before the game's even begun. But they'd become so isolated this past fortnight, her and Joe. That's why she'd made herself turn up, against her better judgement.

'Can I join you?' Ann says, standing before Lauren. She has bolstered herself to say this, in part because there's no one else she wants to sit with: she was always Lauren's wingman and now she's no one's.

'If you must,' says Lauren. The open fire has flushed Lauren's cheeks but her eyes are piercing cold.

Mo and Pat shuffle up nearer to Lauren, making space for Ann at the end of the line. Pat taps the banquette and recruits her entire face into a grin, saying, 'Here you go, love.'

Ann sits, casting a nervous glance along the row, past Pat and Mo's profiles to Lauren, who is watching the game. And a wave of anger comes over Ann, that she's being punished – ostracised – when she's not done anything to be ashamed of. She leans forward.

'Is it warm up there on the moral high ground?' she says to Lauren. Mo and Pat shoot a glance at each other.

'It's nice enough, thanks,' says Lauren.

All four sip their drinks in silence. She doesn't want to sully herself with an argument, thinks Ann. Stuck-up cow. But then

Lauren leans forward and looks down the row at her for the first time. Her expression is hard.

'I took Primrose in, day before yesterday,' she says. 'Gave her a bed for the night. Right mess she was. It's a wonder no one'd been looking after that poor girl. She needed a D&C at Malton General.'

'You had no business taking her in,' says Ann. 'You should'a brought her over to me.'

'She didn't want you. And I don't blame her,' says Lauren.

Mo and Pat have their heads pinned to the banquette's padded backrest. Pat is smiling vainly, Mo's eyes are shining. A ringside seat – Mo can't believe her luck, thinks Ann, but she can't be bothered to rein it in. They are in the mud now, sleeves rolled up, her and Lauren.

'Getting back at me were you?' Ann says to Lauren.

'Getting back at you for what?' Lauren says. 'For throwing yourself at my husband? I don't think so.'

'Now ladies,' says Pat. 'Let's just calm it down, shall we?'

They all take sips of their drinks. Ann's is not deep enough, nor long enough, to cover her shame. She longs to walk out but that, somehow, would be to admit guilt. Or defeat.

'Poor Primrose,' says Mo and Ann can see a ghastly relish in the woman's eyes. She hates her for even mentioning Primrose's name. 'And with that business between Max and Sheryl, too.'

'I beg your pardon?' says Ann.

'Well, Max and Sheryl. You know . . .'

Ann is dissolving. Max and Sheryl? Well, why should that be such a surprise? Sheryl was a trap waiting for any man weak enough to fall in. But oh, the stupid, stupid, stupid boy. To risk all, to throw it away on that.

She is brought round by Lauren's voice, boiling with fury. 'Oh why don't you just button it, Mo? Not enough going on in your life is there, that you need to go meddling about in others? Pilfering the donations from the church bowl not giving you sufficient thrill any more? Oh yes, don't think we don't know about all the money that's gone missing. Father John knows about it an' all.'

Mo has blanched as if she's been slapped. Lauren has stood up and is gathering her cream coat off the banquette. She's so clever, my friend, thinks Ann and she stands and begins gathering her coat at the same time.

Lauren is standing over Mo. 'It's alright to dole it out, isn't it Mo, but not quite the same taking it, is it? Right ladies,' Lauren says, 'I'm off. Give my apologies to Elaine will ye?'

And Lauren marches out of the bar, proud and purposeful, with Ann stumbling on rapid steps after her and nearly getting clocked in the face by the pub door swinging shut in Lauren's wake, hard and fast.

Their feet crunch on the gravel in the black night, Lauren a few steps ahead of Ann and her cream coat glowing. She's standing at her car when Ann calls out.

'Lauren! Wait!'

Lauren stops, her car keys in her hand.

'Thank you,' Ann says.

Lauren nods.

'There's no truth in it, you know,' Ann says.

'What, Max and Sheryl? I wouldn't care if there was. What goes on between folks is private.'

'No, not that. About me . . . and Eric.' Even saying it is sullying, makes it exist, when there never was any truth in it. Not a shred. 'I'd never do owt like that. Not to you, especially not to you. Not to anyone. You know me. You're my best friend, Lauren.'

Lauren nods, but not warmly. More like she's tired.

Ann can see a bruised and damaged thing and she feels the tears prick behind her eyes and then the dam breaks and she starts to cry.

'Everything's falling apart,' she sobs. And it feels rotten to be standing alone in the middle of a car park crying and this makes her cry more, giving way to it, her sight now completely blurred. Then she feels Lauren's arms around her, gathering her up, and hears Lauren say, 'Come here,' and Lauren is resting her chin on Ann's forehead as she holds her close and tight.

ᔆ

Ruby is having a relapse, scrolling through the texts on her phone. Not the Inbox but the Sent box. The stupid torrent of texts she'd sent on Christmas Day.

Even the dog has had too much to eat

Mum and dad asleep in front of Midsomer Murders
Might as well go to bed
Happy Christmas B. Love you.

The next one was a picture of a curved mass in a jumper with two feet poking out and the words 'my stomach' underneath.

Stupid, stupid, stupid cow. Ruby is bashing her forehead with the heel of her hand which also holds a wet tissue. She is in this shabby, unfamiliar house, surrounded by boxes and bin liners. Nowhere is home, except when she's smoking. Smoking is her passion now. When she finishes a cigarette she immediately wants to light another one. Smoking makes a home of anywhere, even a derelict place. Especially a derelict place.

She had stood in front of the house with Dave Garside and looked up. It was absurdly grand. Double-fronted with wide steps and two pillars on either side of the front door. But it was decaying and on a thundering main road – a wide ribbon of cars and lorries – on the outskirts of town. The paintwork was peeling and grey with exhaust fumes. Weeds were springing up around the edges of the steps. The windows were boarded up with ply.

'Shall we go in?' Dave had said, and he'd jogged up the steps and opened the front door.

She'd walked in and the damp had hit her, hanging in the hallway like a wet web. The house was freezing. Dave switched on the lights and she saw a black and white Victorian tiled floor.

'This is massive,' she said gazing up the stairwell. 'Why's he not selling it?'

'Shit location,' said Dave. 'Even in a bull market, no one wants to be on a three-lane motorway out of town. He'll make more from it as a student rental. We're not that far from the university campus here. Needs a lot of work, though.'

They walked down the corridor to the kitchen. Ruby's shoes stuck to the linoleum. She heard their crackling peel in the gloom. A light from the yard shone across the sink and she could make out the jagged silhouette of a pile of unwashed plates and pans. While Dave felt for a light switch, Ruby stepped forward in the dark and her foot crunched into a tray of cat litter which gave off a blast of ammonia. Dave found the light and Ruby saw the darting of black flies above the sink and around the bulb.

'Holy shit,' she said, covering her mouth and nose with her coat collar.

'I did warn you,' Dave said.

He'd stayed and helped her with the washing-up and switched all the lights on. They had explored the upstairs bedrooms – six of them – each decorated with energetic floral wallpapers and all darkened by their boarded-up windows. Then he'd had to go. His mobile phone had been buzzing insistently. 'Sorry,' he said. 'I've got a couple want to complete by the end of the day.'

And she'd felt a pang of jealousy towards the unknown couple and their presumed happiness.

'I'll be fine,' she'd said, standing at the door while Dave descended the front steps in the 4 p.m. February darkness. The minute he'd gone, she searched for her cigarettes and lit one, sitting on a box in the lounge, taking in the room: the television in the corner with the armchair up close to it, its fabric thin on the arms and a greasy dark patch on the back, where a head would lie. There was a large grey-green button-back couch – an antique – with a blanket laid on it; beside it a tiny table with a pair of glasses and a glass of water. Someone had been sleeping in here. Maybe they could no longer manage the stairs. She should have found this creepy but she didn't.

For a week she'd lived in the house's boarded-up half-light, walking to work each day, lying down under the blanket on the sofa each night. Smoking cigarettes. Crying. Looking at old text messages. Remembering him coming into the bedroom in the morning with a coffee for her and then dancing around the bed in his pants while she sat up, squinting into the sun. The queen bee. Remembering meeting him in the freezing street, when she was moving. Not dead, after all. And the shock, new as if it had just happened, that he'd cut her from his life, like a bruise from the flesh of an apple.

'All my love, my kindness, my niceness,' she'd sobbed on Dave Garside's toned chest, 'he's erased all of it.'

'It's not that easy to erase someone,' Dave had said.

'I want him back.'

'I know you do,' said Dave.

'But he doesn't want me.'

'No,' he said, stroking her hair and kissing the top of her head. 'It doesn't look like it.'

She hobbled through her days at work, crying in the toilets, hollow-eyed with customers who could still laugh, shop, talk about films and the couples still together, making their plans. That was the worst of it: couples. Couples moving about freely in their lives. Couples planning holidays. Couples taking joy in the telly and a takeaway, as if there had been a nuclear holocaust outside their window – the grey, charred dereliction that she was living in – but they couldn't see it because they cheerfully had the curtains drawn. The pain of existence didn't touch them. And it felt like the only person – the only person in the entire universe who could make it better was him. How could one person be so powerful? How could one person so expertly reverse into her driveway, dump his truckload of steaming horseshit, and then drive off into the night?

When she wakes, neon strips of day push around the boards that are hammered to the lounge windows. She makes a cup of coffee using some old Nescafé granules she has found in a kitchen cupboard. It is Monday – her day off.

She has found a copy of the Yellow Pages in a sideboard drawer and she sits over it at the kitchen table, smoking. She looks under 'W' for window cleaners and finds 'A Touch of Glass'. Presses the number into her mobile phone.

'Can you come today?' she says. 'Can you come now?'

He says he can. He's in the area with his van.

'And can you bring a hammer?'

'A hammer?' he says.

'Yes, a hammer.'

'I do have a hammer, yes,' he says, uncertain, 'in the back of my van.'

'I'll see you shortly.'

She pulls the Hoover out from the cupboard under the stairs. It is mustard-yellow with a sagging bag. She plugs it in, in the living room, and pushes it back and forth across the carpet. It makes a good job of pulling at the web of hairs and crumbs until they release their sticky grip and disappear. The Hoover makes stripes across the carpet like a bowling green. There is a knock at the door.

'Come in,' she says. 'I want you to take down all the boards and clean all the windows.'

He is still looking around, taking in the vastness. He carries a bucket filled with different-sized wipers and cloths.

'It'll cost you,' he says. 'It's a big house.'

'That's alright,' she says. 'It needs doing.'

'Are you supposed to be here? You're not squatting, are you?'

'No,' she says. And she dangles the bundle of keys that Dave gave her. 'I've got keys. I haven't broken in.'

He levers the boards off one by one and the ground floor of the house fills up, like his orange bucket under the faucet.

'I'll start on cleaning the downstairs windows now. Do the boards upstairs after,' he says.

'Right,' she says.

When he tramps up the stairs, she tours the ground floor, now flooded with light. Some of the windows she opens, bringing in the roar of air and traffic and some faraway birdsong. The musty air begins to dissipate. She mops the kitchen floor. She takes down the living-room curtains. They puff out clouds of dust. She pushes her armchair into a corner and sets a standard lamp next to it.

Her industry gathers pace over the next three days – in the slowly lightening evenings after work. In the hallway there is a green door. She opens it and sees a flight of steps disappear down into the dark. She feels for light switches to her right and left and finds them. She descends. The room is wallpapered with ebullient orange flowers. Against the wall is a brand-new washing machine and beside it a brand-new dryer, their plastic still on. They have been plumbed in but never used – someone's last attempt at independence, too late. Sitting on the surface of one is an open box of detergent. Its powder has coagulated into clumps.

She washes the curtains. She washes the cushion covers. She washes the linen from the upstairs beds. Load after load. She sets an ironing board up in the living room where she pushes and pulls. Her ironing fills the atmosphere with clouds of warm starch. It pushes away the smell of her cigarettes.

The sun has arced over the house, back to front, and the evening light shouts low and orange, its shoulder up against the glass. She has picked up one of the books from a shelf in an upper bedroom. It is by someone called Carol Shields. Out of sheer physical weakness – she has run out of strength for more labour – she reads it cover to cover. She reads standing with one elbow on the worktop in the kitchen, her body curved over and one hand supporting her cheek, the other turning the pages. She reads until her back is shot through with pain and her legs ache. She reads in the basement, waiting for the dryer to finish. Mostly, though, she reads in the corner armchair. Everything inside her begins to thaw, as if she has up to now been locked out in sub-zero temperatures. Ruby is overcome with gratitude, both exquisite and painful, of the kind that gives rise to embarrassing letters. Even this is expressed. 'The sentiment is excessive, blowsy, loose, womanish,' says Carol. 'But I am willing to blurt it all out, if only to myself. Blurting is a form of bravery. I'm just catching on to that fact. Arriving late, as always.' At last, thinks Ruby. Someone at my temperature.

Primrose is kneeling over Claire's avocado bathtub as if taking communion. The water forms two walls over her ears. Despite the torrent, her fringe is still dry. The bath plastic is unyielding but less cold than her enamel one at home. Her knees are sore.

She's been coming here a fortnight now, hanging out in the egg-yolk-yellow warmth of Claire's flat. It's as if she can exhale here, away from the destitution of her own house, where the light is blue and cold; where there are crumbs on the kitchen table and strewn tools; where she and Max avoid each other because the conversation would be too hard and this is their only current means of existence.

'You don't have to wash it,' Claire calls from the bedroom. 'Just wet it.'

She's been recuperating, and they've not gone anywhere, she and Claire, just cooked meals, watched *Corrie* and worked on their puzzles. Occasionally, a kind of shock rises within Primrose about the baby and Max's affair but not often. Primrose is aware she doesn't have many advantages in life: frizzy hair, a solid body with no discernible waist, that tendency she has to be literal in the understanding of things. But she doesn't dwell. It's not in her nature. And now she thinks that might be the greatest gift there is.

She flicks her head up and ticklish trails of water seep down the back of her neck, between the folds of the towel Claire has placed there. In front of her are brown floral tiles. The light in the room is a dirty forty watts and that fitting could take more, she thinks. She stands up and goes through to Claire's bedroom.

The pink floral curtains are drawn and in here, too, there is a low muddy light. Claire pats a stool, set before a dressing table with a three-pane mirror. On the bed is a box with the lid open and in Claire's hand is a pair of ceramic hair straighteners. She smiles at Primrose and clicks them together, like a crocodile snapping.

Here in this flat, she can see something new open up. A place to be herself, or at least find out what herself might be. This kind of freedom – it has never occurred to Primrose at all. Life has always appeared to her as something to be stoic about. Without the baby, even though she holds that memory close as her loved secret from an unhappy time, she realises she is free.

Claire is pulling the hot plates downwards and steam rises and Primrose can smell the human smell of wet hair drying. When the plates have reached the end of the hair, Claire lets it drop. It falls flat against her forehead in a silken curtain. Primrose can't believe it. She shakes her head to make it swish and tickle the side of her face. Her hair has never had any movement before. It has always sat rigidly on her head like a helmet. She puts a hand up to feel it.

''S going to look brilliant,' Claire says.

MARCH

— *Preparation for lambing* —

'What d'ye mean he's not coming?' Joe says as the dogs pant and circle about his legs in the yard.

'Says he's not well,' says Tal, but he's avoiding Joe's eye, he notices, stooping to pat his own dogs as they yap – a criss-crossing, barking mess of black-and-white energy. 'I'm here to stand in for 'im.'

'Well, you've some decent dogs I suppose. I can't pay you, mind,' says Joe. 'This is Max's work and if he's sending you in his place, it'll come out o' his pocket.'

'Understood Mr Hartle.'

'Ah, call me Joe. We've a ten-mile walk ahead of us. Might as well be on terms.'

They set off out of the gate, the dogs straining ahead and Joe in his flat cap and planting his crook. Tal wears a red anorak. Useful, Joe thinks, to spot him across the purple crags of the mountain.

They are bringing the last of the pregnant ewes down off the fell to the in-bye, to build them up in their last weeks. Those carrying twins and any that are ailing are already down. Max did that job at least, though he looked as if he'd been dragged behind a quad bike for a mile or two: dishevelled and bloodshot and smelling of old beer sweats. Joe is sorry for him, and at the same time impatient for him to get over it. Neither of them talk about it – they've worked instead in a sad silence, Max leaving the farm at the end of each day in a great hurry, as if propelled by something. His need for a drink most likely. And all his late mornings accommodated without comment.

If only Bartholomew was here to enjoy the lambing. Such a wonderful time. Granted, the early starts were a pain – out at 6 a.m. every day for a month and still checking them on the field after 9 p.m. But there was no better time when it went right.

Beyond the village, they turn left off the road, through a gate and up into open country where the moss and heather is springy under their boots. They start to tramp the steep incline of the fell, mostly heads down at their wide steps, but occasionally looking up towards the rough grazing and the grey ridge like a spine along the top. Joe loves the fell. There was no arguing with it. He's not sure if that was an idea of his, or if it's something his father thought, and drilled into him. Or perhaps he's just come to an age when he sees it more as his father saw it.

He looks across at Tal, some two hundred metres away, lost in his own thoughts too, and planting his crook in the ground. Shepherds are always loners. He likes Tal – you've no need to make the small talk with him. Joe feels his nose drip in the cold. He sniffs and his Barbour creaks and he hears Tal calling to the dogs, 'Get back!'

He's been as isolated as a shepherd of late. Not that he's fallen out with Eric, just that he can feel his defences flaring whenever the man's mentioned or when he sees him at a distance. It's as if Joe doesn't want too much contact until he's brought it good, the farm. Things are too tight for him to be open with a friend that has everything. He wants the chance to bring the lambs in and make some money, and then he can pick up with Eric – stand as his equal and buy him a pint at the club. Not be looked down on.

Three hours of walking and Joe is out of puff, even though he's fit for his age – near sixty and still tramping mile upon mile each day across his land, chasing sheep and grabbing them and lifting them onto their hind quarters between his legs. They are reaching the higher ground where the ewes are grazing. He sees them, nipping at the grass, big with pregnancy. They set off at an ungainly run at the sound of the dogs. He and Tal stand by a gate which gives out onto the upper moor, begin their whistles and shouts – 'Get away!' – which sends the dogs up the scar and above the sheep to drive them down. Tal is quick. Joe can hear his instructions to the dogs and knows what his plan is. While the dogs work, Joe looks out and takes a breath. The view from up here is magnificent – the slurry colours of the fell, all burnt browns, and then the green fields of the valley and neat walls like stitching.

'Away to me!' Joe shouts and the dogs crouch low in the heather, eyes all on the flock, ears pricked for Joe's voice. Once the sheep are grouped and funneled through the gate – only a hundred and twenty or so – then they'll drive down easy enough, with the odd one straying out to the side which a dog will gather back in.

Joe's steps are larger and faster on the descent. Only three weeks till lambing, when the cuckoos will shout daily, the swallows will return and the house martins will be nesting. They'll come thick and fast, the lambs – every night. Every day, Joe'll walk the in-bye and see more that have arrived. Or he'll see a ewe turning, circling, finding her place to labour and he'll watch till she lies down and births, one then two. Beautiful it is, to see her lick the lamb clean, and then, within half an hour, to see it stand on unsteady legs, staggering, because its every urge is to find the teat. To see that lamb struggle up on its pins can still bring a tear to Joe's eye. And that first-born will be sucking and sucking, its little tail swishing with the pleasure of it, the strength growing in him by the minute, his black feet like nimble socks. And even while he's sucking, the mother'll birth a second on the green field.

He'll be walking the in-bye, early and into the evening, with his crook which he uses to push and pull lambs towards the teat they haven't found yet. He'll watch the ewes that aren't laboring right; step in and pull their lambs out if need be; shove a bit of straw up the nostrils to make them sneeze or swing them by their legs or give their ribs a tickle, all to get them breathing right. He'll watch the ewes that are new to motherhood – make sure they're letting their lambs suckle, because often they won't. Often they walk away. And pen them, if needs be, to make her accept her new job. Ones that have done it before, they're OK. And there's always the dead ones – to a fox or malnutrition. He must skin those, and pull the fleece onto any lamb that's orphaned in the hope the mother will accept it as her own.

Joe is tired now, though the downward tramp is easier and the fell seems at times to be carrying him down and his sheep run out like milk from a pail. It's this time, just before lambing, that he begins spinning the numbers, seeing what sticks. There's four grand to pay in rent next month, the eight grand loan that has all gone to Granville Harris (that sticks in his throat). He'll need at least 450 mule lambs out good this lambing, otherwise he's in trouble. Last year, they didn't make more than thirteen thousand pounds profit and that was before any salaries were taken. And this year, well they'll be worse off because of that fire and the price of feed being what it was. So the odd prize tup wouldn't go amiss. A good one – a ram that got you rosettes at a show –

could fetch anything from a few hundred to several thousand in the bidding.

'Joe? Joe, there's one getting past ye,' Tal is shouting to him and Joe realises he's descended the fell without noticing, his dogs working and his calls coming out of him without his mind on it. Five hours, it's taken them.

'Sorry, Tal,' he says, 'I were miles away.' And his dogs pull in the stray ewe. They are back in the valley now, just outside Marpleton. They must drive the flock across the village green to the fields beside the farmhouse.

'That's a good job, Tal,' Joe says once they are back in the yard. 'Will ye join me for a brew and something to eat?'

'No, you're alright,' says Tal. 'I'd best be off.'

'Primrose?' calls Ann, peering around the open back door of her and Max's house. She checks her watch. 5.30 p.m. She should be back from the Co-op by now. The light is fading, the March wind bitter. Ann has steeled herself to come here and the view of the empty stairwell almost gives her licence to drive back home but instead she steps backwards and turns to cross the yard. She must be somewhere, with the door open like that, tending the chickens or feeding the pigs. I'll find her, and then no one can sayI didn't do my duty.

Her boots curl over cemented-in stones. She carries a plastic bag and in it a fruit loaf she's baked for Primrose. No one can say I'm not doing my best, Ann thinks as she looks over at the mish-mash of sheds to her right, strewn with bits of wood, straw, bags of feed, rusting tools and rolls of wire. Farmyards are messy places, but still. To her left is the chicken coop, with one of its posts at a drunken slant. She notices a dismantled lawnmower spread over a sheet of tarpaulin. Must've been there a while, because pools of rainwater have rusted red in its stiff creases. Such dereliction, Ann thinks. It is a failing this, a sign of some mothering instinct gone awry, to not tend to your place with care. Letting it go to rot like this, she tuts. And then Ann is brought up short. This is the very reason Primrose didn't want her – doesn't like her: her quickness to judge. Ann frowns and her head throbs with the confusion, of feeling she's right in what she sees, but that Primrose might be right, too.

She walks around the back of their small hayrack, to where the pigpens squat at the lower end of a field. Two enormous pigs are asleep side by side in the soup, like a married couple after an excessive meal.

'Primrose?'

She can see Primrose's lower half sticking out from one of the arches. She is lying on her back, the mechanic. She has her arms above her head, tinkering with something in the roof but when Ann calls out, the arms stop.

'I'm not disturbing you am I, love?' Ann says. 'I didn't mean . . .'

'I wasn't expecting you,' says Primrose. She shows no sign of coming out.

'I'm sorry, love. I wanted to see how you were. I baked you a fruit loaf.'

Ann stoops to look inside the pig shelter, raising her carrier bag to Primrose, but she is obscured from the chest up in the darkness of the arch.

'Shall I go and put the kettle on?' says Ann. 'Wait for you in the kitchen? You can come in when you're ready.'

'Alright,' says Primrose.

Ann walks back to the farmhouse and into the kitchen she

always finds cheerless. The light is factory-like, and Ann sees in the worn linoleum and the chipped kitchen cupboards and the crumbs still on the table, more of that domestic neglect which she cannot understand. Open on the kitchen table is Primrose's book, and as the kettle boils, Ann glances at the diagrams of wires and circuit breakers. '*If a three-core flex is being fitted to a metal bulb-holder,*' she reads, '*connect the green-and-yellow wire to the earth terminal on the cover.*'

Ann goes to the sink where she runs a hot tap, her frozen fingers tingling under the water's spreading warmth. She wrings out a cloth and begins wiping the table crumbs into a cupped hand.

'Has the kettle boiled?' says Primrose behind her.

Ann startles and wipes her hands on her trousers. 'Yes, so it has,' she says. She busies herself at the worktop which runs along the wall, getting cups down and filling them.

By the time Ann turns round, Primrose has sat at the kitchen table.

'Are you recovered, love?' says Ann. 'Lauren said she took you to Malton General. That you needed . . .'

'A D&C,' says Primrose.

'I would've taken you, you know. You only had to ask.'

'Lauren was kind to me.'

'Right, yes,' says Ann, turning to fill the cups with boiling water. With her back to the room she says, 'You seem busy with the pigpens.'

'Yes.'

'Is the roof leaking?'

'No.'

'Ah, just routine maintenance then,' says Ann.

'I was fitting a light.'

'A light?'

'Yes.'

'In the pigpen?'

'Yes.'

'In case they want to read?' says Ann, unable to stop herself.

'I'm using parabolic aluminised reflectors. They can withstand outdoor temperature changes. It's quite a tricky job.'

'I can imagine,' says Ann.

'Partly because it's hard to see what I'm doing.'

'Ah well,' says Ann, adding after a pause, 'the light will help with that.'

They both take sips of tea.

'I'm so sorry Primrose, about the baby. Joe and I, we're both sorry. Max has been . . . torn up.'

'Not so I've noticed,' Primrose says.

'How d'ye mean?'

'He's not been here, hardly. And when he is here, he's insensible for drink.'

'He's bound to be upset. Men are not so good with their feelings.'

'There's upset and then there's just plain old pissed.' Primrose says this without sympathy or bitterness, her face holding Ann to account. Is it directness, that makes Primrose speak without flinching, or is she enjoying seeing Ann squirm?

'He's been thrown out of the Fox so I've heard,' Primrose is saying. 'Taken to drinking in Athorpe these days.'

Ann looks to the floor, as if she can no longer stand Primrose's hard gaze. 'You can get through it, you two,' she says. 'You and Max. All marriages have their bad patches. Joe and me . . .'

'He knocked off the local barmaid just after you had a miscarriage, did he?' says Primrose.

'No . . . no,' says Ann. She puts a hand up to her brow, rubs it. 'But he's not a bad lad, Max. Not deep down. He were always a bit closed off. This is his sadness talking, not the better part of himself.'

But Primrose has stood up. 'I think you should go,' she says. All her anger for Max, she's giving it to me, thinks Ann. Both barrels. And fair play to her, because he's not been around to take it.

'Primrose, I'm askin' you. I'm beggin' you. Please don't leave him. He'll fall apart good and proper if you leave him. Joe and me, we'll help, get him cleaned up. Please.'

'I'd best get on,' says Primrose.

'D'you want me to beg? Because I'll get down on my knees now Primrose, on this floor, if it would help. He can't lose you, Prim, not on top of everything else.'

'Really Ann. I must get on.'

'Ah, come on lad.'

Joe looks to the sky with the phone pressed to his ear as he hears Max's recorded voice for the fifth time. 'Come on, son,' he says, after the bleep. 'Worse things have happened at sea. Come home and we'll see a way through it.'

Then Joe kicks his boot on the damp yard floor. 'Well, call us when you can. Your mother's right worried.'

He hangs up and walks to the outbuilding where the feed is kept, to pick up a sack of ewe rolls. They are feeding them constantly, the ewes, now their time is near. He drags a sack out to the yard and heaves it onto the front of the quad bike, and as he straightens, he glimpses the back of Ann's fleece. Almost a stranger, both nursing their bruises and unable to bear the other one bumping up against them. He watches her on the far side of the yard, walking into the field behind the hay barn – the hospital field they call it, for any that are weak or ailing.

He drives the quad bike onto a track running out back across the in-bye. The workload has been heavier without Max these last days, but not half as hard as it would become in the next month or so. If Max doesn't pull his boots up, Joe'll have to hire in help and they can barely afford that.

As he approaches the first field, the bleating from the ewes is loud – louder than it should be. You expect it once they've lambed, the constant bleating, which is a conversation with their young. But not so early. He drives the bike to the centre of the field, distracted by the noise, and stops at the metal manger. He dismounts and hauls the bag of feed over, tips it up and empties it. As he does so, he looks across at the sheep who are calling out in their strange way. One approaches the manger and begins to feed and Joe feels down her swollen belly, saying, 'What's all this noise then?'

Joe is scanning the field and then his gaze stops on something – a pinkish-white blur on the grass, about thirty feet away. He strides over, folding the feed sack as he goes, thinking it a badger that's been half eaten by a fox or some such and he should get rid of it in the sack.

'Oh no,' he says, kneeling beside the aborted lamb. It is pink, wrapped in its amniotic sac as if cellophaned, its little legs out front. He stands and kicks it with his boot. Its mother has not left its side, though she has stopped short of licking it clean. She nips at the grass occasionally, but mostly she has her head up, crying out.

An early one, he thinks. He puts the stiff little body in the feed sack.

It happens.

He thinks to carry on with his rounds of the fields, checking them. Then he sees another whitish blur on the grass, further away. No, he thinks, no, no, no. This is something more. He is walking faster now and the ewes' bleating is loud in his ears. More little blurred bodies on the ground, beside walls or in ditches. A couple have been got at by foxes, their heads torn off. Joe begins stumbling, to see how many there are, hidden, in the dip beside the stream, in grassy pockets, as if the ewes have gone off, private, to deliver their shame. How many more, up on the fell, that he didn't notice? How many more in the next field?

Joe sits down on a rock. A ewe, who still has her lamb inside, nips at the grass beside him. He rubs his forehead. How many? At least twenty dead in this field alone, near a month before term. What have I done? How has this happened? He is rubbing and rubbing his forehead, harder, until he is hitting it with a clenched fist.

The ewes are crying out. He knows them and they know him. And here's death on the field, fresh and raw. Some of these ewes, that were crying out with their loss – he'd rubbed them at birth until they warmed up with life. Fed them careful, kept them with their mothers, clipped their horns, picked maggots from behind their ears. And now this, death all over his field, and who's to say how many more?

What has he done? Made some terrible mistake? He thinks to the year and the decisions he's made. To buy that tup – was it a wrong 'un? To put them out on the fell – too soon? Too cold? He knows what it likely is. Toxoplasmosis. And he thinks to the feed, the stuff he'd bought in from Granville Harris. That knock-down price. Why had they wanted him to take that feed so bad, Eric and Granville, if it wasn't to get shot of it? He bangs his fist against his forehead. He can't bear to check the next field, for what he might find there.

From: ann.hartle@cooperative.coop
To: b_hartle@hotmail.com
Subject: terrible news
12 March 2006, 7.02 p.m.

Bartholomew love,

We need you home. I know you're a grown man and you've a life of your own but we need you home.

I've just come in from the fields and we've had near 200 lambs die on us. Our lives have turned black, Bartholomew. We need you home. Your father is broken by it.

They started coming a week ago, either stillborn or born alive but terrible weak, and then not lasting the night, or the pregnancies have come to nowt, as if the foetus has been reabsorbed. Each day we go out and dread what we'll find. At first we thought it might just be a few, but it's not stopped, the death on the field.

I've never known it this bad, not even with the culls. At least then the lads we knew came from the abattoirs and took away the sheep and we knew it was going to be done right, even though everyone was sad about it. But this. This is medieval. And the ewes shouting from the field like we've done it to them, deliberate. Death is everywhere and each morning we step out and we don't know how many more we'll find.

We've sent some of the dead lambs to the laboratory for testing, to see what infection it is we've got. Joe is sure it's the toxo and has something to do with the feed he bought in from Granville Harris, though to my mind that's a distraction. Just a way for him to get through it.

We had to burn the bodies, there were so many of them. Oh Bartholomew, I'll never forget it. The smell of those lambs burning, it filled up the in-bye. And the ewes in the field – they knew what was happening. They were bleating and circling and bleating. They didn't stop crying out.

And the pyre, the flames. It went on and on. I never knew that bodies take an age to burn. The smoke stuck to our clothes and got in our eyes and our throats. I held his hand while he watched it.

There are still some that seem to be carrying to term – about 150 ewes that we've put indoors, in the outbuildings, because we'll not take any chances with them. But I don't think Joe can lamb them now. He's too broken. I'll have to get Adrian in, I think – that lad from the veterinary college. But we need help – we need you home, Bartholomew.

Mum

Dusk the following day and Joe squints and rubs his eye where the smoke has stung it: blue smoke, which swirls over the pyre behind his hay barn. Still more to burn. No news from the laboratory, but he's sure it's the toxo. At the top of the pile of bodies, bent legs with dainty hooves are silhouetted, black in the burning blue mist.

He walks fast away to his Land Rover, driving at speed towards Lipton. His mind is foggy. He operates out of a visceral, unthinking part of himself.

Joe pulls up outside the club. It is still light – the evenings are lengthening into spring. Glory days, usually, but not now. He wishes it was winter, two months ago, when things could still be rescued, when there was still time, when the dark would have covered him up.

'Hello Joe,' says Eric, without his usual garrulous laugh. He is standing next to Ron Chappell as always, in an otherwise empty room. 'Shall I call Keith to fetch you a pint?'

'I don't want a drink from you, Eric,' says Joe. 'I've taken enough from you.'

'Here we go,' says Eric. 'Keith?' he calls to the bar, keeping his eyes on Joe. 'Keith! A pint for the dark crusader here. What's troubling you this time, Joe?'

'Granville Harris keeps cats,' says Joe.

'Ah yes, that makes it all clear.'

'He keeps cats. You knew Granville Harris kept cats. And you know what cats give to sheep – you've been a farmer. You know that cats and sheep must be kept apart. You knew that feed was bad. And so did Granville. And now my lambs are dead.'

'Ah, so your bad flock is down to me is it, Joe?' says Eric. He jangles his keys in his pocket, shaking his head. 'I've brought down your flock as well as carrying on with your wife? My, I've been busy.'

'Primrose lost her baby,' says Joe. He can't think. The lack of sleep these last two days, the terrible scenes at the farm, and now the warmth of the bar, and the way Eric seems unsullied, makes Joe confused.

'I know Primrose lost her baby,' Eric says. 'I'm sorry for it, man. She should have been kept away from sheep in her condition, but I'm sure it wasn't that. I'm sure there was no connection with what happened to Primrose. You mustn't blame yourself, or anyone for that.'

Joe presses on. 'The two of you plotted against me. "Joe is on his uppers," you said. "Joe will take it and pay for it, too." And now my lambs are dead and there's bodies all over my fields.'

'And how do you know it's Granville's cats that passed a sickness to your sheep? It was Granville's cats, was it, and not any of the strays that wander in? Or your own cats, Joe, the ones that hide in your yard? You know that for certain, do you? Or what if it's some other infection? Are you certain it's the toxo? This is becoming a habit – accusing me. I'm your friend, Joe. But this is becoming too much of a habit.'

Joe is feeling the futility of it all, but he blunders on. 'You wanted to bring me low,' he says. It's as if the room doesn't exist, only the words as they emerge from his mouth. 'You wanted to see me make the choices you've made. You'd see me cook breakfasts and turn down beds like a woman.'

'And why the heck would I want that, Joe?' Eric has put down his pint and is standing tall before him, his patience worn out. 'And less of the "low" I'll thank you. And another thing. I'm not after your wife – I've a very nice one of my own, who spent some nights crying over the rumours you started. Now get out, Joe. Go home. There's no talking to you.'

Eric turns his back on Joe.

He walks out of the club into darkness and climbs into his Land Rover. He takes out his phone and dials Max's home number.

'Hello?' says Primrose.

'Primrose? It's Joe.'

There is silence down the line.

'Primrose?'

'Yes.'

'I said it's Joe.'

'Yes.'

'Were you ever near sheep? When you were pregnant, were you ever out back near the sheep?'

'We haven't got any sheep.'

'No lass, our sheep. The sheep on our farm.'

'I know about sheep, Joe. I knew not to go near 'em or to be in the yard. Not to touch anything. Course I knew that.'

'But Max, he could 'ave brought it home to you on his clothes.'

'Why are you saying this, Joe? Are you saying it were my fault? Do you think we caused it, or that I could have stopped it from happening?'

'Not you, Primrose,' says Joe, and he gulps for air in his too-small cabin of the car. He tries to take a deeper breath. 'Not you, no.'

'Well then, why are you askin' me this?' says Primrose. 'You all think it, all of you – that I should've taken better care of it. Max thinks it were my fault.'

Joe puts his head back. Closes his eyes. The phone is in his lap. 'Not you, Primrose,' he whispers.

He pulls down on the steering wheel and it's almost too heavy for him, pulling the Land Rover out of its parking space outside the club. He eases out gently and as he does so he notices Eric's Nissan Micra parked one space up. Its red paintwork is colourless under the light of the street lamp.

Joe drives at a crawl and his heart begins to pound as he turns the steering wheel a fraction with his left hand. His body is quick with adrenalin and then he feels it, the violence of metal on metal, the rock of his Land Rover as it scrapes and slows. The resistance against the accelerator. And then the alarm, like a small dog yapping, breaking up the night. He pulls away and the resistance stops and he drives fast up Lipton High Street.

ଲ

Bartholomew drives up the M1 in Leonard's fifteen-year-old Peugeot 205, the car rattling ever louder as his speed increases. He has his foot to the floor and he is hunched over his steering wheel, his body stiff with terror. His righteousness has evaporated. What use was it now, when they were in so much trouble? And where had he been, while they were scooping up dead lambs off their fields? Ignoring their calls for help. Sleeping in. Watching television alone with a ready meal.

And his claustrophobia over Ruby – that had evaporated, too. Now, all that was left was her absence. If she'd been with him, she'd have made him his better self, taken one look at that email and bundled him into the car there and then, saying 'You have to go to them, Bartholomew. If you wait, you'll regret it.' But he had waited – a whole day – to square things with Leonard, get cover at the garden centre, pack his bag. What was *wrong* with him?

He forcibly drops his shoulders and pushes out his neck, to stretch the stiffness out, keeping his eyes on the road. He is regretting everything, especially his frozen heart these last two months. He needs Ruby: her help, just as his parents need his. He needs her to make him feel things right. But she's gone. He doesn't even know where she lives any more.

Five hours later, he pulls into Marpleton but instead of parking outside the farmhouse, he turns left onto a track before the house, which takes him across the in-bye. The car rocks and the stones are a tinny hail as they hit the base. Bartholomew has both hands on top of the steering wheel as he squints through the windscreen and out left and right through the passenger windows. At last he sees him, a kneeling figure over on the far side of one of the fields, beside a ewe.

'Dad!' he shouts, but the figure doesn't turn.

As he approaches Joe, he sees the ewe is dead. Joe is holding a newborn lamb in one hand. Its skin is wrinkled in that way that the new have of looking like the very old. It is lying limp in his flat palm.

'His mother didn't make it,' says Joe.

Bartholomew sees Joe's trousers encrusted in mud, his knees sinking into the damp turf.

'Come on, dad. I'll sort this one out. Let's get you in.'

'No, I'm fine,' says Joe. 'I just have to see her right. Get her to the pyre. And mend this one.'

'I'll do it, dad. You're exhausted and you're nearly soaked through. I'm going to sort it all out. I'm here to help you now. I'm here, and I'll get some lads in to help.'

'I can't afford . . .' Joe says.

'Don't worry about that. I'm going to take care of it.'

'I've done a terrible thing.'

'It's not your fault, all this, dad. Could've happened to anyone. Happens all the time.'

'No, not this. I've done a terrible thing. To Eric.'

'Well, we'll talk about that later. Let's get you in and we'll find a way through it. Where's mum?'

'She's seeing to the ewes in the barn. There's still some that could come good. That look well, I mean.'

'And Max?'

'Arh, you don't know about Max,' Joe says, struggling to stand while still holding the lamb. Bartholomew can see how stiff he is in the joints. 'The baby,' Joe is saying.

'Mum told me last night, on the phone. Where is he though?'

'No one knows. He's not worked a day on the farm this last week or so.'

'Come on,' says Bartholomew, over the rain that's getting heavier and the sky lowering in a great grey thumb smudge. He puts an arm around Joe and escorts him towards the car. 'I might as well drive you both back,' he says. 'I have to bring the car round anyway.'

'I'll need to nurse this one,' Joe says, looking down at the lamb that's loose over his palm. 'There's not much fight left in him.'

'Best not get too attached, in case.'

'That's not a way round it,' says Joe. 'You get attached whether you like it or not.'

When they reach the car, Bartholomew goes to the driver door and opens it, expecting Joe to make for the passenger seat. But instead he opens the rear door – behind the driver's – and slides onto the back seat with the lamb on his lap.

Bartholomew looks at him for a moment, sitting on the back seat like a day-tripper, with his grey hair blown about, small and hunched and expectant.

Joe waits for Bartholomew to take him home.

The orange flames of the gas fire rise and lower within its silver cage – like sentinels, thinks Bartholomew, guarding the room. Joe lies on the sofa, lightly snoring. The lamb is splayed on his chest. It sleeps too. Ann has placed a blanket over Joe's legs and over the bottom half of the lamb.

'You used to sleep on his chest like that,' she says, 'when you were new.'

She and Bartholomew are leaning in at the doorway, looking at Joe and the lamb.

'It's good he's sleeping,' he says.

'I'm going to make up another bottle for that lamb,' she says, and she walks off down the corridor to the kitchen.

They both take up their seats at the kitchen table, taking sips of the tea she'd made them earlier, when he'd first brought Joe back.

'I think I should go and find Eric. We need help with all this. Dad can't take any more.'

'I'm so glad you're here,' she says, and he sees her well up, then swallow it down. She folds a tea towel briskly on her lap, smoothing each square with her palm. 'I doubt Eric'll be minded to do owt for Joe right now, love. Not now.'

'Why not?'

'Joe, he's been . . . Well, he lost it a bit, last night. Took it out on Eric. It's a wonder those two put up with us at all.'

'I could still talk to him. And where's Max? Shouldn't we find him?'

'I've been trying his phone all morning,' says Ann. 'No answer.'

'I'll call Primrose and ask her.'

'No,' says Ann quickly. 'No, don't call Primrose.'

'Why not?'

'He and Primrose, they're not . . . It's not right between 'em.'

'We've got Adrian coming today, have we?'

Ann nods.

'And Tal and Jake can pitch in,' he says. 'I'll cover the cost.'

'If you want Eric, you'll likely find him at the club in Lipton. He's there most afternoons. Drives Lauren mad.'

Bartholomew pulls up outside Lipton Conservative Club and parks in a space next to Eric's Micra. When he gets out, he sees the crumpled tail-light and the deep white scar that runs along the paintwork, usually pristine. He pads along the carpeted hall-way and the door to the lounge squeaks as he pulls it towards him.

'Eric?' he says to a figure who has grown rounder and greyer since he last saw him. Eric is standing in a group of four or five other men. He looks at Bartholomew but there is no tight smile or raised pint. Eric's face is dark and slack.

'It's me, Bartholomew,' he says, thinking Jesus, are they all go-ing senile?

'I know who ye are, man.'

There is mumbling from the other men, who shuffle away leaving Eric and Bartholomew alone together. Eric would nor-mally buy him a pint, slap him on the back and talk to him with the affection of an uncle. Instead, Bartholomew feels as if shame itself has walked into the room at his back.

'It's dad. He's . . .

'That bastard scraped my car,' says Eric.

'He's really suffering Eric. If you'd seen what's happening on the farm . . . He really scraped your car? Why?'

'Do I look like I know?'

'We need your help.'

'I've helped him enough, and look where it's got me. No, I'll not help him with owt.'

'We'll pay for the car.'

'Insurance will pay for the car.' Eric holds him with a hard stare, then says, 'Look son, I'm sad for him. There's nothing worse – I had a bad lambing one year and it did me in. Took me years to get over it. But I can't help him. I'm toxic for him. He can't see past it these days.'

'I don't understand it, Eric.'

'No, well. He's a proud man, and I don't blame him for that, I suppose.'

'I don't know what they're going to do, Eric. They'll have to sell up – they'll make a terrible loss on the lambs. They'll be lucky if they can pay off the loan. I don't want to see them renting some hovel and mum taking cleaning jobs and dad care-taking, having to scrimp. Not at their age.'

'Arh, that's a bad lot,' says Eric. 'I wouldn't wish them ill, your folks, much as things have been awkward lately.'

Eric rocks almost imperceptibly on his heels. Bartholomew takes it as a good sign. 'You've always been like an uncle to me,' he says.

Eric smiles now. He rocks back fulsomely and jangles his keys in his pocket. 'I'll get you a pint, son.'

They sit at a table in a corner of the room.

'Course, Joe didn't even want the farm to start with,' Eric says, licking the foam off his top lip.

Bartholomew is eating a packet of cheese-and-onion crisps. 'How d'ye mean?'

'Well, it never came natural to him,' says Eric. 'It were Brian – his older brother, did you meet Brian?'

'Died before I was born.'

'Well, it were Brian who was the natural, not Joe. I remember watching him catch a sheep, calm as you like. That ewe prac-tically ran into his arms. Me and Joe, we were flailing about, hurling ourselves after them.' Eric is laughing and then begins coughing. ''Scuse me,' he says, with his fist to his mouth. 'Joe's dad – did you never think it were funny, that his name was Eric, too? – he'd shout at Joe, humiliate him.'

'He always seemed a nice old buffer, gramps.'

'Had a mean temper, that man.'

'Why did Brian not take over the farm then?'

'There was some sort of falling-out,' says Eric. 'Brian just upped and left and your dad, he was left to pick up the pieces. Well, Ann'll tell you more about it than I can, but it was never Joe's passion, much as he'd have you think it now. He wanted other things from life. But Eric – Eric was one of those men you didn't say no to, however much you wanted to. Poor Joe, he was sort of stuck with it.'

'No wonder he resented me going off and doing my own thing.'

'He was always right proud of you. Talked about your garden centre all the time.'

'We shouldn't talk about him as if he were dead.'

'How's he doing – really?' Eric asks.

'He's lying on the sofa cuddling a lamb.'

They drink their pints silently for a while, Eric smacking his lips and saying 'Arh'.

'What would you have me do?' he asks Bartholomew.

'Help us bring in the good lambs. There's a-hundred-and-fifty-odd that are still to labour and mum thinks they're well and will go to term. We need to keep the farm in good shape if there's to be an auction – give them the best chance of clearing enough money for a house. Max is on the drink by the sound of it. No one's seen him for days.'

'He's fallen foul of Sheryl so I've heard. She gets her claws into you, there's no escape.'

'They were making eyes when I was up at Christmas,' says Bartholomew. 'Primrose must be racked about it.'

'I don't know about this, Claire,' says Primrose, pulling at her bra straps. 'It's too small.'

'No it's not,' says Claire. She pulls the top down, jimmying it over Primrose's back. She adjusts it on Primrose's shoulders. 'I think it's caught on the side.'

She fiddles with a zip which is gaping, just above Primrose's waist. 'I don't want to . . . catch your . . . skin. There!'

'Ow!' Primrose squeals.

'Keep still,' says Claire. She attempts to stand back in the tiny cubicle, then returns to Primrose's shoulder, where they look at the reflection in the mirror together.

Primrose's wide arms bulge out of the chiffon top, her sloping shoulders unable to hold the straps. She is sweating and the inner lining of the top is itchy.

'Best not go near any naked flames,' Primrose says.

At the waist, the top puckers and ruches. Her breasts swell out making the fabric thin. The pattern is an eye-bruising smear of purple and yellow flowers.

'I hate it,' says Primrose.

Claire rests her forehead on Primrose's shoulder. 'Oh Prim.'

'What?' she says. 'Oh come off it Claire. My tits look like two footballs in a string bag.'

'And why is that such a bad thing?'

'Footballs? You'd want your tits to look like footballs? Are you saying you'd go out in this?'

'Alright, no, I wouldn't. You look a sight. All I'm saying is, showing off your assets isn't such a bad thing. I'm just trying to get you out of those Asda jeans and the Sweatshirt of Doom.'

'I love that sweatshirt.'

'I rest my case. Will you let me go and find something else to try on? Please? I won't be long.'

Primrose sees the blue curtain on the cubicle fall as Claire disappears.

They'll go to the Crown again tonight, she thinks, as they have been on Tuesdays and Thursdays and especially on the weekends when it fizzes with chatter and the jukebox and people she doesn't know. All the weeks since February have seemed to speed up in Claire's company, in the bright little home where Claire straightens Primrose's hair, tries out make-up on her (it is a revelation, Primrose can't deny it); where they tackle puzzle after puzzle in the mornings in their dress-ing gowns, with bacon sandwiches to the side and the telly on – puzzles of ancient maps, circus clowns, country scenes, bowls of fruit. They chat about the people they grew up with, the books they're reading (Claire has introduced Primrose to thrillers with raised gold lettering and she's not given Julian Bridgewater a second glance since); the new hairdressers in Lipton and what it has to offer (half-price highlights – Claire won't stop nagging).

Claire had told Primrose about her mother, the black cloud that had descended after her younger brother was born. How her mother didn't get out of bed from one day to the next and the baby screaming and screaming. And her dad walking her to school, grim-faced.

'Is that why you're rescuing me?' Primrose asked.

'You don't beat about the bush, do you, Primrose?'

Primrose doesn't talk about the little bean. She doesn't want anyone saying it was for the best, what happened, even though she's thought it herself.

She crosses her arms in front and pulls the top over her head, struggling with it when it reaches her ribcage. She fights it off over her head and her hair stands up with the static and she throws the top onto the floor.

The last time she'd been home, she'd noticed his clothes piled high in the laundry corner. She is alternating, these days, between Claire's and home, somehow managing not to cross Max's path. She'd looked down on the pile, thinking, 'He's really counting his chickens if he thinks I'm tackling that lot.' But then she'd found herself putting a load in, as if part of her still had the urge to care for him. As if he needed looking after. She had put one of the T-shirts up to her face and grimaced at the smell – beer sweat mingled with human grime and above it a sickly smell like cheap perfume.

'What do you think?' says Claire. She is holding up a hanger and on it is a blouse – dark brown, with a black pattern on it of flowers that's only just visible. It is loose, sort of billowy, but a little bit see-through.

'I love it!' says Primrose. 'Give it here.'

Primrose puts a hand up to her hair and pats it. It lies like a silky curtain down the side of her face. She shifts her head and feels it swish and tickle. She is wearing her new blouse and new black patent boots. ('Fuck-me boots,' Claire had said; Primrose had frowned, 'Claire! Shush!' and Claire had said, 'Oh don't be such a prude.') She'd bought them at Lipton market and they hurt like hell.

She sits on the outskirts of a group – a big round table of men that Claire's befriended. Primrose's too-small stool is set back and she sips her pint of cider and black silently. One of the men has been silent too, and he sits beside Primrose, both of them looking into the circle where jokes are exchanged. Neither is quite engaged in the banter before them and Primrose is aware of his large outline in the blurred periphery of her vision. After an hour, the man gets up and she feels a moment of panic that he is leaving.

'Would you like another drink?' says the man.

'Oh yes please,' she says. 'A cider and black.'

'Right you are.'

When he returns the silence resumes more ghastly than before because Primrose is aware of the spectre of him leaving altogether. She forces herself to say something.

'Do you work around here?' she says, not fully turning her head towards him.

'A little way off usually – over down Malton way – but I'm doing a job in Lipton with Frank over there.'

'What sort of job?'

'I'm rewiring a house. Frank's a builder and he brings me in to do the electrics.'

'Is it a big job?' she asks.

'Not so big,' he says. 'New junction boxes, light fittings, a heating system, the ol' heated towel rail.' He raises his eyebrows at that. Nice eyebrows. Dark and bushy.

'Are you going for a ring circuit or just updating the spur and radial?'

He leans back. 'Whoah, are you an electrician too?'

'I dabble,' says Primrose, blushing. 'I've mostly given it up these days. I used to love it.'

'Love it? Why?'

'I don't know really,' she says. She is telling the truth. 'I used

234

to take things apart as a kid. The most recent thing I did was in-stall parabolic aluminised reflectors in the pigpens.'

He nods. She cannot tell if he's impressed or whether it has put him off.

At the end of the night, she says goodbye to him. She wonders if that is a look of disappointment she sees in his face, that she is leaving. She already can't wait for them to go to the Crown again, to straighten her hair and put on some mascara and hope to see him again, and even the hoping seems to make life more zippy.

Claire loops her arms through Primrose's and they march drunkenly around the corner to Claire's flat, where Primrose now has a stash of overnight things in the spare room.

'You might as well move in,' says Claire.

'You've had too much to drink.'

'Nahhhhh!' says Claire, over-loud. 'You might as well. You're here most of the time anyway. And I could do with the rent.'

Ann is feeding Baby Lamb. She sits at the kitchen table with the animal on her knee. Its bony bottom digs into her lap and the position is awkward – not like with babies, who love to be cradled, looking up at you. Lambs don't like to be up-ended to the world. Their undersides are vulnerable. They like always to be able to run away. White drops slip into Baby Lamb's upturned mouth, which looks like the gaping toe of a black boot. It licks the teat, fast and furious, and white liquid spatters onto its nose and seeps out of the edges of its mouth.

She hears the kitchen door open behind her and Bartho-lomew lays her keys on the table.

'You were a long time,' she says, lifting her head up but unable to see him.

'I had a chat with Eric. Where's dad?'

'Asleep in his bed, where he should be. How was Eric?'

'Cross at first, understandably. But he's a kind man. He'll help us.'

Ann closes her eyes in relief. Then gives the lamb a squeeze. 'This one's been named Baby Lamb. It's official.'

Bartholomew has sat down opposite her, his coat still on.

'You not stopping?' she says.

'Baby Lamb?'

'I know. Wretched, isn't it?'

'Like the Diana Ross song?'

'You what?'

'Baby Lamb, my Baby Lamb, I need you, oh how I need you,' he sings.

'I hadn't thought of that.'

'Eric told me all about uncle Brian.'

Ann says nothing. She is looking down at Baby Lamb.

'And about gramps. I never knew dad didn't want the farm. That gramps made him.'

'I don't know as it were that cut and dried,' she says. 'Eric – he was just one of those men who made you bend to his will. Hard as nails, that man. I remember they never had any heating on in this house – I used to die of the cold when I came here to stay. Used to beg Joe to say something but he never would because Eric always made him feel he wasn't tough enough.'

'Did you ever want it? The farm, I mean.'

'I wanted your dad,' she says. 'And the farm came with him. And I wanted you boys. I got what I wanted.'

'But you could have gone off together – done your own thing. Made your own life.'

She can feel herself bristle. 'There you go again, Bartholomew. Always wanting us to be better than we are. Always looking down on us from such a great height.'

'I didn't mean it like that, honestly, mum. I'm just sorry for him – that he didn't have the freedom I had.'

'Well, we didn't do so badly,' says Ann. Baby Lamb has stopped feeding and is trying to right itself in her arms. She tips it off her lap and it scrambles away, out of the room.

'He's going to shit everywhere now,' she says. 'We'd best keep him in the kitchen. Go and get him will you son? I'm tired.'

Bartholomew goes out in search of Baby Lamb and Ann rubs her forehead. He comes back in and she hears the kitchen door shut behind her. He puts the lamb in one of the dog baskets and sits back down.

'Why did you never tell me all this – about dad?'

'You were never interested, son,' she says, sighing. Impatient. 'You never asked.'

'What would he have liked to do?'

'I don't think he ever really asked himself that. He never had choices – not like you. He was into geology, when I first met him. Used to read books about tectonic plates and the continental drift. Bored me rigid with it. But there was no chance of him studying or leaving, so he put his back into it.'

'I just find it so sad,' Bartholomew says.

'Good god, Bartholomew. It's just ordinary.' She gets up and stands at the sink with her back to him so he can't see her face. 'And anyway, the farm gave us a lot of happiness, more after Eric died, I'll grant you. We loved it when you two were little. It was a wonderful place for bairns to grow up in. You were always outside with Joe, riding on the tractors or climbing in the hay barn or feeding the animals. That was Joe's happiest time, I think. Children – especially boys – need the outdoors.'

'I s'pose,' he says.

'You don't remember it like that?' she asks, and she sees the man there, at the kitchen table.

'I don't really remember it at all,' he says. 'Does anyone really remember being a child? I mean, it's not like there's times that I could bring back and tell you how old I was or what we were doing. There's the odd memory – like dad walking me over the field and telling me about sowing and harvesting. I can remember his voice and looking down at the stubble and my blue wellington boot treading on it.'

She nods.

'But I think it's with me more when I'm at the garden centre and I'm planting or watering. I think it's there – in my work.'

'You'll be sad to see it go,' she says. 'As sad as us.'

She sees tears in his eyes, sitting unburst on the rim.

'I'm so sorry mum,' he says. 'About not being here, not helping you. I didn't want to face it – I don't know why.'

She goes over to him, cups his head against her body and kisses his hair.

'I've been awful to Ruby,' he says, breaking out of her arms and looking up at her as if she might be able to absolve him. 'I've been cruel to her.'

'Well,' she says. 'You'll need to make it up to her then.'

'She'll never take me back. Why would anyone want me, mum? I'm so . . .' He shakes his head and then looks up at her exactly as he did when he was five and she'd say to him, 'I could eat you up I love you so.'

'I think you're about ready, son. Once you feel you'd be lucky if someone put up with ye – then you stand a chance of making it work.'

He lies in the single bed in the back bedroom. He can hear Joe snoring and his mother in the bathroom. He wonders what Ruby is doing, who she's with. He gets out of bed and picks his jeans up off the floor. Feels in the baggy pocket for his phone and climbs back into bed with it. He lies, holding the phone above his face and scrolls through the inbox. So old, they are now. Down the list he goes, remembering.

> Want 2 go camping? We cld use my pants as a tent!

> Just scoffed last of black forest gateau. Hate self.

> Folk festival on campus this wkend. Let's grow beards and go!

> I've got some bells you can jangle later

He hasn't recognised it before – the thing that always seemed to him like hectoring. He was so busy avoiding her pressure, that he didn't see it for what it was.

He presses 'Create Message'.

> I've made a terrible mistake. I want you Ruby. I need you.

Within seconds his phone vibrates. She never delayed in reply-ing. She was never out of range. His heart is thudding as he sees the little envelope sign.

> It's a bit late for that. I'm with someone else now.

APRIL

— *Lambing* —

Bartholomew stands outside Winstanton Estates on the high street. In the window is a huge flat screen, rotating property details, and below it, among the screen's trailing wires, is a row of potted orchids. He'd been to the café in search of her, of course – yesterday, as soon as he'd driven back from Yorkshire. But the girl who straightened from loading the dishwasher wasn't Ruby. It was Magda, from the Ukraine. Ruby had gathered up all her days owing, she told him, and taken a break. Wouldn't be back at work for a fortnight. 'Got new place. Needs very clean. I no say more.'

So here he is. Desperate times, desperate measures. Inside, he can see two young men in suits sitting behind desks, one on the phone, the other on his computer. Chancers who've stumbled on the good times, Bartholomew thinks. He pushes open the door.

'Name's Wayne, how can I help?' says Suit One, not rising but holding out his hand across the desk to Bartholomew.

'Actually, I was wondering if Dave Garside was here.'

The two men shoot a glance at one another.

'You go, Gary,' says Wayne, and Gary immediately gets up, walking to the back of the shop, his tasselled loafers sliding on the laminate floor, his suit jacket flicking out behind him.

Wayne answers a phone that has begun to ring. 'Winstanton Estates. Yep, yep, no, that one's gone. Went for a hundred thou over the asking price. I know. Four days after it came on.'

Dave Garside emerges from the back of the shop, following

Gary. He catches sight of Bartholomew and rolls his eyes.

'This better be good,' he says, 'I've come off my break.'

'I thought you went to Ruby's for your break,' says Bartholomew. Not a brilliant strategy, when he's after Dave's help.

'On holiday isn't she?' says Dave.

Wayne has ended his call. ''Ere, Gary,' he says, nodding at Dave and Bartholomew. 'Lovers' tiff.'

Gary smiles to himself as he sheafs through papers on his desk.

'This your boyfriend, Dave?' says Wayne. 'You going to introduce us?'

'Back in your cave Wayne,' says Dave.

'Oooh!' says Wayne, holding up an imaginary handbag with two hands. But then he trails off. Gary laughs, more supportively this time.

Bartholomew is bewildered. Boyfriend?

'I need to see Ruby,' he says. 'It can't wait a fortnight, really it can't. It's really important, but you see I, I don't know . . . I don't know where she lives.'

'I don't think you'd be her number one choice of caller right now,' says Dave.

'I just want to explain, to talk.'

'Look,' says Dave, 'you've really put her through hell. I don't think she'd appreciate me giving out her address. Sorry mate. I can tell her you were looking for her when I see her.'

'I really need to see her, Dave. I've fucked everything up.'

'Well, like I say,' Dave says – and he's a big man, standing taller than Bartholomew – 'we can't give out personal contact details I'm afraid. I can pass on a number.'

He turns to feel for a post-it pad on Wayne's desk. 'Would you like to write down your details?'

'No, she's got my number. She hasn't answered my calls.'

'Well, p'raps she doesn't want to see you then. Now if that's all –'

Dave's body is angled towards the back of the shop.

Bartholomew says nothing, can't think of an argument in his favour, and Dave strides away, disappearing through the back door.

What now? Bartholomew is thinking, his hand on the door's handle.

'Here, Gary,' he hears Wayne saying, rather theatrically, as he's about to pull on the door, 'has that new tenant – Miss Dalton – settled her rent for this month?'

Bartholomew stops, his back to the room.

'What, Miss R. Dalton, of 43 The Vale, you mean?' says Gary, over-enunciating. 'I don't know Wayne. I'll check.'

Bartholomew pulls the glass door, fast, using all his weight, and steps out onto the street.

He stands outside a grand double-fronted house, the traffic roaring behind him and rings the bell. He steps back and waits.

Nothing.

He rings the doorbell again. To his right is a broad bay window, so clean it is all reflection of sunlight and tree. He presses his head up to the glass, cupping his eyes so he can see inside. There is a pale-grey button-back sofa and on it a book, splayed open. He recognises one of Ruby's blankets over the back of the sofa and one of her mugs on the side table. He is shocked that she has settled into a place he's never seen before, a new life he doesn't know about. It is neat – he can see the Hoover stripes on the carpet. He steps back and takes out his mobile phone, the millionth time he's stared at the small screen since he'd received her text, but it never vibrates into life, except with the word 'Mum'.

It's a bit late for that. I'm with someone else now.

It wasn't like her – it was so terse. And then there were all his calls, which she hadn't answered. That wasn't like her, either. This person he loves has become a stranger to him.

He tries the door one last time but without much hope. He looks at his watch. 9.30 a.m. Should've been at work an hour ago. He walks down the steps. Defeated so soon. He approaches his bike where it leans against the peeling front wall, then stops. He reaches into his pannier for a scrap of paper and a pen.

Ruby, I just want to talk, that's all.
  I just want to explain. Please call me. B

He pushes it through the letter box and cycles away.

Ruby throws her cigarette onto the ground – her third of the morning and it's only 9.30 a.m. – and grinds down on it with the toe of her plimsoll. A shaft of watery April sun slants low across the scant little back yard and warms her face.

She thinks she should go back to her book, develop that air of poise, but she's read the same paragraph several times without the words forming any meaningful pathway into her brain. So she's been pacing, room to room, another Nescafé; another cigarette; taking out her mobile phone which has registered all his missed calls. His text had thrilled her, then infuriated her, then saddened her and then all three over and over again. She had stopped herself from following up her masterful hammer blow of a response – she wanted it to resonate, like a dagger to his heart. At the same time, stopping herself from sending more text messages or answering his calls was a personal agony. But she stood firm: striking up a dialogue would be tantamount to an overthrow. And anyway, where was he now? That message – so urgent and passionate – had been nothing more than a whistle in the wind. Where *was* he now? And where were the flowers? His trusty steed seemed to have developed a limp. Typical. It was never the way it was in films.

She hurries inside, through the back door and into the kitchen which smells of lavender floor cleaner. She has stopped smoking inside since she's been cleaning the place up these last weeks, doesn't like to sully the lovely starchy smells of laundry and furniture polish. Another Nescafé, and then my book, she thinks, peeping through to the lounge where the spring sun is warming the room through its broad windows. It has annoyed her beyond measure, the effect of his text, because she's been sad for three months and then, with that message, something within her became rectified, as if she's been righted just because he has righted her in his mind. And how pathetic was that, after weeks and weeks of crying? It was a terrible thing to realise how much one existed in the mind of another person, how much love – or was it good opinion? – could demolish or resurrect. To be lovable – wanted, appreciated – it was everything. And yet it was no more controllable than the weather. She feels as if she's been in Siberia and now, with one text, she was back in the sunny uplands, only independent now she can feel his gaze. Is that all that exists? His version of me?

She carries her mug across the hall to return to the sofa and in the doorway to the living room stops, and steps backwards. There on the mat inside the front door is a folded piece of paper. She picks it up and opens it. He has been here. At her front door.

'Looks great, Leonard,' he says, aware of how much ground he has to make up. Guilt – it seems to be everywhere, in every corner of his life. They are standing at the lower boundary, looking up towards the warehouse. The view is a myriad of paths, white with new gravel, which are bordered by greying oak troughs.

'And I've started off the annuals in the cold frame.'

'I can see,' says Bartholomew.

'The grasses are coming on, too. I thought I'd do a whole border of grasses. They look great with the astrantias and alliums but there's something about a single variety all running together. Just seems to have more impact.'

'How've you managed all this by yourself? You've done so much.'

'Worked the weekends, stayed late,' says Leonard. He still sounds huffy, but can't help wanting to show his work to his boss for approval. 'Once you're into it, you can't stop,' Leonard is saying.

'Those spring troughs are amazing, Len,' says Bartholomew, and they both look at the display – a series of star magnolias, underneath them pots of euphorbia and bleeding hearts. Leonard has arranged a simple palette – white and green – but gathered in such swathes so that the euphorbia form a thick ribbon of lime and the stellatas meld overhead in a canopy of loose flowers like torn tissues and then the white dicentras, arching with their little bells.

'I'm sorry I left you in the lurch,' says Bartholomew and he notices Leonard shifting awkwardly. 'It's an important time.'

'Yes, well.'

'What happened about all those orders for accessories, you know, what I said a couple of months back – the toadstools?'

'Never got round to it,' says Leonard. 'S'pose I got waylaid.'

'Thank god.'

'Made a decision about selling then?' says Leonard. Bartholomew can see he can't bear to look at him. He is stiff with nerves.

'I'm not selling, Leonard. I'm sorry. I'm sorry I was like that. There was stuff going on at home.'

Leonard shifts again foot to foot. Bartholomew turns away to pick off some dried leaves from a stem.

'How are the trousers working out for you?' asks Bartholomew.

'Oh they're magic,' says Leonard. 'You just wash them, and they're good to go. No ironing required. I might order some more.'

'Well, I probably owe you a few days off.'

Leonard is hopping now. He taps his watch. 'It's that time,' he says. 'I shall pick up the paper and venture in, if it's all the same to you.'

Some things never change, Bartholomew thinks, as he watches Leonard hurrying up the main path to the warehouse. He glances at the entrance gate, where his eye is caught by a pea-green coat. Ruby's hair is glowing in the sunshine. The sight of her makes his body quicken. She hasn't seen him yet, and he watches her familiar form, grown strange over three months of separation. He is filled with desire and reluctance. Some part of him – and not a small part – would like to remain where he is, full of unrequited longing, unblemished by the real person. He is not sure he can absorb any more guilt. But he walks briskly up the main path towards her. He has a hand over his eyes and is squinting when he says, 'Hello, stranger.' He smiles at her. She doesn't smile back.

'You left me a note,' she says. Her face muscles are barely moving. She looks haughty and elegant. She is so pretty, her face like home to him.

'I'm glad you came.'

'Yes, well, here I am, then.'

'Can I make you a tea?'

'No, you're alright.'

'Um, shall we go and sit on that bench?' he says, pointing the way with one arm, the other hovering over her back. He daren't touch her. How have I got us here, he thinks, to this impossible place?

She sits rigid, looking ahead at the plants, and he sits beside her, his body turned towards hers. Above them, a white cherry is in blossom, its nodding flowers lit by the new sun.

'It's looking well,' she says, nodding towards the beds and paths.

'Thanks. Mostly Leonard's work.'

'What did you want to say?'

'I don't know where to begin,' he says. He pauses. They sit, for a moment, looking out together. Then he turns to her, saying, 'Who are you going out with?'

'I'd say that wasn't your ideal starting block.'

Her eyes are steely – sad-looking. They've lost their usual Ruby sense of amusement.

'No, sorry Ruby. I'm really sorry, about what happened.'

'Yes, well. Water under the bridge now,' she says. 'I've got a new place. Fresh start.'

'I saw.'

'It's better – I feel better. I don't think we were suited, to be honest.'

'Oh don't say that,' he says. 'I don't know what got into me at Christmas. I was cutting myself off. There was stuff happening at home.'

'Well, like I say,' she says, 'there's no need to worry about that now. We've both moved on, ha'n't we?'

'But I do worry about it,' he says. 'I mean, I don't want that to be, it.'

Her back is straight as a rod.

'There was a fire, at Christmas I mean,' he says. He slumps back on the bench. He feels exhausted. He just wants to tell her everything.

'A fire? At the farm?'

'Everything's turned to shit. I mean everything. They have to sell up – mum and dad. Primrose lost the baby. Max has started drinking. Really couldn't have got any worse.'

He can feel her processing what he's said. He rubs his eyes with both hands.

'You've been dealing with all that. By yourself?'

'Sort of. Made me realise things.'

'What things?'

'That I was an idiot. That I need you.'

'You want me back so I can help look after your mum and dad? How could a girl refuse?'

'No. I want you back because I love you, because you're a good person. You want it like a romantic film, Ruby, when all that stuff's just crap. I want you because it's better to be together. I want you because you're different to me, better than me, and because, because I need you and I couldn't admit that before. Why is that so terrible? To realise you need another person, to realise you're not as good without them?'

She is frowning now and he sees that there are tears in her

eyes – hot angry tears and her chest is rising and falling. She is pushing it all down, he sees, not wanting to dissolve in front of him.

'You lost all your kindness,' she says in a wobbly low voice. Her hands are fists in her lap. 'You hurt me and you didn't even feel it.'

'I know. I do know that, Rube.'

She swings round to face him. 'You don't call me that. Not now. It's not like that now between us.'

'I'm sorry. Please, I'm trying to say sorry.'

'I've spent three months crying and feeling wretched. I've had to move out of my flat because I couldn't stand to be in the same street as you. And every time I reached out to you, I just got nothing. You were cruel. That's not how you treat someone you love.'

'I know. I'm sorry.'

She has stood up and is looking down at him. 'I've got to go. Good luck with everything.'

'Please Ruby, let's talk some more.'

'I told you, I'm with someone else now.'

All the energy has drained from his body. He is letting her go because he is too exhausted not to, and because his destruction is everywhere, irreparable.

A moment passes and she is still standing there, as if she's waiting. 'Right, well. I'm off.'

He looks up at her with his hand over his eyes to shield them from the low sun. 'Don't let me keep you,' he says.

'Don't try and contact me again.'

'No, if that's really . . .' he says, his head hanging down, elbows on knees.

'You can text me maybe.'

'I know how you like to text.'

'But just as friends.'

'Right you are.'

She is still standing there, tightening the belt around her pea-green coat. She really has lost a lot of weight. She looks ridiculously pretty.

'Is that it then?' she says. 'Is that the sum total of what you have to offer me?'

'You just told me you're going out with someone, Ruby. What do you expect me to do, spear him with my sword?'

'Yes! Yes! I do bloody expect that. Or at least more than "Sorry Rube, fancy giving it another go?"' (She has put on a moron's voice. Bit uncalled-for, he thinks, smarting.) 'It's like you want me to wait and wait and wait. Like I have to constantly pretend that it's all fine and I don't need to get on with things. This is my life Bartholomew. I can't keep gambling on you. And here's a newsflash: women can't have babies at 105!'

'You're not 105.'

'No, but I'm not twenty-one either. I'm thirty years old. What about the things I want?'

'God, you're always pushing aren't you? You never stop pushing. Forgive me for not showing up with a ring!' he shouts. 'I thought a chat first might be an idea. But it's never enough for you, is it Rube? Nothing's ever enough!'

He gets up from his bench. She is silenced by his outburst and he marches away towards the warehouse, thinking that's it then, it's all gone to hell in a handcart. I wanted to beg her forgiveness, win her back, I even want to marry the stupid cow, and I've ended up telling her to sod off.

☮

The metal ring-pull handles clatter as Primrose pulls open a drawer and lays her folded T-shirts inside it. Her suitcase is open on the bed and she turns to unpack the next layer but stops and stands in the centre of the room. Her own room. She has never had her own room before. It is small – a single bed up against the wall with the window above it, a chest of drawers and a wardrobe which is far too big. There is a lamp on the chest of drawers and beside it her keys – her own set of keys to Claire's flat. Claire is out and Primrose is marvelling at the silence and the feeling she has of possession: being alone in a little flat that she has, temporarily, all to herself.

She feels beneath the lampshade and pushes its hard little button to turn it on though she doesn't need to – it's bright outside. She sits down on a sliver of bed beside her suitcase. She looks at her watch. She hasn't much time, she's meeting Jacob at the Malton job in an hour and wants to change into her new outfit first, but she sits for a moment and looks at her little pink room. Should have brought that rug, she thinks, but I can't go back now. There's no going back now.

She'd been surprised how quick and easy it was to pack – how little she'd wanted to bring away with her. Just her clothes really, some towels and bedding. She'd tidied up the kitchen and packed away her tools – there was no room for them in Claire's flat and she barely touched them these days anyway. They seemed like a cumbersome dead weight as she pushed the black boxes into the cupboard under the stairs, then returned to the kitchen to write Max a note.

Dear Max,

I've gone to live in Lipton with Claire. I'm sorry it didn't work out with us.

*There's a fresh ham in the fridge – a nice one from Alan.
I've fed the pigs and chickens but you'll need to see to them
now.*

Primrose

She should go. The bike ride to Malton is forty minutes at least,
but she can't tear herself away from this private place, even for
Jacob with his bright eyes and energetic eyebrows. Oh it's lovely
how he listens to her with so much going on in his face, listening so hard and smiling and craning to hear what she might
say next. But Jacob is poor competition for the joy of this box
room with all her things just where she wants them. She thinks
back, with regret, to Ann Hartle's attempts to get her interested
in homey things – market-stall tea towels and Coopers peg bags.
She never understood it then but she does now. Now she wants
to shift that lamp a little to the left and lay her book beside it;
buy a rug; position her wash bag on the bathroom shelf. She
wants to mark out her space in the world, and she wants this
more than she wants Jacob.

'Prim?' calls Claire from the hallway.

'In here,' shouts Primrose.

Claire peeps round her door. 'How's the unpacking?'

'Good thanks.'

Claire steps in, rustling in her anorak and out of breath from
the stairs up to the flat. 'Here, you've made it nice,' she says.

'I might buy a rug.'

'You couldn't look at the ignition on the stove could you?' says
Claire. 'It's not worked for a year and I'm that fed up of using
matches.'

'Course I can,' she says. 'I'll borrow a couple of tools off Jacob.'

'When are you seeing him?'

'Ooh bugger it, right now. I'm late. Supposed to be in Ribble-head at two.'

'OK, well, I'll see you later on. Fancy the Crown tonight?'

Primrose nods. 'And I'm making us lasagne for tea.'

'La-di-da,' says Claire, walking off down the hallway. 'You'll be shaving your Parmigiano next.'

She walks into the Ribblehead house which is thick with dust. Her new boots clack on the raw wooden floorboard and Prim-rose steps carefully over the holes and cables and the mess of tools.

'Hello,' she says.

Jacob backs clumsily out of the cupboard under the stairs and settles back on his haunches.

'Hello, Primrose,' he says, and she is reassured by the fullness of his warmth towards her.

'What are ye working on?'

'Just finishing off the kitchen circuit. I've put it on a separate system to the old one.'

He is rubbing his hands on his overalls.

'You look nice,' he says to her and she squirms a little under his gaze. He is so bald about looking at her. Honest maybe. Or shameless. Whichever it is, he takes in her clothes, her body, without apologising for it. She's not used to it.

'Come on,' he says. 'It's all dusty here. It'll ruin your new boots. I'll treat you to a tea round the corner.'

As they walk he places a hand lightly on her back. She thinks he would probably like to hold hands, but she keeps hers firmly in her coat pockets.

They sit across the pale Formica table in a café which is filled with the other builders on the job, who seem to like him. He has friends. Her tea is too hot, so she just sits, looking at him and he talks – about his van, saving for a new one, whether he might take her to the cinema to see a Harry Potter film (she nods), the next job across the dale which hasn't been confirmed yet, but there's plenty of work – a boom time in construction. He says he's keeping his head down, working and saving for the future when he'd like a place of his own (but not at these prices). How what he'd really like to do is keep animals – on a smallholding maybe. The irony, she thinks, but she doesn't say anything, just smiles at him and nods. She can see how hard he's working to impress her – and how available he is, in the moment. But his words zone in and out to her, muffled behind a kind of ambient fog, as if she can't stop herself detaching from it all. You have all sorts of ideas about me, she thinks as he talks – all sorts of ideas about what I might provide for you, all the fantasies I'm going to fulfil. But it's only a matter of time. She realises that she has little hope. And that she feels sorry for him. There he is, working his socks off with that charm offensive, basking in the perfection of them both in this new thing. But she knows that soon enough it'll shatter down. They will both emerge, as they are.

For now, though, she goes along with it, carried along by his hope and enthusiasm, which is unsullied by a marriage gone wrong.

Max pushes open the door of the Crown in Lipton. It has a different feel this one – more hushed, more genteel than the other boozers he's become familiar with. Lately – since Tony Crowther barred him from the Fox – it's been the Plough at Athorpe, one of those anonymous places on a trunk road out of town, with tringing fruit machines and the air so full of fag smoke it made your eyes sting. There were several like him in the Plough – men sitting alone, their roll-ups next to their pints. He knew he was joining their ranks, with their sheen of sweat and shaking hands.

Every day he woke saying, no more, today is the day I stop, and then the day would reach such a pitch with this need in his body – like a fist tearing at his insides. This need eclipsed every other thought in his head. And his mind, filled up with it, would trick him, saying, 'It's just the one'. Just one, to steady things up, because he definitely would be better. And he'd find himself among the men (and the occasional woman) in the Plough, for whom a pint was no longer a social event. And then, after the sheer joy of holding that amber glass and taking that first sip, and the pleasure and relief which seeps through his body with gulp after gulp; then the revulsion would come, his mind saying, that's the day shot, all turned to shit: you gave in, you weak fuck, you pathetic pile of . . . Well, in for a penny, in for a pound. Might as well go the whole hog. Tomorrow, after all, is another day. And he would abandon himself to it because there's no saving him today. Not today.

But this is not the Plough, it is the Crown, where the door closes ever so slowly, its bristles dragging on the soft pile of the carpet. And the room smells, not of failure but of home-cooked food. Steak-and-kidney pie. Yorkshire pudding with gravy.

Max scans the room. His gaze stops at a group of men and women at a table close to the fireplace. At its edge is a woman with glossy brown hair. She has one hand on her glass and isn't saying anything. She wears a brown and black floaty blouse and a big necklace. Something about her is familiar. He approaches the group.

'Primrose?' he says.

Her face falls. She gets up hastily and shuffles out past jutting knees to where he stands. 'What are you doing here?' she whispers.

'I got your note,' says Max.

'Over there,' she says, nodding at a table at the back of the room, far away from the group.

They sit down and he stares at her though her eyes are on the table. Then she looks into his face, holding him to account, her expression blunt as a mallet, and he flinches under the directness of it. She's wearing make-up – her eyelids are shimmery. He's never seen her wear make-up before. And her hair is different, her clothes. He takes in her new look and sees in it a life that has gone on without him. Her new interests – new friends – pursued while he's been drinking his into oblivion. She's not lost, as he is. They are not lost together after the failure of their marriage. No, he's alone in that. He feels speared by envy, right through his heart.

'You look . . . you're different,' he says, and even he can hear how bitter it sounds. 'What've you done to yourself?'

She flushes and touches her hair. 'What d'you mean? I've just straightened my hair.'

'You look,' he says, 'you look ridiculous.'

She fiddles with her necklace. He sees her shoot a glance across the bar to Claire and a man standing next to Claire. Both are looking over at Primrose. He sees Claire mouth 'Are you OK?' across the room and Primrose nods back, in her shy way. The man is staring.

'Who's 'e?' asks Max, nodding towards the man.

'Why d'you want to know?' asks Primrose, weary of him. Her

eyes are dead. She's just being patient, he thinks, waiting for me to have my say and then hop it, so she can go back to him. And he settles into it, the wounded party.

He finds himself examining her again. Her shirt is slightly see-through. 'That new clobber?' he says.

'Did you come here to say summat?'

'Just thought we could 'ave a drink together after five years married.'

'Right,' she says softly. 'How's Sheryl?'

'Oh god, Primrose. Sheryl, I didn't mean . . . That were a mistake. It's finished now. Sheryl never meant anything.'

'If it never meant anything, then it were a foolish thing to end a marriage with. More fool you.'

'You were always doing your wiring.'

'Pardon me for having an interest.'

'You never looked like that when we were together.'

'Looked like what? Ridiculous? Good thing too. You wouldn't want to be married to someone ridiculous, now would you?'

'I didn't mean that. You look good. You look great, Prim.'

'Jesus Max, what does it matter? Are you really that dense? I was there, day in, day out, breakfast, lunch and dinner. I was there. Couldn't you have used your imagination? Look, you went for summat else and to me, that let's me off the hook.' She softens. 'I'm sorry. But you and me, we were never . . .'

'Never what? We rubbed along.'

'We were never love's young dream, were we? Come on, be honest.'

'I can make it up to you,' he says, but even he is aware how lacklustre it sounds. A damp squib, this. 'I can make it right. Cook more dinners, take you out once in a while. It'd never happen again, that thing, that stupid thing.'

'You'll be alright,' she says. 'Give it a bit of time.'

Primrose joins Claire and Jacob at the bar, saying 'I'm OK,' in answer to their worried expressions. She takes a deep breath but cannot draw it deep enough. She tries again and begins to gasp. She clutches at the bar as the room spins and she's gulping for air, bigger and deeper but still not getting any oxygen. Jacob rubs her back, saying, 'Come on, let's get you outside for some fresh air.'

She sits on top of one of the wooden picnic tables which over-look the Crown car park, her feet on the attached bench. He stands beside her, his hands in his pockets.

'You haven't got a cigarette have you?' says Primrose.

'I don't smoke.' He is frowning hard – those beautiful eye-brows forming a dense canopy.

'No, course,' she says. 'Sorry. Don't know what that was.'

'Panic attack by the looks of it,' he says and he climbs to sit down beside her on the table top and she feels it creak under his weight. He smells nice, of Freshly Washed Man. He leans for-ward, his elbows on his knees and she looks at the brown suede coat covering his big back. 'What did Max have to say?' he asks.

'Oh, you know, "Come back, there's chickens need feeding."'

'He's not looking too good,' Jacob says.

'That's what drinking in the Plough does for you.'

There's a pause. 'What did you say?'

'You've nothing to worry about,' she says. She feels irritated by his questions, putting himself in the middle of this.

'I didn't mean . . .' he says. 'I don't mean to put you under any pressure.'

'He's still . . . I don't want to go back to 'im,' she says. 'But it were five years.'

'It's a big thing,' he says, looking out across the car park. 'I know. I've been there. Not married, but I were with someone for a long time. Takes a while to get over.'

He's quite something, she thinks. Quite a catch. 'You're a nice man,' she says, and she reaches forward to take hold of his hand.

⌒

Ann strides across the yard to where Adrian, from the veterinary college, and Eric have fashioned a makeshift lambing shed under the charred arch of the hay barn. She steps in and breathes the familiar smell of straw and sheep – a clean, mammalian smell – and she takes in the sight which never fails to cheer her. This is what she'll miss most.

They have carpeted the open barn with straw, with bales set about the edge and in between as hurdles – little walls for the sheep to bed against. There are metal partitions and within their various pens, groups of ewes blink patiently while their lambs suckle with flicking tails. The noise is of bleating and rustling – mothers and lambs talking to one another and all their conversations new. She is always struck by how similar it is to her own first days with her babies: the nuzzling with hard, pushing noses and the low chat.

Yes, this is what she'll miss, and Joe will too. If he'd just come out and take a look, see how well they're managing, and Bartholomew down south getting regular updates on the phone from Eric. But Joe, he can't bring himself to come outside and see, not with Eric taking the reins, though she thinks it's not rivalry keeping him away but shame over what he did that night, to

Eric's car. You had to forgive the man, because what Joe had witnessed on that field – that was more than any man should have to take, and now he was keeping quiet, nursing Baby Lamb. Letting it seep into his bones. There was no longer any question about selling up – Joe knew it and she knew it. They would just have to come to terms, as Barry Jordan put it, and hope the auction would clear enough for some place half decent to live.

She sees Eric stride over the straw towards her with high lifting legs.

'This is more like it,' she says, smiling to him, but careful not to be too friendly.

'It is,' he says, beaming. 'Haven't had this much fun in years. They're doing well, this lot. Lambing like beauties. Reckon we'll have more 'an two hundred in by end o' t' week.'

'How's Adrian doing?' she asks. She has her hands in the pockets of her padded jacket and nods over to Adrian, who is on his knees next to a labouring ewe on the far side of the barn.

'Very good. Aye, he knows what he's doing. We're quite a happy band when all's said. Hadn't realised how much I miss it, lambing.'

'And Tal?' Ann says.

'He's over on the in-bye feeding the fattening lambs and the shearlings. You've nothing to worry about of the ones as are left. It's a good flock.'

'Yes, well, won't be ours much longer,' she says as they look across the shed together. 'I've given notice to the water board. Six months they need. We have to be out by mid-October.'

'Mrs Hartle,' says Tal, coming up behind them and touching his cap to her. Always had lovely manners that boy. 'Eric,' he says. 'There's a tup I want you to look at on the east field.'

'Ah no,' says Eric. 'P'raps I spoke too soon.'

'No, no,' says Tal quickly. 'Nothing to worry about. He's a big boy, is all. Turning into a fine ram. Got a sweet head on 'im, good legs. I think we might have somethin'.'

'Right well,' Ann interrupts, 'I think I'll leave you boys to it, if that's OK. Keep Bartholomew up to speed, won't you.'

'I will Ann, I will,' Eric says.

And she walks back to the house, hearing Eric say to Tal behind her, 'Come on then lad, show me this tup then.'

'There's a sheep I'd like you to take a look at,' says Eric, on the phone to Bartholomew that evening.

'Oh no,' says Bartholomew, frowning at his feet, the phone in his hand. He is sat on the edge of his bed, back hunched, looking over his outstretched legs. He can hardly bear to hear it. Scrapie? Vibrio? 'If you need antibiotics, I can pay,' he says.

'No, no. It's not ill, this one. Far from it. It's a good 'un. When are you next up?'

'Weekend,' says Bartholomew. 'Just for the one night. I don't like to leave mum on her own at the moment.'

'You're a good lad,' says Eric.

'No I'm not, Eric. I've not been good at all. Think I should help them set a date for the auction.'

'Aye, well, your mother's already informed the water board.'

They are silent for a moment, as if to absorb the finality of it.

'She's started looking in the paper – at houses. Your mother,' Eric says, as if to brighten the mood. 'Looking ahead she is.'

'Tell her not to get her hopes up,' says Bartholomew. 'We'll be lucky to clear thirty thousand pounds in the auction, and then there's the loan to come off that. How's the car, by the way?'

'Back from the garage and good as new,' says Eric.

'I don't know how to thank you,' Bartholomew says and his chest expands, with that pushing cloud of feeling. It's been happening a lot lately, a very unmanly tearfulness. 'I don't know how to say –'

'You've no need to say anything,' says Eric. 'Not to me.'

'Right, well, I'd best go, Eric. There's someone at the door. Yup, right you are. Bye now, bye.'

Ruby stands on the front step, having rung the bell with her elbow. She can hear him walk down the hallway and the door opens and there he is, distracted. Surprised.

'Ruby,' he says. 'What's that? A pie?'

'Yes, a pie,' she says, looking down at it. 'With chicken and mushrooms. And a bit of humble in there somewhere. I might have been a bit . . .'

He stands back, holding the door open for her, and she steps inside.

'I'm so glad you're here, Ruby,' he says. He is in shadow in the hallway, but she can hear he is crying. 'I'm so tired. Sorry.'

'Come on,' she says. 'Through to the kitchen.' And she leads the way down the hall, carrying the pie dish before her.

He sits down at the kitchen table and she sees him press into his eyes with his fingers to stop the tears. 'Urgh,' he says, almost growling. 'I'm such a girl.'

'I didn't realise what you were going through,' she says. 'How difficult it must've been. Even when you told me yesterday, it didn't sink in – I was too angry. But it must've been awful – having to juggle things down here with going home. It probably still is. Still going on is it?'

'Well, yes. I'll have to go up after work on Saturday. Eric's helping me, and dad, he's sort of submitting to the whole thing.'

'I'm sorry about it all.'

He nods. They are awkward and it's like they're nervous strangers.

'I don't know how you put up with me,' she says.

'I don't put up with you. I love you,' he says.

'I do know what I'm like.'

'We have to put up with each other, don't we? At least, I hope, I wish –'

She takes his face in her hands and kisses him on the lips.

'What about your boyfriend?'

'Yes, my boyfriend,' she says with a worried look. 'I'll have to explain things to him.'

'Where is he?'

'Oh, he'll be at work – at his merchant bank, or maybe driving back in his Porsche. Or at his club in London.'

He looks at her. 'He's a bit made-up, isn't he?'

'A little bit maybe.'

'Come here,' he says, putting his hands around her waist underneath her top. 'Where have you gone? You're disappearing. What am I supposed to grab hold of?'

'Oh there's still plenty of me,' she says, and she leads him out of the kitchen by the hand.

The little Peugeot rattles as Bartholomew changes up a gear and his eyes flick to the left, then quickly back to the road.

'You can always put that on the back seat,' he says.

'I don't want it to spill,' says Ruby.

She looks out of the window again, at the M1 slipping by in the darkness: the orange lamps overhead and the cat's eyes in the road and her reflection in the passenger window – she finds motorways at night soothing, reminding her of all those sleepy journeys back from holidays as a child.

Her goulash soup is still warm in the big Tupperware box on her knees and she holds it with both hands. On the back seat is a crusty white loaf in a plastic bag, because goulash soup should always be eaten with fresh bread, white and springy, and a slather of salted butter. She has cooked this soup – a beef stew really – for hours, so the meat is loose and flaking in a thick sauce flecked with paprika and bobbing with carrot and potato chunks. She glances at Bartholomew, whose face, lit green by the dashboard, is fixed on the road.

They walk up the front path to the door. Ruby holds the Tupperware box with both hands. She can smell wood smoke on the air and the farm smell which is like creosote.

'What's that?' she says.

'That's the video entryphone,' he says. 'I'll tell you later.'

Ann is opening the front door, her distracted face smoothing into a bright smile at the sight of them.

'Ruby love!' she says. 'What a lovely surprise!' She steps back from the front door and throws her tea towel over her shoulder. Ruby is overtaken by shyness and hangs back. 'Come in, come in,' says Ann. 'And you, Bartholomew. Give us a kiss.' She pushes up her cheek and he bends to kiss it.

'Hi mum. You alright?' he says.

'Yes, yes, we're holding up. Come through,' she says, waddling down the hall to the kitchen.

'Where's dad?' he says when he reaches the kitchen.

'I think he's nodded off in front of the television,' says Ann. 'I'll let him rest if that's OK.'

Ruby sets her Tupperware box down on the kitchen worktop. 'I've brought you some goulash soup,' she says to Ann. 'Well, it's beef stew really. I thought you might need a break.'

'Bless you, you good, sweet, lovely child,' says Ann. 'Goodness, what a treat. D'you know, I don't think anyone's said that to me in thirty-five years. Oh how lovely to be cooked for.'

'Do you have a big pot I could heat it in?' asks Ruby. She catches sight of Bartholomew, looking at her.

'Shall I do some potatoes?' asks Ann.

'No, you're alright. I've brought some bread. You sit down. I can sort it all out.'

'You're a good girl,' says Ann. 'She's a good girl.'

'I know, mum,' says Bartholomew.

Ruby and Ann stand in the doorway to the living room, looking in. In front of the fire is a dog basket and in it is a lamb. His dainty black legs are bent under him. He appears to be asleep but one eyeball stares upwards and he blinks. Beside the lamb is a dog bowl and rested in it is a baby's bottle filled with whitish liquid, tinged brown on its surface.

Joe Hartle lies on the sofa on his back, with a blanket over him. The lights from the television play across his face.

'Sometimes I wake up grumpy,' says Ann, 'and sometimes I let him sleep.'

☙

Bartholomew knocks on her bedroom door, then opens it and peers round it. 'Can I come in?'

Ruby is imprisoned in the tight single bed, the counterpane tucked in tight as a brace. The attic room has all the chill of a place where the radiator is permanently switched off. Ann has put Bartholomew in the back bedroom, one floor below, with his Bananaman bed set.

'OK,' she says. 'But no funny business.'

He hops through the cold wearing only his pants. 'Shove over then.'

'There's no room in here for you,' she says. She is smiling at him, but the temperature of their relative ardour has changed. Ruby is all held back. Not cold, not unloving exactly, but keeping some part of herself in reserve. Mistrustful of him. He feels at once terrible guilt – that he's caused her natural effervescence to cool – and yet, at the same time, it has only served to increase his enthusiasm, as if there is space now for his desire. They were like one of those cuckoo-clock couples, he thinks, where one figure is out only when the other has backed inside.

'Come on, I'm freezing,' he says.

'Should'a worn more 'an your pants then.'

He pulls back the blanket and she shimmies over saying, 'Oh god.'

They are crammed into the single bed, limbs knocking.

'Mmm, lovely and spacious,' he says, snuggling into her with his face in her neck. 'We should get Baby Lamb up here too.'

'I like the name Baby Lamb,' she says.

'It's not going to last him long.'

'It could. It's got a sinister thing going on – a bit mean. Like he's a despot or a mafia boss.'

'You mean like Baby Doc or Baby-face Nelson. I hadn't thought of it like that,' he says. 'I don't think the mob would have him. He's had his balls chopped off.'

'Seems a bit harsh.'

'Least he won't end up in a casserole.' Bartholomew has his

eyes closed, breathing her in. 'I should call that auction chap,' he says. 'See what dates he can do.'

'Isn't that down to them?'

'It's better if I take care of things, if it's done quickly.'

'It's not your farm.'

Bartholomew shifts his body so he can put his arms around her under the sheets.

'That's really uncomfortable,' she says.

'Shurrup, it's sensuous.'

'Ow! Get your arm out.' But he can feel her smile against his cheek, her skin so warm, her smell everything to him, his whole world.

'Listen, Rube, I've been thinking. What about you coming to work at my place – trying out that café we talked about. Wouldn't take me long to do up the lean-to. And the farm shop idea – there's no way me and Leonard can take that on with everything else. You could be in charge of all the food stuff.'

'Your elbow is really digging into me.'

'What d'you think, Rube?'

'Shouldn't you find Max? Tomorrow, I mean.'

'What about my idea? I could make you Head of Nutritional Strategy. Or Head of Strategy, brackets Nutrition. Which would you prefer?'

She has closed her eyes, her neck cricked at an angle.

'Rube?'

'Let's just slow down a bit shall we? Now go back to your own room and get some sleep.'

She rolls over in an almighty lunge, pulling the blanket with full force around her and the bed lurches downwards and there is a loud thud as Bartholomew hits the floor.

He pulls up on the road outside his brother's smallholding and walks through the wide gate to the back of the house, thinking of what Ruby had said at breakfast.

'It's taken a while for anyone to see to Max.'

She was sat at the kitchen table among the detritus of breakfast. They were alone. Ann had gone out and Joe was reading the paper in the living room with Baby Lamb. She'd watched as he'd spread jam on his toast, then said, 'Why has no one gone to find him, talk to him?'

'Thought he needed time, that's all – to get over things and give him and Primrose a bit of space.'

'Was it?' Ruby had said. 'Or maybe you've been enjoying your spell as golden boy and him being the lost cause. Maybe you don't want Max back in the fold.'

He looks now at the shabby yard. The outbuildings seem derelict. Blown sheets of tarpaulin and old hessian sacks have gathered rainwater. There are banks of mud and straw. The vegetable patch is barren earth with some brown top-growth. The chickens peck about in their shabby coop. Bartholomew approaches the back door and knocks. Steps back and waits. Then he bangs on the door again. The April sun is gaining confidence and he can feel it burn the back of his neck.

He knocks again.

'Alright, alright,' shouts Max from inside and Bartholomew hears a clattering and a key turning on the other side of the door.

Max opens the door. He is wearing tracksuit bottoms – crumpled, as if he's slept in them. His hair is matted. His face, also slept in, is puffy and he has thick grey stubble across his chin. Max says nothing but shuffles away down the hall, leaving the door open. Bartholomew follows him in.

When he reaches the living room, Max has already resumed his place on the sofa, lying beneath a navy sleeping bag. The room is dark and thick with the smell of night halitosis and sweat – a sweet and acrid smell which makes Bartholomew want to retch. On the coffee table are two cans of Newcastle Brown Ale.

'Come on, get up,' says Bartholomew, his heart thudding loudly in his chest.

'Fuck off,' says Max, rolling under the sleeping bag.

Bartholomew walks across the room and scrapes the curtains open. He opens a window and is relieved by the spring air which buffets in.

'Get up. Go and have a shower. I'll put some coffee on.' He is shaking but he covers it with big movements, striding across the room and down the hall to the kitchen.

The room is a mess. The sink is full of washing-up, the wide farmhouse table littered with plates, crumbs, mugs, silver takeaway trays still gloopy with food, apple cores and bread ends. Bartholomew hears Max pad up the stairs and is shocked that he has obeyed him. He hears thudding in the ceiling above him and then the shower going on.

He washes up the dishes in the sink wearing yellow Marigolds, and searches through drawers and cupboards for a black bin liner. He clears the table and sets the percolator onto the stove.

'You've been busy,' says Max in the doorway, rubbing his head with a hand towel.

Bartholomew pulls at the rubber gloves, turning them inside out as they peel off; the fingers amputated. 'I'll get you a coffee,' he says. 'Sit down.'

Max again obeys him. Bartholomew avoids his eye, busying about the room. He doesn't know where to begin.

'So,' says Max.

'So,' says Bartholomew, setting two clean mugs down on the table.

Max is bent over, his arms crossed over his belly.

'Mum and dad are selling,' says Bartholomew, his back against the kitchen counter. 'Auction's going to be end of September most likely.'

'You got what you wanted then.'

'I'm sorry?'

'Your share. You wanted your share.'

'What share would that be? You think there's some inheritance to be had?' He hits his forehead with the heel of his hand. 'No, of course, while you were off getting pissed, the whole flock went down. They could've done with your help.'

'He was going to sign the farm over to me and this is your way of stopping it.' Max has got up from his chair. He has started to clench his fists, open and shut, by his sides.

'What is it you want, Max? A handful of lambs that are worth less each month? A burnt-out barn?'

'It's alright for you,' says Max.

'Why is it alright for me?' Bartholomew asks, and he feels strangely calm. He can see the fury bubbling inside Max and it makes him calmer.

'You're so fucking smug.'

'No, come on, why is it alright for me?'

'Because, because.' Max has begun to pace, clenching and unclenching his fists. 'You're all set up, aren't you Bartholomew?' he says, walking around the table. A bubble of saliva has gathered at the corner of his mouth.

'Am I now?' Bartholomew says, watching his brother.

'You've got your income, your business.'

'That's right. It's all been so easy for me.'

'This was my livelihood,' Max shouts and the back of his hand sweeps low over the table and the two cups go flying against the wall, the noise a violence in itself. The cups bounce to the ground unbroken.

'Take it easy, Max,' says Bartholomew. He walks to the end of the room to pick up the cups off the floor. 'Let's just calm it down, shall we?' he says, but as he turns, Max is upon him. 'Come on now, take it easy.'

Max is not shifting. He's big, his face above Bartholomew's and Bartholomew is backing against the wall and Max is inching forwards.

'Archangel Bartholomew, back to save us all,' says Max and droplets of his saliva land on Bartholomew's mouth. Max is breathing hard, close to his face and his breath is so rank – sweet with stale alcohol – that Bartholomew feels violently sick. 'I should kill you,' Max whispers.

Bartholomew turns his head away, holds his breath. 'You're a fucking lunatic,' he says, his eyes closed, his head to one side, pinned against the wall by the putrid smell. Then he feels Max's hot breath retreat away and he opens his eyes.

Max has returned to the table, lowering himself down on a chair. He looks exhausted.

'So,' he says, 'you've been right in there, 'ave you? Golden boy, picking up the pieces.'

'That's right,' says Bartholomew, exhaling but still leaning against the wall. 'I'm the Prince fucking Regent. It's all about me, Max. Don't you care about them at all?'

'Yes I care.'

'Doesn't look like it.'

'I've got troubles of my own.'

'So has everyone you selfish, self-pitying fuck. It's always me that has more, isn't it? It's all one big measuring exercise with you. There was never a conversation that wasn't about lining up our ducks on the side of the bath and seeing who has more. And you never saw me. All I ever wanted, all I ever wanted . . .'

'I'm sorry I disappoint you so much,' says Max.

'You do. You do disappoint me. Everything I do, Max, you're always there, daggers drawn. Did you ever think about coming down to see my place, not to measure it up, but to be interested? In me? Or askin' after Ruby?'

'She's back on the scene is she?'

'Yes she is, not that you'd notice.'

'When did you ask me about Primrose – about being left by my wife?'

'I never thought Primrose was right for ye.'

'You don't say owt about her,' Max says sharply. He pauses, rubbing the stubble on his chin. 'I went to see her at the Crown. She's got a new look. That's what leaving me does – gives you a whole new look.'

Bartholomew hurries to the back door, opening it to let the air in because the room has become so airless he cannot breathe.

'She didn't leave you over nothing. She had reason. She would never have gone if it weren't for Sheryl.'

'Sheryl's a bitch. Sheryl trapped me.'

'Aye maybe. But it was you that shat on your own doorstep. Sheryl'd take anyone.'

The spring air gusts in, lifting some papers on the side by the sink.

'I've got nothing now,' says Max.

'Oh come off it. You never had anything before. It were all dad's. You were just hitching a ride. Go get yourself something of your own.'

'With what?'

'With tuppence-hapenny, like the rest of us. What, d'ye think I won the lottery? I'm up to my eyes in debt. You're a daft fuck, Max. You think everyone's riding their millions. If you could just see . . .'

He stops. 'I've got to take you back with me for a family meeting.'

'Gimme a moment, will ye?'

'I'll get you a coffee.'

'Fuck coffee. Wait there.' Max goes out of the room. He comes back in with two cans of Newcastle Brown Ale. Hands one to Bartholomew, who takes it. Max sits at the table and they open their cans simultaneously, the click, then fizz a release.

'Cheers,' says Bartholomew, holding his can up.

'Here's to the farm,' says Max.

'Good riddance,' says Bartholomew.

'You don't look too good,' says Bartholomew, glancing at Max as they drive towards Lipton. Max doesn't answer. He is gazing out of the passenger window at the fields going by. 'You need something to eat,' says Bartholomew. And then, after a time, he says, 'Have you thought what you might do?'

'Take off somewhere,' Max says, without any enthusiasm. He is still looking out of the window.

'Where?'

'France maybe. Sell the Land Rover, get a summer job picking fruit or summat. Jake might come along.'

'Isn't that taking the old crap with you?'

'I'm not brave enough to go on my own,' Max says, looking at Bartholomew at last. 'I'm not like you. Striking out was never my strong suit.'

'There you go again,' says Bartholomew. 'You're always thinking I've had it easy. You think I didn't shit meself, setting up on my own?'

'There's some folk like a risk, that's all – thrive on it. I'm not one o' them.'

'Bullshit, Max. You see the outside of people and think that's all there is.'

They are under the canopy of trees now, in bright spring leaf and its reflection playing on the windscreen. Past Eric's Nissan Micra, back in its driveway, and around the curve of the village green. They can both see the Fox and Feathers, not yet opened for the lunchtime trade.

'Can't stay round here,' says Max.

'Probably not,' says Bartholomew, pulling up the handbrake. 'Come on, let's go in.'

'Hiya love,' says Ann, rustling into the kitchen and lifting her shopping bags onto the table.

'Let me help you with those,' says Ruby.

'Where's Joe? How's he been?'

'Fine. He's resting in the living room. Doesn't half have that fire on high. I was sweating in there.'

'Oh I know. I find meself sitting there in a T-shirt, perspiring, and Joe's sat next to me in two fleeces and a blanket over his knees like he's ninety. Where's Bartholomew?'

'Gone to find Max.'

'Ah,' says Ann, stopping for a moment, holding a red pepper in one hand and a bag of tomatoes in the other. 'I thought we'd have a cold collation for lunch – ham and cheese and bread, that sort of thing.'

'Where do these go?' Ruby asks, holding up a packet of biscuits.

'Empty them into the tin on the side, would you?'

They both hear the front door open but they continue attending to the shopping.

'Hi mum,' says Bartholomew, walking into the room. 'Look who's here.'

Ann sees Max trailing behind, grey-haired. Ill-looking. He has washed, at least, she thinks. 'Oh Max love,' she says, walking over to him and reaching up to his face with her hands. He bends so that she can cup his face and kiss him. She wants to do more – cradle him, cover him with kisses like when he was a bairn and he fell and she was able to make it all better. But now even their bodies prevent this.

'You sit down, lovey,' she says. 'I'll get you a tea. Would you like a tea? Or coffee p'raps? Or a biscuit. You've probably not eaten. Ruby and me, we're just getting lunch. Nice bread – I got a bloomer from Greggs – and cheese and ham. I could slice you up a tomato and there's the Branston pickle you like. Are you hungry? You could have a lie-down if you're tired. I could make up a bed for you to rest in, love.'

Max has sat down at the table. 'Don't fuss mum,' he says. 'Where's dad?'

'He's resting. I'll get him when lunch is ready.'

'No I'm not,' says Joe. He is standing in the doorway with Baby Lamb by his side. 'Hello son,' he says to Max.

Bartholomew and Ruby stand with their backs leaning

275

against the kitchen counter. Joe and Ann look down at Max.

'We're a right pair, aren't we, son?' says Joe, smiling at Max and rubbing his shoulder with one hand. 'All lost we two, aren't we?'

Ann puts her arm around Joe and kisses his cheek. She has her other hand on Max's back and she kisses the top of his head.

'Right,' she says. 'Come on. Lunch.'

'I can do it,' says Ruby. 'Leave it to me.'

'Thank you, lovey,' says Ann. 'Bartholomew, you can lay the table.'

Joe has taken a seat at the head of the table. Ann is placing jars of chutney and mayonnaise at its centre. Ruby is busy at the counter, with her back to the room. Bartholomew walks around the table, putting a plate in front of each seat.

'I do think we need to set a timetable,' Bartholomew says, and the room erupts into groans. 'For the auction.'

'Here we go,' says Ruby. 'Could you clench those buttocks a bit tighter?'

'What?' says Bartholomew.

'Excuse me,' says Ann. 'That's enough from you, Bartholomew. Let's get the lunch out shall we?'

'I just think we have to sort it out,' he says.

'You sort out your dahlias,' says Joe. 'Leave the farm to us.'

'I don't know why I bother,' says Bartholomew.

Ann has a hand on the bread loaf and is sawing it on a chopping board. She places a thick slice on each plate.

'Everything alright with Primrose?' Joe says to Max. 'Is she coming?'

Everyone stops for a moment.

'Primrose,' Max begins. Ruby puts a cup of tea down in front of him and he lifts it to take a sip. 'We're, she's . . .' He rubs his palms on his knees.

'Not feeling well?' says Joe.

'That's right,' says Ann. 'She's not well. Stomach thing.'

'Ah well,' says Joe. 'You can report back to her.'

The activity in the room resumes, Ruby washing tomatoes in the sink and setting them on the table in a bowl. Bartholomew reaches for the packet of ham and puts a slice on his plate.

'No,' says Max loudly and all eyes are on him. 'Primrose left me,' he says to Joe. 'Gone to live in Lipton with a friend.'

The table absorbs this statement with a criss-crossing of arms fetching ham, cheese, butter, knives clattering, gulps of tea. Ann notices how slow Max is to fight his way in. He's no appetite, she thinks sadly. 'Is there anything I can pass you, Max love?' she says. 'Something for your bread?'

'I'm alright with tea for now,' says Max.

'You all know we're going to be selling up,' says Joe, gruff and powerful.

'We want a bit of a retirement,' says Ann. 'Take things a bit easier.'

'We talked to Talbot,' Joe says to Max. 'He says there's a position for you there if you want it. Nothing grand, but not labouring. Land management, he said.'

'He'll see you right,' says Ann.

Then Bartholomew says, 'I don't think that's what Max . . .'

'No, you're alright,' says Max. 'It's a good idea – to work for Talbot. He's a decent enough chap.'

Ann sees Bartholomew cast a look at his brother and Max avoiding his eye.

'Autumn,' she says into the room and everybody stops. 'Auctioneer says late September would be about right. Once lambs are weaned.'

SEPTEMBER

— Weaning and harvest: the end of the farming year —

'Here we are,' says Lauren, pulling up the handbrake.

Ann sits in the passenger seat while the car ticks and looks out at the wide cul-de-sac. Bilious clouds scud over a series of lurid red roofs. The newly tarmacked road is lined with bungalows, flat and low. There is too much space between them, as if they're sharing some pretence of detached snobbery. Bland rectangles for windows, bricks that are a sickly shade of yellow. Noddy boxes, Joe would call them.

'Right,' says Ann, and they both get out of the car. They follow a black, glistening path to number six where the agent greets them at the door.

It takes about ten minutes to clack around the empty rooms.

'And how much did you say it was?' Ann asks at the end of his tour.

'£137,000,' says the agent.

Ann's eyes bulge. 'Lauren,' she says, but Lauren stops her arm.

'Thanks ever so,' Lauren says to the estate agent, 'do you mind if we take a minute?'

'Not at all,' he says. 'I'll wait for you outside.'

They wait for him to leave the room – a bedroom, he called it, but barely wider than a double bed. The rooms are boxy, all of them. Mean, with low ceilings. Yes, there are down-lighters, but they don't seem like Lauren's. Some of them are wonky, so the hole's exposed and you can see how cardboardy the plasterboard ceiling is. And the doors are thin, and the floors are orangey and in places they creak in a sticky way.

'That's a hell of a price for a rabbit hutch like this,' says Ann to Lauren, who is by the window looking out to the garden where a postage stamp of newly laid turf is surrounded by bare fencing.

'It's a bit steep, I'll grant you,' says Lauren. 'That garden's charmless.'

'We'll not get near that price,' says Ann. She pats her collarbones. 'Everything's so expensive. God, Lauren, we have to be out in less than six weeks. Auction's in two. What a mess.'

'Calm down. We'll find you something. Come on, let's get out of here. I'll buy you lunch on the high street – just to cheer you up, like.'

'You don't have to keep saying that,' says Ann. 'I'll let you buy me lunch.'

They walk together up the steep incline, Ann's arm looped in Lauren's, towards the Wooden Spoon café at the top of the high street. To their right, on the opposite side of the road, is the Conservative Club. To their left, the grand old Victorian shop fronts, dark-grey stone, blackened around the edges, cut in big old slabs. Same colour as the pavement, as the dry stone walls out on the fell. Past the newsagents, the bakery, the bicycle shop, Drapers, which sells hiking boots and expensive anoraks to walkers. Ann looks up to where the old clock hangs between the upper windows and there she sees a 'For Sale' sign, above the bookshop.

'Look at that,' she says to Lauren, pulling back on her arm.

'What? Oh yes. Must be a flat. Shall I ring? See if we can see it?'

They climb the musty stairwell. Dark, it is, the stair carpet maroon, laced with dog hairs and thinning at the treads.

'Doesn't bode well,' says Lauren, her face turning back to Ann from a few steps above.

The agent is up ahead, shoving his shoulder against the door. 'It's recently vacated,' he says – same chap as earlier. Happened to have the keys on him. 'Not as good nick as the place I just showed you.'

They walk through to a room which stinks of dog. The walls are the colour of cigarette tar, the old gloss woodwork yellowing too, and the carpet is patched. But it has the highest ceilings Ann has ever seen, lined with a cornice of carved roses – the stately proportions of a Victorian drawing room. Two enormous arched windows stretch up, big as a church's; impossibly bright and warmed by the sun. A view of the sky, and below them the bustle of the high street. Ann immediately pictures a Christmas tree in the corner.

'It's on at £75,000,' says the agent. 'Not been that much interest because it needs a bit of work. Two bedrooms above and a bathroom.'

'It's a maisonette?'

'Yes.'

'But no outside space.'

'No.'

Lauren and Ann look at each other. 'Baby Lamb,' they say in unison.

'Oh, but Lauren it's so beautiful,' says Ann, feeling excitement bubbling in her chest as if she might lift right off the ground with it. She runs up the stairs, where the bedrooms have the same elegant proportions, with little cast-iron fireplaces, and there is a shabby avocado bathroom. Ann walks slowly back down the stairs in a daze.

'Bit grubby,' says Lauren from the hallway. She disappears and Ann hears her shoes tap on linoleum. 'You'll need a new kitchen.'

Ann joins her in the small galley room next door to the lounge, with beige units, an exposed old fifty-pence meter and torn-up floor. 'Yes, but the rooms,' Ann whispers urgently. 'Lauren, the feeling of it. Right in the centre of the shops, too. Joe could walk over the road for a pint at the club.'

'That's all I need,' says Lauren. 'Eric at the club more often.'

Ann's not listening. 'Just needs a lick of paint is all. Me and Joe and the boys could do it.'

'Slow down. It's still a lot,' says Lauren. 'God, look at you. We've got to see what the auction gets you first. Come on, let's go for lunch, I'm starving.'

'Five more minutes,' Ann says. 'Let me have another look upstairs.'

Ann stands beside an industrial-sized tea urn, borrowed from the church kitchen. It rumbles and spits. The trestle table before her (also borrowed) is spread with cakes and sandwiches wrapped in cling film; Kit Kats in their box, the cardboard lid folded back and '10p' written in marker pen on the lip; sausage rolls on a white tray. It is a bright day, with a playful wind and delicious unexpected heat to it: a real Indian summer. She feels the dampness under her arms and on her forehead. She can smell her lavender bubble bath rise off her too-warm skin. She glances at Lauren, standing next to her, immaculately turned out as always in a white sleeveless shirt and pearls.

She looks out across the in-bye, now the auction site. Over in the yard, their vehicles and equipment are lined up: the tractor and its various attachments, quad bike, gates, lamb adopter, sheep bars and metal mangers, sorting pen; each with a lot number. Joe is there, she's sure, has been all morning. Pacing among the lots with Baby Lamb on a lead. Earlier she'd seen him standing too close to those that were looking around. She watched him frown, as Granville Harris picked over the metal, Granville saying to a man next to him, 'Bit o'rust on that one,' and Joe had muscled in, saying, 'There is not. It's in perfectly good nick.' She'd had to pull him away or they'd not sell anything.

Here in the field, the sheep are penned, also in lots. Lambs just weaned earlier in the month, now ready for sale. Adrian and Eric had brought in around two hundred and fifty mules at lambing, twins and singles. And there's another two-hundred-odd pure Swales that had lambed on the fell by themselves. And a few tups. They can't sell the dogs, not yet. That's more than they can take. The field is thronging with men in jeans and T-shirts and green Hunter boots. There are overweight women, their arms wide in vest tops and cropped trousers, and children climbing on a parked tractor which has been brought in as a plaything. The toddlers are petting the lambs or running in circles.

They come for the day out, as much as anything, for the chat and the cakes and to see how low the prices have sunk. They did it themselves – her and Joe – when the boys were small. She puts a hand up as a visor over her eyes and squints as the sun burns dry and powerful. Sees Bartholomew standing chatting to Adrian and Tal beside the sheep pens. He has his arm around Ruby's shoulders – he always seems to have an arm around her these days. Holding on tight. She's a pretty girl, Ann thinks, in her jeans and that bright-orange flowery shirt. She's pleased for Bartholomew, to see him settled and happy. She scans the field, sees a small girl, maybe six or seven, in a blue dress running circles around the pen, pursued by a friend. Our field – same field the boys played in – and the one next door which had the perfect pitch for rolling down. Max must've been that girl's age, Bartholomew about four, and they'd clasp onto each other and roll, one over t'other, giggling so hard that Bartholomew wet himself and she'd scolded him for it. No one'll want to play with you, if you keep pissing your pants. And Max pushed him off, saying 'Yuk'. She'd never imagined a moment like this would come. Never thought she'd get old. And she has an urge to shout 'No, I can't do it, I'm not ready.' But to whom? And who could make it stop?

'Yes, love,' she says, sensing a customer in her peripheral vision, waiting in front of her table. 'What can I get ye?' And she turns to the man and squints as the sun obscures her view with its shards.

'Tea please,' says Joe, 'and a slice of that beautiful sponge. It looks light as air does that.'

'Oh Joe,' she says, and she walks out from behind the table and puts her arms around his shoulders, burying her face in his neck which is as much home to her as this place. 'Oh Joe.'

'Come on, now,' he says, his hands on her hips. 'We'll be alright, Annie.'

To their left is the auctioneer, holding his loudhailer in one hand and stooping to find the face of Brenda Farley, whose debilitating hunch has forced her eyes to the grass. Ann lets go of Joe. She stands beside him and the two of them look out together. Groups of people chat in huddles. They sip their drinks. They wolf down Ann and Lauren's cakes. She notices a couple of teenagers talking awkwardly to one another. The boy is flushed red all along his jawline, just like Bartholomew when he was that age.

'Where's Max?' she says.

Joe nods to his right. 'Over there, talking to Talbot.'

Ann follows his gaze and sees Max, his body angled towards the older, bigger man who is in full countryman uniform despite the heat. Max is listening to Talbot, cocking his head, alert as a sheepdog. He nods and listens again.

'Think you might have to give up your position as font of all wisdom,' she says to Joe as they both watch Max.

'Gladly,' says Joe.

'Right,' Eric says. They turn and he's standing with an arm around Lauren, on the other side of the trestle. 'I think we're about ready to begin.'

'You've done a grand job, Eric,' says Joe. They stand, the four of them, looking out across the field at the cheerful scene. Here she is in her summer dress, serving tea and cakes, thinking how glorious the field looks filled with her community, standing here with her best friends and greeting all the many nice people they know . . .

She frees herself from Joe's arm and looks out across the field behind them, where the cars are parked in lines. Hot as August it is. She sees a family sitting at their open boot, eating sandwiches and passing around a flask. How the English love to sit at the boots of their cars. The mother unwraps a foil parcel and hands some food to two children who sit cross-legged on the grass. The father, sitting low in his foldaway chair, reaches into a bag and pulls out a newspaper. Ann thinks she can see the woman frowning. Why is it, she thinks, when they went to events like this – a country show or an auction or a church fair – times when they were younger and the farm was still going and the children were young – why hadn't she enjoyed it, in the way she was enjoying this one? Tasting it. Noticing. She had so often been angry or tied up with how the boys were misbehaving and not getting enough help from Joe. Oh the mind is perverse, that she should feel pleasure on this funereal day which is trussed up like a garden party and peevish when it had been there for her to enjoy. Why must it take a lifetime to learn to live in the present and to have the knack of it arrive just when the present is running out?

Behind her, she hears Joe's gruff voice saying, 'Eric, I don't know how to say –' And she hears Eric stop him, saying, 'Shurrup man. Buy me a pint later when you're rich.'

And then another voice, distorted by the funnel of a loudhailer, saying, 'Ladies and gentlemen, I shall be opening the bidding on Lot 32 of the Hartle estate.'

'Am I bid fifteen pound, fifteen fifteen. Come on lads, gimme fifteen pound. Sixteen, sixteen, sixteen pound. Fine Swale stores these, come on folks, seventeen pound, seventeen, seventeen, eighteen, let me see eighteen, thank you sir, eighteen pound.'

Joe and Ann close their eyes against the auctioneer's rotten song of numbers, a mean reckoning on the animals they've cared so much for.

'Not sure I can listen to much more o' this,' says Joe.

'It's the breeding ewes next,' says Ann. 'They'll get more.'

Lauren crosses two of her fingers in the air.

Bartholomew and Ruby have wandered over to stand beside them, and Max too, to the other side, and it seems to Ann as if they're forming some circle of protection around her and Joe. Joe's gaze is on the ewes and she knows what he's thinking – that he knew them, from birth many of them, when they followed their mothers up onto the fell; that they were his – his flock, his family. And which stranger would they go to? And would they look after them right? And she thinks people don't understand it, because sheep are reared for meat, but if you're not looking after them well, you don't feel good in yourself.

'Forty pound, forty pound, forty pound. Can I see forty-five? Good ewes these, fine breeding animals, forty-five, forty-five, forty-five, thank you sold!'

He lowers his face so she can put her forehead against his forehead and they both have their eyes closed as the auctioneer says, 'Four Swale tups . . .'

'We'll be alright, Joe. We'll rent somewhere,' she says. 'Get jobs, both of us. I can get some cleaning, you can do odd jobs, shepherding if we keep the dogs, help w' harvests and what have you. Not the end o' the world.'

Against the black of her eyelids she pictures the lovely flat on Lipton High Street. No hope of it now, not with these numbers. That lovely drawing room where a Christmas tree would have looked . . .

'Oh Annie,' Joe is saying. 'At the end of our lives, nothing to show for it. What would your father say?'

'Well fortunately, he's dead, so that's one less thing to worry about.'

'I feel like someone's moving my guts around,' he says.

'Nine thousand, am I bid nine thousand? Nine thousand thank you. A fine ram this, first prize at Leyburn show.'

Ann and Joe lift their heads up to stare at each other. Eric is rocking fulsomely on his heels, the grin all over his face.

'Nine thousand and fifty am I bid? Nine thousand and twenty five, then, nine thousand and fifty? Thank you, nine thousand and fifty, nine thousand and fifty, nine thousand and fifty. Gone. You've done well there, Dugmore.'

'What the hell was that?' asks Joe.

'A prize tup you had among your fattening stores,' says Eric, hopping up and down, dancing, giving Lauren a hug. 'Adrian spotted him back in April, checked the parentage in your log. Took him to the country shows earlier this month and he got more rosettes pinned on 'im than Miss World.'

People around them are hugging. Eric walks around the table to clap Joe on the shoulder. 'You were always good, Joe – there were never a better man for breeding sheep. I think I'll hold you to that pint now, if it's all the same.'

Bartholomew and Ruby are hugging, Adrian and Eric are hugging, even Bartholomew and Max clap each other heartily on the shoulders. Ann is standing in a daze, looking across the trestle at Lauren.

'Suppose that flat's a goer now,' says Lauren.

'Yes,' says Ann, 'suppose it is.'

Ann is sat on a folding canvas chair behind the trestle table, so low that her bottom almost touches the grass. She shuts her eyes, enjoying the light burn of the sun on her forehead. Four prize tups – three that they'd bought last October and the one found in the flock by Adrian. That's brought us thirteen thousand pounds alone. And another twenty thousand for the remaining sheep. And ten to fifteen thousand for hardware and vehicles – that's what the auctioneer's going through now. Minus the loan they've got. Should clear forty thousand give or take. Enough for that flat and a mortgage that won't cripple us. Max can pay his share. We've survived, she thinks.

She looks at the crowd of backs, which is all she can see from a place so low. All these people, she thinks, I should be more of a host. She makes a move to heave herself out of the canvas chair but feels Lauren's hand applying pressure on her shoulder.

'No you don't. Here, drink this.' Lauren hands Ann a steaming cup of tea in a chipped, rose-covered mug.

'This has seen better days.'

'Haven't we all?' says Lauren, opening another canvas chair in a blur to the side, and letting out a huge sigh as she heaves down into it. 'Flamin' heck,' she says, 'might as well 'ave sat on the grass.'

At the edge of the group of backs, Ann can see Brenda Farley, pushing her face upwards against the lowering force of her hump. Her hair is so white it is almost luminous. She is wearing a navy cardigan over a floral shirt which is buttoned to the neck. Her best for a day out, bless her.

'Farm machinery, implements and sundries now,' says the auctioneer. 'Bomford Scimitar pasture topper, Graham Edwards livestock trailer – about twelve foot this one – complete with foldaway sheep decks.'

Ann watches the strain on Brenda's face, her creased forehead. She is listening intently, as if the auctioneer is reading out her own will and testament. The strings of her neck are pulled like strands of dough.

'Quad trailer,' continues the auctioneer, 'sheep troughs, ring feeders, electric-fence unit. And one for your mutton chops, Granville – Lister sheep shears.' Ann hears the crowd laugh. She watches the delayed reaction on Brenda Farley's face: the mouth still slightly open, the laughter drifting towards her; the smile as she looks to the people surrounding her and sees them laughing. It is as if this woman lives on a distant shore and everything laps onto her beach that little bit later than it does everyone else.

She feels Lauren put a hand on hers.

'I'm going to give that woman my chair,' says Ann, making to get up.

'She's alright,' says Lauren, stopping her arm. 'Any road, if she got in it, she'd never get out again. You rest a bit.'

'Christ Lauren, is that all that's ahead of us?'

They both watch as Brenda attempts to lift her head again, her jaw slack with fresh confusion.

'Not such a bad life,' says Lauren. 'Gas fire on the full setting. *Countdown* on the telly. Incontinence pants on, nice and snug up to the armpits. Could do worse.'

'But for time to run out, Lauren,' Ann whispers. 'I never expected it. Thought I'd be thirty for ever. It's like I didn't see it coming. And now it's here.'

'I don't think we'll be carrying you out in a box just yet,' says Lauren. 'We've got that flat to sort out first.'

Evening the following day and Ann thinks the washing-up will never end. This must be her sixth lot at least. Her hands are dry with it, reptilian when she'd looked at them in bed last night. Must get some of that Vaseline hand cream, she thinks, but that's another trip into Lipton I haven't got time for and then her mind goes to the flat, as it does constantly, and she smiles to herself while looking out the window because soon, touch wood, she'll be able to walk to the shops.

The evening sun is everywhere, casting the yard in an orange light that seems artificial, and sliding in through the window. It bathes Lauren's face so that she looks impossibly tanned as she stands next to Ann, drying a cup with a tea towel that's as good as sodden. Ann is feeling about in the sink, noticing the silky suds as they coat her hands. Pleasing it is, the slide of it as she turns the cup in the water, much as it dries out her skin.

Their silence is amiable, through all the rounds of washing-up they've done together. Lauren has been by her side these last two days, helping with the catering marathon that accompanied the auction – all the cups and plates from the day itself, then the folk that stayed on past the afternoon into sunset, either sat in her kitchen or taking tea out to the yard. And then the smaller group who stayed to dinner – Ruby cooked another of her excellent stews with baked potatoes to feed the five thousand (that girl is really a marvel in the kitchen): Max and Bartholomew of course, Max sullen but she thought that was because he was off the drink and feeling the pull of it, Bartholomew eating as usual like it was his last; Eric and Lauren; Dennis Lunn, who'd helped so much with the penning and moving the sheep about. And on it went, even today – every time another person arrived to pick up some livestock or machinery, they popped in for a brew and a slice of fruit cake or a bacon sandwich.

'Only this stack to go,' says Lauren, bringing a pile of plates over from the kitchen table and putting them next to Ann on the counter.

Ann had managed, late this morning, to peel Joe away from the to-ings and fro-ings and take him to Lipton to see the flat. He'd harrumphed all the way up the stairs, complained about the smell, the size, the state of the place but she could see some sparkle in his face, a covered-up interest in it when he said, 'I'll have to pull this lino up.' She could see him thinking, 'There's a job for me here,' which was a pleasure to him (much as he wouldn't admit it) after saying goodbye to so much.

'Look Joe,' she'd said, standing at the window. 'You could go to the club in your slippers.'

'I'm not that old yet that I can't put me shoes on,' he'd grumbled. But he'd stood next to her looking around the room and she could feel it coming off him – something similar to what she felt, a new start, a new type of life that would be interesting and different to the one they'd had.

Upstairs, they'd stood in the second bedroom with the sun streaming in through muddy glass and she'd said, 'Max could go in here, you see.'

'Is he going to be back with us till he's fifty?' Joe said.

'No,' she'd scoffed. 'Don't be daft. Just till he's back on his feet, settled at Talbot's, and off the drink. He's hurt, Joe. We have to look after him.'

'You've changed your tune.'

'Yes, well,' she'd said, venturing back down the stairs.

She wasn't stupid. She knew they'd struggle with it: leaving Marpleton and the house her children had grown up in and the work of the farm and that connection with the land and the fell. But she also had the sense that the worst was behind them, and that the changes were most painful when you resisted them or in the run-up. It was gone now, and a rest would do them no harm. They could be snug in this place, without auction or feed prices to worry about. She'd even snuck into Al's Electrical to see about the price of halogen down-lighters while Joe went for a loaf to Greggs.

She hands Lauren a plate and the drips tickle down Ann's bare forearm.

'That's doing nothing,' she says, nodding at the sodden rag Lauren is holding. 'There's a clean one in the drawer.'

Lauren turns and while she's bent over the drawer she says, 'There's some news actually.'

Ann looks at her friend but she's only half present, her mind feeling its way endlessly over the new landscape she's moving through. She says, 'Don't tell me, you're pregnant.'

'That's it,' Lauren says, shaking out a tea towel with sheep breeds on it. 'I'm just pretending to be in me sixties. Hanging out with you geriatric old farts makes me feel good about meself.'

'What then?'

'Sylvie's pregnant.'

Ann stops, both wet hands in the air. 'Oh Lauren!'

She puts her arms around her, keeping her hands out and feeling tears prick in the corners of her eyes.

'A baby, Ann,' says Lauren. 'A baby that's just a little bit mine.'

'More 'an a bit. A quarter.'

'After Jack . . .'

'I know.'

'I thought,' Lauren is breaking up, 'I thought I'd never hold a baby again and be that in love wi' it.'

'And now you will.'

Lauren is sobbing now, heaving with it. It's come sudden, out of nowhere –perhaps she's been turning it over in her mind with all the drying-up she's been doing.

'When it happened,' she is saying, between little gasps, 'when it happened, Ann, I thought life would never go on, and now . . .' She sniffs, laughing at herself. 'I'm already scared. What if he gets sick? What if I love 'im too much and he gets sick?'

Ann shakes her head at Lauren as if to say, 'Don't be daft woman.'

'I don't even think Sylvie wants this baby,' Lauren blurts, in the relief of tears that are better out than in. 'I think she's doing it for me and I don't care, I want it that much.' She wipes her eyes with the tea towel.

'Well, it's the least she can do after you bought her that car.'

'Yes,' says Lauren. 'Absolutely.'

They return to their positions, Ann at the sink, Lauren waiting with her tea towel for the next plate.

'Where's Ruby got to?' asks Lauren.

'Gone upstairs to read her book.'

They are silent for a time, then Ann says, 'Happen I could get that baby gym back off Primrose.'

'Don't you dare. I can afford another baby gym. God, you're tight. Any road, sounds like Primrose might need it herself before long.'

Ann turns to her in surprise, and Lauren holds up her tea towel in defence. 'Only a rumour,' she says.

'Poor Max,' says Ann sadly.

'He'll be alright Ann. He will. He'll be better off at Talbot's. He'll meet someone, someone more suited. I've always thought Max needed a right bossy woman – someone to knock him into shape. Take charge.'

'Someone like his mother you mean,' Ann says.

'Not that bossy, no,' says Lauren, giving Ann a squeeze about the shoulders. 'Here, shall we go back and see the flat again to-morrow? Do some measuring?'

ᘒ

'You can't take Baby Lamb to that flat,' says Bartholomew.

'So your mother keeps telling me,' says Joe.

They are leaning on a fence looking out across the in-bye, each with a boot on the bottom rung and Baby Lamb nipping the grass at their feet. The field is set with empty metal pens, the stock having been loaded into various trailers and trans-ported to new farms. A burger van stands like a stranded white box with its hatch padlocked, waiting to be towed away.

'When's Alan coming for that?' asks Bartholomew.

'Dunno,' says Joe. 'Said there was no hurry.'

'What'll you do wi' it then? Baby Lamb, I mean.'

'What'll I do with *him* you mean?' says Joe. 'Max says he'll tek him. Says Talbot'll find a spot in his farmyard with the petting animals. Very progressive is Talbot – tamed animals for kids to stroke. A visitor centre he calls it but I've seen it – just a yard it is.'

'You get good subsidies for that, teaching schoolkids about hedgerows and lambing, all that,' says Bartholomew. He notices his Yorkshire has become thicker since being home, or perhaps just in conversation with his father.

'Aye and grows fuel crops,' Joe says. 'Tries out all sorts does Talbot. There's no flies on him.'

There is something in Joe's voice – is it impatience with his son, or contempt for Talbot? Bartholomew can't quite make it out – some cynicism as least, about other people's efforts. Understandable, he thinks, Joe's defensiveness towards Talbot, the farmer who is still farming and soon to be the focus of Max's needy gaze. Yes, he should be understanding, but instead he says: 'Still doing your bidding then, Max.'

'How d'you mean?'

'Well, taking Baby Lamb off your hands. Staying on up here, farming with Talbot, moving into the flat with you and mum.'

'You'd have him leave us too, would ye?'

'No, I . . .'

'We can't all be as perfect as you, Bartholomew. Some of us know our limitations. Important that – to know your limits. We all have them, you know. Even you.'

'What you mean is, *you* know our limits – mine, Talbot's, Max's. No one's allowed to exceed you.' And as he says it, Bartholomew feels he's trespassing where he shouldn't – on the rightful order of things – but he can't stop himself. He looks nervously across the in-bye, avoiding Joe's gaze.

'Exceed me? Big word that,' Joe says.

'Do well then, do better. Would that be so terrible?'

'Yes, it's terrible. Wonderful and terrible.'

Joe hangs his head low between his shoulder blades and kicks the base of the fence.

'Happen I'll have more time to travel now the farm's gone. I could come and visit maybe, see what you've got down there – your place.'

Bartholomew looks back at him and he thinks he's never felt so small and so sorry and so much full of love and also a kind of sorrow that might be the new order of things.

'You'll have to let me get it ready. Tidy the place up a bit. For the royal visit.'

'Oh aye, I expect the red-carpet treatment.'

And he shakes Bartholomew at the neck, like an apple tree, and Bartholomew submits to it.

ACKNOWLEDGEMENTS

My thanks go to Alexandra Shelley for being a most attentive reader, and for cheerleading when all seemed lost. Thank you to my agent Sarah Ballard for taking me on and being unflappable. And to my editor, Sarah Savitt, for enthusiasm and faith and careful reading.

For help in my research, thanks go to Steve Dunkley at Eblex and Paul Harper of The Farmer Network. Mistakes or licence taken with the details of fell farming are mine, not theirs.

For various kindnesses, thanks to John and Deborah Steiner, Eve Happold, Jane Milton, Laura Godfrey, Daniel Burbidge, Sian and Joel Rickett. Thank you Maggie O'Farrell, Andrew Cowan and the Arvon Foundation for early encouragement. My thoughts go to Sarah Didinal, who came with me on the first research trip for this book and whom I still miss.

Thank you George and Ben for being the sweetest distraction at the end of the writing day. Above all, there was one person who believed in this book before anyone else did, and who was its greatest champion: love and gratitude go to my husband, Tom Happold.

ff

Faber and Faber is one of the great independent publishing houses. We were established in 1929 by Geoffrey Faber with T. S. Eliot as one of our first editors. We are proud to publish award-winning fiction and non-fiction, as well as an unrivalled list of poets and playwrights. Among our list of writers we have five Booker Prize winners and twelve Nobel Laureates, and we continue to seek out the most exciting and innovative writers at work today.

Find out more about our authors and books
faber.co.uk

Read our blog for insight and opinion on books and the arts
thethoughtfox.co.uk

Follow news and conversation
twitter.com/faberbooks

Watch readings and interviews
youtube.com/faberandfaber

Connect with other readers
facebook.com/faberandfaber

Explore our archive
flickr.com/faberandfaber